PORTLAND ZIONISTS UNITE!

AND OTHER STORIES

WRITTEN BY
ERIC FLAMM

INKWATER PRESS

PORTLAND•OREGON
INKWATERPRESS.COM

Publisher: Inkwater Press | www.inkwaterpress.com

Paperback ISBN-13 978-1-62901-598-9 | ISBN-10 1-62901-598-9
Kindle   ISBN-13 978-1-62901-599-6 | ISBN-10 1-62901-599-7

1 3 5 7 9 10 8 6 4 2

PORTLAND ZIONISTS UNITE!
AND OTHER STORIES

CONTENTS

MAUSER KARABINER

DECEMBER 1995, HEBRON, WEST BANK

YONI TAGER

I STUMBLED OUT of the Humvee with six other soldiers. The guys looked as pissed off as I felt—our uniforms disheveled, shirts and pants twisted off-kilter on our slender builds. We all lacked sleep. I had known when I lay down I would have less than two hours rest and so hadn't even bothered to take my boots off. I stood there and squinted in the sun, looking at the dusty Hebron street, the flat cement buildings, the garbage— feeling raw at the effort it took to take it all in, but numb to the world two steps beyond.

The air still had the crisp smell of morning coolness, and through my haze I nodded in recognition that all was the same as it had been yesterday, and the day before that. The street was capped by three square cement blocks, three feet thick, meant to stop cars. On the other side was the Israeli Defense Forces fight position, a half-moon of sandbags piled to waist height, against which another six Golani soldiers lounged with their flak jackets open, helmets off, rifles propped up against

1

the sandbags. They looked like weary commuters on a bus whose air conditioning had unexpectedly broken, and they threw off irritation with every gesture. Nothing to be said— no greetings or explanations. We were all here, with all the common grievances, very much in the grinding present.

"*Allo habbi*," Dror Harel said with a smile. He hadn't been summoned for extra duty and so had grabbed a few more hours sleep, now having the luxury of good humor. He carefully attended a battered gas burner with a *finjan* coffee pot, sitting haphazardly on a green jerrycan. Harel carefully poured the coffee into four dirty glasses and handed them out, the guys letting the grounds settle before languidly sipping. Boaz Kubovich paced on the far side of the sandbags, zipped up and by the book, chin strap secure, cradling his loaded rifle. He kept his eye on the far end of the street and the small crowd of Palestinians slowly drinking their own coffee, smoking, chatting, and getting ready for the day's activities.

A green IDF cargo transport had been backed up near our position, tailgate down, showing a pile of plastic riot shields and ammo boxes containing the full spectrum of projectiles—all the flares, tear gas, live ammo, and rubber bullets for the entire West Bank and Gaza and then some. We would be gearing up soon for another round of riot control, as each day brought a protest of rocks and bottles. Today was starting slow; the Palestinians slept in or watched Al Jazeera, not yet assembling on the street in force. Kubovich stood sharp-eyed and vigilant while we pulled ourselves out of our haze.

A soldier handed the glass back to Harel, who splashed water on it from the jerrycan and flung the grounds indiscriminately onto the street. He refilled it with coffee and extended it in my direction. I took the glass and caught a strong whiff of body odor from Harel—reminding me that I, too, stank, as I had slept in my uniform more nights than I could remember.

David Ostrov, my buddy from South Africa, sat down

beside me and leaned against the sandbags. He'd been selected, as I had, to go on the supplemental mission—either as punishment or confirmation of competence, I couldn't tell which. We had both spent most of the night riding around to help arrest a possibly fictitious Palestinian suspect deep in the city. Two jeeps, two Humvees, and almost eighteen guys joined the party. We drove all over fuck—our twenty-something commanding officer, Alon Carmeli, was not proficient at map reading. We even stopped and asked directions from two beaten-down Palestinians in work clothes who were on route to a checkpoint at four in the morning. One, who wore a sweat-stained Yankees cap, pointed out the street, not pausing about giving assistance, probably fearing reprisals should he not answer or be elusive. I knew none of this was supposed to make sense, but I was nevertheless surprised to discover that it really didn't.

When we had gotten to the house, I didn't have to go inside until later. I just had to stand guard outside, which was a reprieve of sorts. A squad of eight entered the house and turned it inside out, throwing everything on the ground: wedding pictures, *Star Wars* pajamas, a bin of onions, a bottle of aspirin, an orange plastic cup— random items from an ordinary life. I never learned if this was one of our "show dominance" tactics that Carmeli regularly enjoyed, or if we were truly searching for a security suspect.

This was the third time I had participated in one of these shakedowns. The first time I had to stand over four terrified kids—all younger than seven—and try and remain unbendable. In all the screaming and crying, I deliberately didn't want to say "it will be okay," because at that moment, it didn't seem even remotely likely. Always plenty of drama, with the hysterical women and children, everyone awoken to their worst fears, the IDF at their doorstep to trash the house and arrest anyone who didn't like it. Last night, we had found no weapons or terrorists, but, as I said, we may not have been looking for any.

Now watching Ostrov sip his coffee, I instinctively felt he shared my growing contempt and incredulity that what we were doing had any enduring value to the IDF, to Israel, to anybody. I swatted this away, because out of all my army buds, Ostrov was the most gung-ho and the biggest army asshole, someone who kept his eye on a prize that had become increasingly invisible. I liked his fitness and aggression, but his lack of cynicism worried me. When I volunteered for the IDF from my snug little Long Island suburbia, I knew part of the bargain would be to grow suspicious of the security framework, as tough experience with guns and bureaucracies colored my thinking. We were still the good guys, but now I had to think harder, hoping for a clearer concept of who I would be at the end of the tunnel.

I stood up, stretched, ambled over to the truck, and took out a few shields, leaning them against the sandbags where we sat. I like to slowly gear up, making sure all the straps and Velcro are to my liking, weeding out happenstance and error. The shields stood ready for the order to push the Palestinians back to their side of the street, or just disperse them—a distinction with no difference from my end. The way we had been doing it was to pair up—one guy held the shield, protecting his buddy from the hail of rocks and bottles, which allowed him to fire with a steady hand. I kicked the gravel with my boot and looked around at the dilapidated buildings—I wanted whatever we would do to begin already. I was also angry. The feeling had been with me so long it had melted into me, and I couldn't remember what life would be like without it. The yellow winter sun warmed me and brought awareness to my aching fingers, as the cuticles were cracked and infected from the dryness. I pulled off a sliver of dry skin, satisfied when it hurt and bled.

I sat down and closed my eyes to test how strong the fatigue pulled. I was content when my lids flipped open—I would be plenty awake for the next several hours at least. Yehuda Alkana told us a settler group was on the move today and would roll into the town for the modest pleasure of pissing off the Palestinians and tweaking the nose of the IDF, all in the name of a grand statement promoting the virtues of West Bank settlement.

"Yoni, you did your bit yesterday. Today I'll take my crack on the shield," Ostrov said in his clipped South African English, underscoring that neither of us had much enthusiasm for shooting anymore. Given the eternal and ambiguous nature of the mission, which was to keep everything at a simmer, we knew that nothing we did or did not do would bring any improvement. Maintaining a shitty stalemate was the best possible outcome. I felt comforted by the fact that Ostrov, too, was a volunteer, and had arrived on these shores with an economics degree at the advanced age of twenty-three. I was a few years behind him, with no college, coming to Israel with my own weird concepts of Zionism and duty. I knew what Israel meant to my former high school classmates back home in Westbury, New York. For them, Israel would always be a hyper-idealized place of beautiful contrasts and manageable conflicts—a land of undisputed excellence, and always the refuge from any future Holocausts in the United States or Europe. More broadly, we all tacitly acknowledged Eretz Yisrael as the undisputed warehouse of every possible manifestation of the Jewish soul and longing. These thoughts still burned true, but other ideas had begun to creep into the mix.

The bullets we now used were metal slugs coated in hard rubber to reduce their velocity, fired by jamming a packet of three down an enlarged tube anchored to the ends of our rifles—the shot powered by the gas emitted from a blank cartridge. The bullets, black cylinders half an inch wide and

5

three-quarters long, could embed themselves deep in the flesh should they hit at close range. After thirty yards, they would usually bounce off skull or bone, leaving a jagged cut. When we fired the rubber bullets in packets of three, each slug drifted in its own random trajectory as it tumbled through the air, further allaying any fears we personally were responsible for the injury we inflicted. It had come down the grapevine that if you needed to take down a troublemaker, you could break open the cellophane holding the three bullets and load the gun with just one, ensuring greater velocity and accuracy. Alkana had tried this several times with the envisioned results—but as a new immigrant, I felt obligated to do things by the book.

"I'll set up for the rubber," I told Ostrov. "More theater of the absurd." I scanned the dusty street past our barricade toward Arab Hebron and looked at the drab concrete buildings with rebar sticking out of the top, streaking the gray cement with brown rust. The stores had their shutters pulled down, steel doors firmly in place, entire facades dilapidated and rusted. The knots of Palestinian youths who patrolled the end of the street might as well have been rusted, too, given their overall look of poverty and slack expressions. Political setbacks, settler violence, and the endless drone of shuttle diplomacy were all just a background hum when I looked down my gun sights as young Palestinians ran to the end of their courage to throw Molotovs or rocks. Usually, the hulking presence of our squad would ensure that the missile landed short of its mark. But once a day the protesters' anger would boil and the level of confrontation reached fever pitch, the mob boldly advancing down the street. We aimed for the legs and let loose. Head injuries were not uncommon, nor suspect, given the chaotic nature of the encounters. Afterward, an ambulance was called, and we chased down the lightly injured, the others fleeing back to their homes or hiding behind old women in the *souk*.

The next day the sun rose, all players took their mark, and another day unfolded with the same ritualized symmetry.

I had been in the army two years, spent time in Lebanon, and now had to reconcile that any chance of being a soldier as I originally conceived it had passed. In basic training, I imagined how I would cut down Hezbollah fighters by the score with precision shots from the mortar or light machine gun, the poor suckers ill-informed about the deadly and efficient IDF fighting forces. When I was finally up north and on patrol, my mind was anesthetized from the crushing boredom of sameness day after day. When the attacks came, the Hezbollahniks proved to be savvy fighters. They expertly hid devastating roadside bombs, blew up our convoys with Sagger anti-tank missiles, and always melted away into villages the moment I could draw a bead on any of them. I figured Hezbollah knew exactly how fucked up everything here at occupation ground zero was, adding Hebron to an endless list of grievances that no doubt kept them warm all winter and sharpened their resolve to fight.

Despite all the difficulties in the Lebanon Security Zone, I felt proud that my guys stood tall. We maintained tight discipline even after months of bunker living, remembered our training when things got hot, fought hard, and looked out for one another. When bad things happened, we ran the wounded to the helicopter and aggressively secured the perimeter, keeping everything tight and dialed. I felt close to my guys—even the assholes who weren't pulling their weight in training—all of us bonded in acknowledgment that this was real soldiering. We were true warriors with our guns and artillery; I fired my rifle at shapes and shadows, satisfied when I didn't shit my pants.

Now in Hebron, I reluctantly lowered my expectations. After the first week's duty, I concluded that despite Hebron being an historically important city for the Jews, with patriarchs and matriarchs buried here and there, it was now a patch of dust and dirt inhabited by two hundred thousand Arabs who didn't want us around. Today I knew I wanted to be far away, but it troubled me that I couldn't think of the location, either in Israel or the wider world. I believed, somehow, that the arbitrary nature of my service would suddenly take meaning, direction, and purpose, but it was slow in coming. Nobody I knew or had read in the media was smart enough to disentangle and make sense of the handful of soldier deaths that occurred each month like clockwork. If the heavens fell, or if I got shot or blown up, my death would contribute nothing to any cause, philosophy, or movement.

Safe to say that all this was the usual experience of any starry-eyed schlub enlisting in the IDF. I pled guilty to wanting a test of my mettle, an adventure—and I received it in spades. I realized that when I shared my frustrations about our assignment with the folks back home, they could have a good belly laugh at my idiocy. But what the folks at home wouldn't get was the nature of my discomfort. I was fine with all the boredom, fatigue, hunger, and thirst—but on the bad days, it was the discord from what should be and what was that threatened to overwhelm me. Every morning when I got up—although some days it took longer than others—I realized that the world had changed. No longer were the Jews, Israelis, and IDF of the same body and mind, breathing the same air. These things had become nuanced and removed from one another, like three circles of a Venn diagram moving in opposition, where the point in common grew smaller each day.

As I looked around at my fellow soldiers, I remembered how Yitzhak Rabin was assassinated by a fellow Jew only a month ago. Yigal Amir, a young religious fanatic and a law student at Bar Ilan University, had chatted up the security people at the Tel Aviv Oslo Accords rally, earning their trust. When Rabin came by, Amir walked up right behind the prime minister and fired three hollow-point bullets, two hitting him in the back. Despite being a kick-ass soldier early on, Rabin never found it prudent to wear a ballistic vest—no matter how loud the crazies pounded on the barricades and got in his face, as they had in the weeks leading to that rally.

The television stations spun in crisis mode for days. Any time I looked at a television it showed the footage of a knot of policemen swarming Amir and frog-marching him off. More disturbing, and also in frequent rotation, was a clip filmed outside Ichilov Hospital, where Rabin had been taken. It showed a group of bearded men with *kipas* and dowdy women in long skirts, having long prayed for this outcome, gleefully chanting, "Rabin is dead!" I recoiled with disgust and disbelief yet could not look away. I watched hours of television as reporters repeated themselves, and the same footage recycled again and again. "With horror, grave sorrow, and deep grief, the government of Israel announces the death of Prime Minister and Defense Minister Yitzhak Rabin, murdered by an assassin."

Rabin's murder underscored that whatever feelings I held about how Jewish people the world over were united in fraternity and humanity, I needed to adapt to new realities. Any goodwill toward the dour religious Zionists who made their homes here in Hebron—and our mission was to protect them—was gone. We were mercenaries now. No more righteous crusades or purity of arms to avenge the spilled blood of Jewish children from bygone pogroms. The assassination brought to the fore the idea that the army carried out orders—withdrawing from areas of the Occupied Territories, going on joint patrols with the Palestinian Authority—that a significant portion of Israelis couldn't accept. Now every last patrol in Hebron felt like a political statement, and I had to suck it up, obey orders, and run out the clock in this deranged soap opera.

When news of the assassination had broken, our unit was at a large training base in the north. The mood of the camp lingered in sadness and dark, agonized introspection as the shameful act sank in. Despite the robust pro-settler stance of the officer corps, Rabin received eulogies for being the heroic commander of the Palmach, a legendary unit in the War of Independence, and his later support for Oslo was glossed over. That Amir had, like us, been a Golani soldier just a few years before made us suspicious that the public would soon assume we were equally violent and ideological. Amir had been most "un-Golani" because he had accomplished his deed through guile and stealth rather than good marksmanship, using dum-dum bullets that exploded on impact and firing at point-blank range.

We didn't have to wait long before hearing scuttlebutt about what kind of soldier Amir had been—the sort who shot Palestinians' rooftop water heaters for sport when on patrol in Gaza, or cut their clotheslines, always looking to ensure that the enmity between us and the Palestinians never stopped festering. As a Golani, I learned that this behavior was tolerated, if not encouraged, especially if your sector drew heat. But even in this environment, Amir was repeatedly told to knock it off.

We spent about ten days being teary-eyed crybabies, all sadness and solemnity. And then a "boys will be boys" mindset and black humor returned. When President Clinton eulogized Rabin, he concluded his remarks with the memorable statement, *"Shalom, haver"* ("Goodbye, friend"), which instantly became a bumper sticker and all-around catchphrase. For us, the tagline replaced *"Hasta la vista*, baby" when we wanted to indicate a painful finality for our enemies.

Now, as I scanned the street and sipped my coffee, I tried unsuccessfully to think about what life would be like out of the army. Today would be another long, tedious day, and the moment arrived that I went from being cold to uncomfortably hot. The Palestinians would soon start their chanting or the settlers would burst on the scene and initiate whatever stupid shit they had planned. Rubber bullets would be fired, blood would flow, and another journal entry would be logged for humanity.

A dented and dirty red Mitsubishi Lancer slowly pulled to the side of the street and parked behind the truck with our gear. The occupants were trying to pass as civilians, as the car bore yellow Israeli license plates—red or black plates would have loudly broadcast a police or military vehicle. But nobody was fooled.

"Your girlfriends arrived," I said to Ostrov, who clenched his fist and probably wanted to hit me. I was still drinking my coffee, so I appreciated his restraint.

The two swarthy and athletic men who emerged from the car looked like they had jumped out of a Shin Bet catalog for activewear—both were styling cool shades, dark shiny Adidas warmup jackets, and blue jeans, with holstered nine-millimeter pistols over the back-right pocket. Ostrov held jealous anger for any member of a security force who he believed operated at a higher level than his—and as his friend, it was my duty irritate him as best I could.

"Our lot never gets better with these blokes around," Ostrov said after the men had drifted down a side street.

The Palestinians picked up on the semaphore of the new arrivals and threw rocks, some of which rolled up against our sandbags. I smelled the smoke of a burning tire and heard the volume of chanting and cursing spike—the curtain was going up! I peeked over the sandbags and regarded the news cameramen crowded together in an alleyway, checking their cameras and microphones, aware now that the orchestra played an introductory tune and things might happen. The journalists, mostly men, wore athletic shoes and stained, collared shirts, and several had bicycle helmets with wrinkled "PRESS" cards taped to the front. All looked pale and out of shape, with cigarettes dangling from their mouths and concerned expressions.

Half of our guys wanted to shoot all members of the media. The other half, myself included, regarded the cameramen and reporters as pains in the ass who deserved to be shot, just not on purpose. It wasn't right that we were out here all day, every day, but for the thirty seconds things got out of hand— with soldiers shooting and screaming, whacking Palestinians to the ground with rifle butts, lining up the day's catch in riot cuffs—it was all over the BBC and CNN what a bunch of war criminals we were. Don't even ask about the Arab media. And no matter what the Palestinians did, they were always the victims. The cameras and reporters never mentioned the rocks, Molotovs, and occasional bullets that the *shabab* hurled at us. Those fucking pundits got up in the morning *surprised* that Israel continued to exist, even though we had been here, on this crappy street, going on thirty years. Absolutely I felt misunderstood. At the end of the day, Hebron was an ugly city full of zealot whack jobs. I wanted to save my blood for a battle that counted.

I heard grinding and the low throb of an approaching diesel engine, but didn't feel the need to rouse myself to peer over the sandbags. "The circus has arrived," Kubovich said.

I needed to get my head out of the clouds. I slowly stood and picked up a rock—throwing it hard down the street, and frowning when it landed short. I resolutely inhaled and closed my flak jacket. "Jim, jim, jimalaya," I said, kicking Ostrov in the boots, making him twitch his lips with the old Palmach work chant.

Despite growing up in South Africa, Ostrov was like me: raised with an idealized Zionism fully divorced from modern realities, and which expressed itself in his Jewish day school, pious *schul*, even his family's *pushke* for gathering coins for tree planting. Ostrov's entire family had made *aliyah*—risen—to Israel in 1993, I guess to escape the violence and lawlessness of majority rule that had come to his beloved Cape Town in 1994. Last April when the elections made majority rule official, he announced to the platoon that anyone cracking wise about the new government in South Africa would answer to him. Things felt more normal a few weeks later when Ostrov came close to a smile from a joke about cheap Johannesburg real estate. But when Sergei Chaimovich called him "Mandela" during a soccer game, Ostrov coolly doubled him over with a punch to the gut.

The elder Ostrov had taken a job as a high-level tech executive, so the family enjoyed the good life—"posh," as Ostrov called it—in Ra'anana, north of Tel Aviv. My family was all back on Long Island, but when on furlough, I stayed with my uncle who lived in Giv'atayim, a working-class neighborhood east of the city.

A group of old Arab men and women cautiously ambled past our position on their way to the *souk*, eyes downward. They carried baskets and folding, wheeled shopping carts—the type old people in New York City use. I picked up my rifle and hung it around my neck, absently tapping the loaded magazine, reassured that I took no chances. I looked at Kubovich, Alkana, and Chaimovich for a sign of needing to do something, and not seeing any officers, sat down again.

My mind ruminated out of habit, and excitement or boredom brought no answer or cessation. It was always the same question: how had I ended up here? What was the chain of events, both lofty and ridiculous, that allowed me to exist at these coordinates of place and time? As I mentioned, I had craved true experience, a test to understand myself better, to know my soul in granular fashion, to follow the logic of my commitment to Israel, the IDF, the righteousness of aggressive Zionism. Back in Westbury, other guys from the neighborhood had done similar stints in the IDF, coming home looking stoic and mature, as if having gained a hard-fought truth. When I pumped them for information, encouragement, shortcuts, and insider tips, a few tried to clue me in, saying I wouldn't be a good fit. With the Oslo accords, the modern Palestinian

Authority, and the quagmire in Lebanon, the age of the IDF hero had passed. But I didn't listen, believing they referenced only my physical fitness, or my nascent concept of politics. Perhaps they misread current political events that would cast aspersions on the IDF. I don't think they were discouraging me because they knew me personally—they didn't—but were talking to earlier versions of themselves.

Born to Binyamin and Tova Tager in Westbury—a leafy, quiet place—my upbringing was the usual for a family of observant Jews: synagogue on Saturdays, taking it easy on Shabbat, and the parents growing weary promoting the consumption of kosher food. On all points, allowances were made if life became impossible—"I'm having an argument with God," Dad said if he needed to go into the office on a Saturday, or if the office pizza was vegetarian instead of kosher. My dad was a chemist by training, working as a product design and development manager at Pollux Pharmaceuticals, a contract manufacturer of nutritional supplements and over-the-counter pills.

Binyamin, or "Benny" as he was known at work, enjoyed being righteous in the dictionary sense of the word and did all the thankless synagogue stuff of *gemilut hesed*—bestowing kindness—to those in need as well as leading daily *minyan* prayers. Tova, my mother, fit in well with the orientation of our community but with less outward enthusiasm than Dad, resigning herself to fundraisers, the Tikkun Olam Committee, and Sisterhood meetings at our Conservadox congregation of Shaarey Tefilla.

I attended the Zacharias Frankel School in nearby Williston Park, a Jewish school covering grades K–12. Sure, we had daily prayers, and all food was confined to *parve* and kosher dairy, but

most classes were secularly academic. The best among us went on
to the Ivy League rather than become Torah scholars and rabbis,
although each grade had its share. The school boasted that critical thinking and an inquiry-based approach was the essence of
academic excellence in addition to the Jewish way of the ages.

Along this path, I learned about Israel, and how great
it was just to walk and breathe Jewish air, on Jewish land,
knowing the Jewish government ensured nobody had to work
on Yom Kippur and kosher food could be found everywhere.
In fifth grade, I carefully made a drawing of Masada, using as
reference the cover of the Yigael Yadin book, which had rested
for time immemorial on the coffee table in the living room.
The next year, I had the assignment of creating a model of a
historical synagogue or another site important to the Jewish
people. I rendered the Western Wall plaza out of dried maca-
roni glued to cardboard—a big hit with my mom.

When seventh grade started, I threw myself wholeheart-
edly into the Israel curriculum set by Rav Abramov, a round,
middle-aged instructor of religious studies. He taught us about
the history, character, and temperament of modern Israel:
how Israel would do anything for peace—even give up the
endless empty defensive distance of the Sinai Peninsula, as
Menachem Begin had done with the Camp David Accords.
When Abramov covered this, a misty disbelief drifted across
his face, like Jews had landed on the moon and lit Shabbat
candles. He told us that Israel forewent $17 billion in invest-
ments, turning it all over to Egypt. "For *what?*" he yelled. "All
those farms, factories, apartments, irrigation systems, roads,
thrown away"—a reference to Sadat's assassination in 1981.
I heard this and shook my head, dumbfounded at how things
could have turned out so wrong.

Abramov and the other teachers enthusiastically set the
stage for when we took our eighth-grade class trip to Israel.
We learned the geography, the rudiments of how the Knesset

differed from the US Congress, the agriculture and industrial products—illustrated with cherry tomatoes and Elite chocolates—the ingathering of exiles from all over the world, and, of course, the wars. We even used class time to watch the 1979 classic *Raid on Entebbe*, suspending our disbelief with Charles Bronson as Dan Shomron, the paratrooper commander who executed Operation Thunderbolt. Bronson's gruff voice may have lacked any nod or wink to Hebrew-accented English, but such a trifle didn't impact our enjoyment. We boys celebrated the message that Bronson was chosen for the part, because nobody did righteous anger and vengeance like him. I watched *Death Wish* and *Death Wish II* on videocassettes at a sleepover at Kevin Weinstein's house, gleefully bouncing in my sleeping bag when the odious muggers got their brains blown out for their evil ways.

Abramov, usually jovial and smiling, became solemn when he explained the relationship between the Jewish people and Arabs. He relished intricate *gematria* and the delicate nuances of religious observance the way a gourmet savors an exquisite morsel—yet he offered no gradation for the Jewish-Arab situation, defining it as *sinat chinam* (baseless hatred) by the Arabs toward the Jews. In a long, rambling lecture, he explained how Yasser Arafat needed to wear a military uniform and pistols when he addressed the United Nations in 1974, and how the true Arab culture of violence and anti-Semitism was represented by the pistols.

When Abramov brought up facts about Israel—how Haj Amin el Husseini collaborated with Hitler, or how the Arabs terrorized Jews in British Mandate Palestine and pressured the British to keep the Jews out, especially during the years of the Holocaust—he liked to conclude with a "just so you know." He said this in a slightly sinister way, inferring that not to know was to be ignorant of a significant, perhaps transformative, truth.

For my bar mitzvah, my father's brother, Mordechai, who emigrated to Israel a decade previous, sent me a copy of *Myths and Facts 1982: A Concise Record of the Arab-Israeli Conflict.* He inscribed it with these words: "Being Jewish is like being a gun-slinger in the old West—got to have a fast draw and plenty of ammunition." The book was arranged with "myths"—inaccurate platitudes—followed by "facts"—lengthy answers full of scrupulously researched quotes and data. I threw myself into learning the material, and tried to read a few pages each night, convinced the information was of vital importance and I could help push back the curtain of ignorance about Israel that enveloped the world. The book, a bit too advanced for my thirteen-year-old brain, had a reference section that I studied carefully, perusing the different maps, timelines, chronologies, and texts of important documents such as the Camp David Accords and UN Security Council Resolution 242. I spent the most time looking at a data table that compared the Arab World against Israel, covering leaders, land area, population, literacy, life expectancy, estimated gross national product / gross domestic product, annual defense expenditures, combat aircraft, tanks, and armed forces. All the data reinforced the resounding miracle of Israel—militarily, culturally, and economically. But my favorite appendix by far was "Arab Attitudes towards Israel." This was a compendium of everything hateful an Arab leader had ever said about Jews or Israel over the thirty-four years of Israeli existence the book covered. The first quote from Arab League Secretary General Azzam Pasha in 1948 set the tone: "This will be a war of extermination and a momentous massacre which will be spoken of like the Mongolian massacres and the Crusades." Like Bronson's movies, the bad guys were clearly identifiable and deserved only violent destruction.

In eighth grade, as our winter trip loomed in our minds, the curriculum on Israel stepped into high gear. Perhaps the capstone lesson, and the one I anticipated most, was meeting Mr. Pinchas Levine, affectionately known as "One-Armed Pinchas." Pinchas enjoyed an ordinary life as a furrier in Brooklyn in the mid-1940s until he boarded a boat to British-mandate Palestine to fight in the Haganah—the paramilitary force that later became the IDF. He spoke to the students departing for Israel every year but was also a cheerful presence at our community Kabbalat Shabbat services and Holocaust Remembrance Day.

A few years previous, Pinchas still had a grandchild enrolled in the school, which made his effusive good nature part of the pick-up and drop-off scene. He had a craggy face and a nose too large to bear any exaggeration, accented with heavy-framed glasses long out of fashion. He had a penchant for pinstriped slacks and rarely wore a jacket, his white dress shirt revealing straps underneath that held on the scuffed and faded yellow prosthetic device that extended below his right bicep. In the afternoons in front of the school he insisted on getting out of his maroon Buick to pick up his grandchild, even though this was not required, and it delayed the other parents, who stayed in their cars. Parents, teachers, students all treated Pinchas warmly and with a cautious deference due to his heroic status.

Abramov talked Pinchas up for two weeks as we studied Israel's War of Independence. "That would be a good question to ask Mr. Levine next week," he might say to a question about an early battle. Or, "Remember to ask Mr. Levine, as he probably was near Jerusalem at that time."

I arrived at school extra early on the day of Pinchas's visit, worried that I would miss any opening remarks by the great man, who was destined to be regarded as a historical figure by future generations. Soon the gaunt man strolled into our classroom, his bald head reflecting the fluorescent lights, his warm simile infectious.

"Hello *kinderlach*," he said in a raspy voice. He slowly scanned the rows for students he recognized, greeting them with a brief nod. "A real experience, as you kids might say. Arriving in Israel in 1946, prehistory. First boat when it was safe to travel there at the end of the war. *Ach,* that's World War II. Did I know anything about Israel, Palestine, the British, Arabs? Only the price of a pelt in Toronto, I did. The Haganah—so much marching! Always so hot."

Despite having done the same presentation every year for decades, Pinchas still needed prompting from Abramov to tell his more historical anecdotes. After accepting the offered chair, Pinchas tried to focus on what we might want to know, his broad smile settling into one of sly amusement. He started with stories about what illegal immigration and general subversion looked like under the British before the fighting broke out. "Remember all radio transceivers were banned," he said, wagging a finger. "I mean, it was okay to have a radio, some great songs then. Irving Berlin, 'Dancing Cheek to Cheek,' good song. But the radio couldn't broadcast. So, of course, my nudnik cousin, Shaul, had a transceiver. He was a big Haganah muckety-muck. A real pain in the *tuchas* for the British. Every night he would make his broadcast, tell the units, agents, hidden in Tel Aviv, what was going on, where to go, what to steal. The British, they knew. *Of course!* But they knew only what area of the city had the illegal radio. They didn't know where it was hid. Shaul got word when the Brits were launching a raid to look for the radio. Who knows what 'Shaul' means?"

"A fox!" we chanted in unison.

"*Ach,* that's right," Pinchas said. "He was smart like that fox. Shaul took that radio apart, broke it down into twenty pieces. He gave me half the pieces, told me to go to the Zonsteins, the Levys, the Mograbis, and others, and give each of them a piece."

"Where did the families hide the radio parts?" Ruthi, the girl who sat in front of me, asked excitedly.

"The *balabustas,* that's who I gave the parts to. Every *balabusta* has a special place in her kitchen or house. A place her husband, the kids, the British, nobody can find. I didn't want to know. Nobody knew. We just handed over the parts, and a few days later came back and picked them up. Those *pishers* never had a chance."

Pinchas became more somber when he spoke of how when the fighting broke out his unit mobilized, first moving south to Lod, then working slowly up the Jerusalem corridor. I realized this was the special moment, and hung on his every word, so excited to have living history in our midst. "We had casualties every day in the beginning," he said, telling how his unit of twenty guys advanced on an Arab village when a sniper shot him, a flash of pain and regret echoing across his face.

"And I was taken all the way back to Tel Aviv that night. My dear wife, Malka, *zichrona livracha*, was back in Brooklyn. She couldn't get to where I was for almost four months. And when she arrived and saw me, guess what?"

Our minds raced, trying to find the answer.

"*Ach*, she couldn't recognize me—I had grown such a *lux-ooorious* mustache. I looked like someone else." He twisted the tip of a huge, imaginary mustache with his left hand, six inches to the side of his clean-shaven grin.

"What gun did you carry?" I asked.

"I had a Mauser Karabiner along with a few of the other guys. My buddy, Izzy, had a Lee-Enfield. But there were rifles from Spain and Czechoslovakia, too. Always a problem. The day after fighting, we'd need more bullets. Never knew what ammunition would show up. If we could even use the bullets. I laugh about it now, but I cried back then. *Ach*, how can a war be fought when the bullets don't fit the gun? But we got through it. Everything turned out okay."

Pinchas looked grim for a few beats but then perked up and launched into an anecdote underscoring the irrationality of his officers, regaling us with tales of how he would emphatically tell them in Yiddish to "*gai kukken aften yam*"—go crap in the sea. Abramov would have scolded us for using strong language, but for One-Armed Pinchas, all was permitted. Pinchas further explained how he got away with cursing the officers because none spoke Yiddish—being *sabras*, they spoke Hebrew. Pinchas and his fellow foreign-born soldiers mainly spoke Yiddish, emphasizing that nobody had any clue as to what the hell was going on.

Pinchas good-naturedly fielded further questions about the food they ate, the songs they sang, and how it felt to be in Israel the first few months of its existence. We were all elated, wondering if our own lives would ever shine so brightly, and envious of Pinchas' hardship and sacrifice.

The fall of that year dragged on forever as I dutifully went to the *b'nei mitzvot* of my friends and relatives, eagerly awaiting my chance to get on a plane with my class and fly to the modern, almost cosmopolitan, State of Israel as well as Eretz Yisrael, the conceptual homeland of all Jews the world over. This was to be my first trip "by myself"—glossing over the teachers, guides, counselors, drivers, and armed guards all making sure no harm came to us. A comprehensive itinerary included soaking in the syrupy waters of the Dead Sea, peering at Syria through binoculars from Mt. Hermon, crying at Yad Vashem, praying at the Wailing Wall in Jerusalem, and learning various lessons from local rabbis, archeologists, and naturalists. Although I had been to Israel twice before to visit Uncle Moti, who immigrated in the 1970s, the latest trip represented a departure from lazy days with the family on the beach at Herzylia, introducing a higher level of understanding of how Israel had come into being, survived, and flourished. This trip was to learn about Israel in a holistic way: religion fusing with history and emotion as you stood on the land and breathed it in deeply.

Out of all the exceptional things we saw, one stood out further than any other: the revered grounds of Latrun. The dusty spot amid agricultural lands wasn't a synagogue or a biblical site but a dynamic piece of history, its importance in my spiritual awakening surpassing any pieties a house of worship might imbue. The battered old police fort built during the British Mandate strategically overlooked the road that connected Jerusalem with Tel Aviv. The modest stone structure vaguely resembled a small crusader fort, a turret with slit windows rising above the two-story rectangular building. The façade, bullet-pocked and weathered, spoke of the furious fighting that had taken place during the War of Independence when Jordan's Arab Legion repelled two full assaults by the Haganah—the troops being poorly equipped Holocaust survivors who took high casualties. Ariel Sharon, then a mere platoon commander who would become prime minister, was wounded in the first assault ten days after Israel's declaration of Independence.

Off to one side of the police station sat the armor museum with twenty-five tanks and artillery pieces parked in chronological order. When our tour bus opened its doors, we raced to the tanks and tentatively stood upon them in reverence and awe of the heroes and villains who had operated this machinery. Soviet-made armor captured in the various wars was also displayed. Our fingers traced the twisted metal of their battle scars as we imagined the explosions and screams. Our guides, Oren and Gershom, radiated a profound sense of destiny as they dramatically made the landscape come alive with the battles of Latrun throughout the Biblical, Crusader, Ottoman, British Mandate, and modern Israeli ages. The vaunted Merkava (chariot), the IDF's main battle tank, got the premier slot in front of the police station, the historic landmark a perfect photo backdrop for this awesome weapon of aggressive self-defense. Oren told how the Merkava had performed brilliantly in Lebanon three years earlier, animatedly explaining that its 1,500-horsepower, turbocharged diesel engine sat in the front to provide greater protection to the crew. His voice lowered a notch, saying that in Israel, a small country, every soldier counted, and no effort or price was too big to bring our boys home.

The history of the weapons, the fort, and the land was only the warmup. As the day wore on and we got our fill of battles and glory, I became aware that adjacent to the parking lot, an amphitheater and parade grounds had been decorated for a ceremony. IDF transports were nearby, and a crowd of soldiers milled around the parking lot, looking happy and relaxed in clean uniforms. Gershom told us we would have a picnic dinner that night and observe the induction of soldiers into an IDF armor unit.

When the sun sank, an IDF band struck up hits I recognized by Foreigner and Madonna. The musicians played with precision as the lead singer, an energetic young man, did an excellent job, even if his English phrasing was slightly off. We put on our sweaters as the evening chill settled over the grounds, the encroaching darkness concentrating our attention to the lighted center of the amphitheater. The soldiers to be inducted stood outside the grounds in formation with a rigid solemnity etched on their faces. Officers puttered around the lighted area, organizing two tables with books and M16s. I noted fancy insignia on a few older men and figured these were the high-ranking officers who ran the show.

An officer called out a crisp command, the band played a martial tune, and the soldiers marched into the amphitheater and stood at attention. Proud relatives in the audience enthusiastically pointed out their young men and shared loud comments with family members, while younger siblings stood up and waved, even though they had been instructed moments previously not to directly regale the troops. The soldiers stood like statues, solemn and unflinching, instructed to show ultimate decorum. Periodically a father stood up to snap a picture, looking satisfied, while the mothers appeared grim. Another officer came to the lectern and told us all to stand for Hatikvah. I sang the words unconsciously, thinking only about the bullet marks on the building, the tanks, and how when there was a need, Jews picked up arms, figured out how to use them, and gave the evil of the world one hell of a fight.

After Hatikvah, the brigadier general, a portly fellow wearing a khaki shirt with his olive beret under an epaulet, walked to a lectern and commended all the young men for embarking on an extraordinary journey of self-sacrifice and patriotism. When our schoolboy Hebrew failed to hold up to the difficulty of the speech, Gershom translated the main bits in a loud whisper.

"Look around at your comrades, and keep it first in your minds that we are the sons and daughters of one Eretz Yisrael," the brigadier general said, taking his time to let his eyes linger on the troops. "There is no other country in this world, no other place under heaven—not that we would desire it. The village in which my father was born was utterly destroyed. I journeyed with him back to Hungary to look for the spot where his house once stood. Nothing remained. Even the stones of fences and fireplaces had been taken away to be used for other purposes by the gentiles. The village was long gone, an overgrown and forgotten patch of countryside. Standing there, I felt its absence, the void like a lead weight on my soul, and I wept. I heard the shrieks of terror from my grandfather and grandmother as they watched their home, their village, burn. In my mind I saw every atrocity. As I stood and looked at the landscape, felt the history, and heard my father's memories, one wish stirred my thoughts like no other: to whisper into the ears of my grandparents, to tell them about our prosperous, wonderful country. To tell them about the miracle of the IDF, about Dimona, about Entebbe. About the honor given to their grandson of contributing to the rebirth of our people, of putting the force of steel and fire into the oath 'Never again.' This honor will now be yours. Long live the Israel Defense Forces! Long live the State of Israel!"

The brigadier general finished his remarks to cheers and applause, taking two steps back into the line of the other dignitaries. Lightheaded, I felt the immensity of the responsibility these soldiers were undertaking, answering their country's call without discussion, naysaying, or equivocation.

An officer stepped to the lectern and read the names of the soldiers. One by one, each soldier progressed to a table where he stopped and saluted the commander and brigadier general. He was presented with a palm-sized Bible and an oily M16, the diesel fuel coating for storage having been cursorily wiped off. The soldier transferred the Bible and rifle to his left hand and pressed the two tightly together, so to shake the hands of the commander and brigadier general.

The name "Shimon Lapinsky" came over the loudspeaker. One teacher whispered that he was an American who had volunteered, his efforts even more outstanding because he was a *hayal boded*—a lone soldier—with no immediate family in Israel. This was the pinnacle of devotion: someone who wasn't compelled to serve, the way Israelis are, but had chosen to volunteer, be away from family and friends, open his life to the unknown dangers of service and life in a country far from the comforts of home.

When every soldier had received their Bible and rifle, the commander walked up to the lectern and scowled—his voice filling with rage and awe, close to a yell. "Dear fighters, you are about to accept the mission of protecting the people of Israel—Am Yisrael—and its legacy. Know that today we are still challenged to live in our homeland free and unopposed. Our enemies will continue to provoke us on numerous fronts. As you start your life as a soldier, a member of Am Yisrael, remember the Bible is the source of our power, the strength of our union, the flame that burns in our hearts. Today you will pledge your allegiance to the IDF. As your voices rise and become one, the Jewish people will live and flourish. This is the response to Babylon and Rome, who exiled our nation; the response to the Nazis, who almost annihilated us; the response today to our enemies who, with all their energy and ability, attempt to kill and demoralize us. In every generation our enemies come forth with evil intent. We will answer them—*Am Yisrael chai!* Today you will join the IDF's Armored Division, the vital force which will be the front line to shatter any enemy's advance. The duty to defend the State of Israel rests on each and every one of you. With strength and ultimate courage, rise up and go with success."

After a pause, the commander's tone grew more somber and his cadence slowed, indicating that he would say the oath to be repeated by the individual soldiers. The soldiers extended their right hands to their sides, holding their rifles vertically while pressing the Bible against the handguard with the left hand. The commander looked off to the farthest corner of the amphitheater before intoning:

> I swear and commit to maintain allegiance to the State of Israel, its laws, and its authorities;
>
> To accept upon myself unconditionally the discipline of the Israel Defense Forces;
>
> To obey all orders and instructions given by authorized commanders;
>
> To devote all my energies;
>
> Even sacrifice my life for the protection of the homeland and the liberty of Israel.
>
> I swear!
>
> I swear!
>
> I swear!

A great cheer went up. I was envious of the adventure the soldiers were embarking upon. The training, the physical punishment—these were the essential ingredients to being who I imagined I wanted to become. Not a devout person, I put little thought or emphasis on prayer or spirituality every time I sat in synagogue, seeking any diversion—often imagining going with Charles Bronson to Entebbe, or being part of the paratrooper unit that captured Ammunition Hill in Jerusalem.

Seeing the soldiers with their rifles and Bibles underscored how deeply I loved Israel and the IDF more than I'd loved anything else in creation. I wondered how incredible it would be to look the brigadier general in the eyes, get in the truck, and head to Lebanon or wherever the battle was. With the force of history, the Bible, and the world celebrating the miracle that was Israel, how would any enemy ever find a foothold? We would bring the region to heel, showing all countries of the world that Israel was a light unto the nations—like the Bible said. The gun and the Bible proved the American soldier had left the world of the Diaspora for good, shedding all the materialism, weakness, confusion—spiritual rot—that comes from living in a wealthy country with secure borders. He was gaining the innate wisdom so obviously apparent in Israelis, but that no professor, course, or book could ever teach a teenager stuck in Westbury. My classmates and I had only the option to go home, maybe say a prayer, write a school report, or make a presentation, but this soldier could now pull the trigger himself and hasten his transformation.

With a diesel throb, the settler bus pulled up to the makeshift parking lot near our position. The arrival sparked our Palestinian counterparts to action and brought a spirited round of chanting accompanied by a higher volume of sling-shot-launched gravel that pinged and popped ever closer to the sandbags. The media started filming. The show had begun.

"Give me a fucking curfew," Chaimovich said. "Lock those bastards down. Blessings for everyone."

"Which bastards?" Ostrov asked.

Chaimovich looked darkly at Ostrov before muttering, "Your mother's cunt."

"A hundred years, that's what it will take," Ostrov said, ignoring Chaimovich, fastening his helmet strap. "Then the Messiah will come. Or maybe not."

I sat on a sandbag next to Ostrov, and we watched the settler bus make its final maneuvers before stopping. The bus said *Unitours* on the side, looking every inch a sleek, modern tourist machine with all the heat, A/C, and video that any traveler could wish for, the dark windows merging into the roof to provide maximum sightseeing. Looking at the luxury I was reminded of how nice it would be to go on furlough, get on a similar bus, fall into a seat, and let the road noise lull me into a deep sleep. Someone else could deal with all the responsibilities of the world for a few hours. I thought of a hot shower, sitting down to a table of Aunt Smadar's *kubbeh* soup, and eating an uninterrupted meal. A rock came flying toward me, and I quickly scooted off my perch, the action bringing me abruptly back to present circumstances.

The bus door opened with a hiss; the settler men came out, then the women. The men stood with hands on their hips and calmly regarded us soldiers, the chanting Palestinians, the dusty street, and the journalists as if it were a beautiful day to launch their sure-fire program to win friends and influence people. They had the usual knitted *kipot* on their heads, and dark pants and white shirts with the *tzitzit* fringes hanging out. They sported large machine pistols in neoprene holsters, or small-caliber pistols in their waistbands. They looked pale, hot, and greasy under their beards; the women looked not much better in their long dresses and head coverings.

Yaacov Kodesh, a soldier from our unit who had ridden on the bus as a guard, walked over and accepted an offered cup of coffee, nodding hello. "A hot one," he said. "Last night a trailer took a few bullets. No one hit."

"More goddamned Jewish charity," Ostrov said. "A full company to protect seven families on that hilltop. Fuck."

"Those caravans were Shamir's parting gift," Kodesh said. "Those assholes are pissed when the bullets miss. For every Jewish victim, the true Zionist reaction, according to them, is to build more settlements, plop down more caravans on hilltops, bring more crazies here, so even more shit can be stirred up."

Carmeli came over and scanned our faces, eyes lingering on the gas burner and *finjan*, probably about to inform us how we had transgressed some facet of military protocol. He looked at the settlers and then at us and frowned. He ordered us to gear up for a foot patrol, as the squad now had the great honor of escorting the settlers past the *souk* and to the *yeshiva*. I put on my helmet and picked up the shield, throwing it back into the truck, returning to the sandbags to remove the rubber-bullet launcher from my rifle. I would leave the tangible hazards of the street protest for those unseen, the possibility raising its head that here was an opportunity to prove my worth as a soldier. I closed my flak jacket, picked up my gun, and walked over to the settlers, trying not to look anyone in the eye.

The men, robustly middle-aged, spoke loudly, occasionally clapping one another on the shoulders, defiant and happy, radiating confidence and menace as they stood tall and casually surveyed the street. One man, whose clothes looked newer and cleaner than the rest, talked about Islamic Jihad leader Fathi Shikaki and how the Mossad had gunned him down in Malta in October. "Shikaki's walking in the street. The boys come by, two on a motorcycle. The one in back takes out his pistol with a silencer, shoots Shikaki twice in the head." The man paused, making his hand into a gun and pointing it at the imaginary corpse. "The motorcycle stops. The guy shoots one more time for insurance. They make sure no shell casings are left behind, then jump back on the motorcycle and speed away."

I drifted close, hoping for more exciting details—the man conducting himself with an air of languid self-assurance with his erect posture and head aimed upward. His beard was cropped close with the borders neatly trimmed. He rocked on his heels and tried to point his words to the larger group. He must have been a leader, as he sounded well-versed in *hasbara,* or explaining—the Israeli version of propaganda. The man knew about the security services, telling the assembled how the Mossad Bayonet Unit had sent Islamic Jihad into total disarray with the assassination. "Of course, those bastards don't have any succession plan. It's not like anyone wrote up a job description or can call the employment agency."

The women ranged from teenagers to *balabustas,* whose tight, cruel faces showed nervous excitement. I knew not to talk to them or even stand too close, hoping to be quickly done with the lot. I put a magazine in my rifle and chambered a bullet. I had that acid feeling in my stomach that I could taste in my throat, but the adrenaline kept it in check. I walked over to Alkana and punched him in the arm. "Gum?"

I waited for Alkana to fish out a stick while I looked at my boots and the sky with a growing sense of agitation. We'd be walking down narrow streets where any shithead could drop a cinderblock or Molotov on us from a rooftop. No chanting, no loud protest, no nothing—just serious injury for a bunch of assholes still fighting the War of Independence. They'd go to their *yeshiva*, and pray, sing, lecture, or whatever—all in the face of a crowd of pissed-off Palestinians, floating ten feet off the ground in the euphoria that here was the great victory promised. Already I sensed that the assembled settlers teetered on the verge of congratulating one another for the mere fact of reaching this dusty Hebron street, even though they had accomplished this under military escort. I bounced on my toes, trying to let go of emotion and sink into fighter mode.

"Tager, Ostrov, Aloni, Levy, Alkana," Carmeli yelled out, assigning us positions around the twenty-odd settlers. I checked my gear one last time, smacked the bottom of the magazine in the gun out of habit, and nodded to Ostrov, who grimaced in return. The settlers decided for themselves the time was right and started walking, forcing us to jump into action as we fell behind. I glanced at Carmeli, who looked as bitter as any of us but said nothing. We walked away from the barricades and chanting, and made our way down small streets toward the souk. The settlers sang a psalm as I scanned rooftops, my rifle tight in my hands, running my finger over the safety, imploring myself to be vigilant every few seconds. We scrutinized blank-faced men and women, a boy leading a donkey carrying firewood, and a junk merchant. We wondered if this was the enemy as they passed by.

When we reached the souk, a long street of open stalls with vendors showing wares on small tables or tarps spread on the ground, no angry crowd greeted us—just a bunch of people getting on with their lives. I slowly took in the buildings and market, feeling the worst had passed as the street opened and allowed us to spread out and enjoy better visibility. The ordinariness of the scene—men and women calmly doing their daily shopping, tending stalls piled with fruit, vegetables, clothing, household goods—felt like a reprieve from serious punishment. We walked a few steps, and I exhaled, realizing that I had been holding my breath. The settlers stopped singing, and all eyes turned expectantly toward their leader, who clapped his hands together and yelled, "*Yallah!*"

The settlers sprinted off in different directions, shouting and cursing, overturning tables, scattering produce, sweeping stacks of pots and pans to the ground. "Bastards and whores!" shouted one settler, apoplectic, as if every Palestinian man, woman, and child in the souk had personally fired the bullets that had landed in their compound the night before.

"Bring everyone back here!" Carmelli screamed, standing impotently amid the unfolding chaos. He raced after a settler and pushed him away from his assault on a shoe stall. I gritted my teeth, slung my rifle across my back, and gave chase to a large settler. His *kipa,* held to his hair by a clip, had flopped to the side from throwing his weight against a stall loaded with turnips and potatoes. I grabbed his neck and shoulder and flung him with all my might, riding a furious spike of adrenaline, which landed him hard on his ass. He looked up with an almost childlike expression of genuine surprise, as if he had never expected to be rebuked, and calmly said, "Easy, brother."

"Back to the street!" All about me, settlers and soldiers were grappling, yelling, scuffling, the Palestinians looking on in mute horror as their livelihoods were trampled. I guessed that they knew their resistance would break the momentary war between the settlers and soldiers, uniting them against a common foe. Stall keepers were forced to resolutely step back and witness their goods scattered and trampled in the street.

A middle-aged settler woman wearing a beret found a stick and gamely had a go at a housewares stall, flailing at the pots and pans, and aggressively landing her blows near the glaring shopkeeper—a woman about her own age and stature in a *hijab.* I grabbed her by the waist and pulled her away as she screamed and kicked, scratching my arms. "You have no right to touch me!" she yelled. "You're not my husband! You're not even Jewish!"

I threw the woman down and looked up to see Ostrov struggling with a large man who appeared suntanned and stronger than the rest, as if he did agricultural work. I sprinted over, leaping the last few feet to hit the settler high, and landed heavy on top, butting him in the face with my helmet for good measure. He looked stunned as blood flowed from his nose. I felt my acid stomach turn into a warm glow—if a fight was required, I was pissed off and happy to oblige. As Ostrov and I grabbed him by his arms and dragged him off, I realized that if this was all that was left of being an IDF soldier, then here I stood, ready to rock 'n roll with all takers. The brooding anger continued to spill out in a torrent, consuming all thoughts as I raced from one settler to the next, figuring out what needed to be done. I could have ridden the wave of rage longer as the purity of the anger felt cathartic, but I held it back and brought myself under control. I wanted to punch these fat settler fucks in the teeth, kick them hard in their soft bellies. The Palestinians would hate us forever—they were our consistent, unfaltering brethren who we were locked together with in eternal hate—but these other idiots were supposed to be on our side. We were supposed to be working together.

I took a deep breath and realized I instinctively knew the mission. Our squad needed to be the padded cell, the gentle restraint, the responsible adults who would prevent further destruction until the settlers felt they had punished the Palestinians enough, or ran out of energy.

I looked over the assembled as they started to brush the dust off their clothing, wondering why no one had been shot or seriously hurt. The settler whose nose I had bloodied had recovered himself, and all looked like we now could proceed. Somehow everyone in our squad had kept their worst natures under control. We regrouped and pushed the settlers past the shopping area and toward the *yeshiva* with a subdued aggression. I knew I had skirted the edge of propriety—too far in that direction would have meant problems later. The notion that the settlers were not completely wrong in their actions also danced in my consciousness.

Two young settler women with faces of mischievous

defiance abruptly pivoted and sprinted past me down a side street back to the souk, pumping their arms to gain distance. I doggedly ran after them and caught them attempting to overturn a watermelon stand. Both frantically pushed melons off the stand and swept the bags and string and other items onto the ground. I grabbed their arms and pulled them back without too much effort, turning them around and shoving them in the direction they had come.

"Bastard!" one screamed, spitting in my face. "Idiot! Goy!"

They upped the volume for a few beats, and walked back to where the others were congregating. They stopped to look once more at the watermelons—maybe to savor their destruction or test my resolve—and I loomed close, ready to grab them again. Out of the corner of my eye, I saw a Palestinian run close—a gleam of metal, a blur of motion. I turned, hunched my shoulders, and instinctively drew my arms close, bringing my head down.

The knife flashed quickly, aimed for the back of my neck. In the instant, I turned a few degrees and caught the blow on my flak jacket. The women screamed and sprinted toward the soldiers. The knife deflected, and I shielded my face with my left arm as I fished for my rifle with my right. I whipped around hard with my left elbow, catching a slashing strike across my forearm and feeling a burning pain. I blindly grabbed my rifle and lunged at my attacker, terrified and flailing, doing what I had trained to do by default—my mind a searing blank of panic before it erupted into pandemonium. I struck the guy hard in the chest with serious intention, almost knocking him off his feet.

Unfazed, the kid came at me again, bobbing the upturned knife in front of him, eyes on fire. He was sixteen or so, with a downy mustache. He wore a faded yellow T-shirt with the logo of the Brazil World Cup team. He jerked his head left and right and wildly looked for an opening. With a grunt he swung the boning knife at my head. I made to strike him again with the rifle, and he jumped backward, a look of eager pursuit and concentration passing over his face, like a kid in the school-yard playing an intense game of hoops. Whatever deep hatred and loathing he held I couldn't see it—he was just a kid. His rigid black eyes expressed anger and fear and I took this in as if it would tilt the balance one way or the other. I stepped back and pointed the gun, flipping the safety off. I still hoped he would wake up and run, drop the knife, or show any indication of where we were headed. No reaction.

Fuck, fuck, fuck. Nothing else came to the surface in the riot of thoughts.

Locked together, the outcome was preordained. Despite the gun leveled at his chest, the kid made a low noise and leaped forward, trying to bat the gun's barrel away as he lunged and swung the knife. I took a half step back, blipping the M16 twice, a few feet separating us, resolute, unflinching. The kid stopped and lowered the knife with an absent expression, as if he didn't inhabit his body anymore, collapsing on the ground and holding his chest as dark blood oozed between his fingers.

The chaos in my head settled into silence as I froze, my ears ringing. I noticed the perimeter of Palestinians; they had withdrawn during the rampage, but now they were pressed forward with dark, angry faces. Maybe they wanted to help the kid, maybe they wanted to rip me limb from limb. I stood there at a loss for what to do and tightly gripped my rifle as the kid gasped and coughed. Bystanders yelled and screamed and I prepared for the sky to fall or the kid to leap up and have another go. Alkana jogged up beside me, taking a combat stance with gun lowered, yelling in Arabic. The crowd retreated. "Let's get out of here," he said.

Blood flowed liberally out of my left arm with every pulse, yet I couldn't feel it.

"C'mon, man, time to get the fuck out." Alkana cautiously came next to me, pivoting around with his rifle at his hip, putting an arm on my shoulder, pulling me toward the others. We backed away from the watermelons, the wailing screams, making our way to the souk entrance. The shots had ended the settler's rage, and they now donned their cloaks of pious respectability, congregating where they had started their tear.

"What the fuck," Carmeli said, his face inches from my own.

"I shot someone, sir," I said. Hearing this, the settlers cheered.

"Medic!" Carmeli yelled. He grabbed a compress bandage out of his pocket and applied it to my arm.

Chaimovich came over, dropped his medical kit to the ground, and unpacked. Before he could do anything, one of the settler men came over, sweating and dirty.

"I'm a doctor," he said. "Let's have a look."

The quick change of hats from adversary to rescuer felt oddly normal, as if our game had officially ended and we were all friends again having a beer. He peeled back the compress, saying, "Need to get stitched up."

I limply leaned against a building, hoping this would be my last day in the army, my last day in Hebron, but knowing I would become familiar with the city as if it was my own neighborhood, coming back to the souk day after day. I watched as the doctor taped the compress into place, and thought how great it would be if he and his group existed someplace far away, leaving only us and the Palestinians to wage our eternal war. I shuffled slowly to the Humvee and slumped into the back as waves of disbelief and weariness washed over me. I closed my eyes with the clear hope for something better, aware of the abstract longing but nothing more, as I waited for the ride to the hospital.

COMMUNIST PARTY CRASHER

MAY 2014, WEST HILLS, PORTLAND

SARAH GUTMAN

I WALKED INTO our federation's conference room to have a big-boy talk with Mr. Sorehead himself, Yoni Tager. He hadn't arrived yet, allowing me to gather my thoughts and take in for the thousandth time the framed and faded El Al poster depicting a sunny Tel Aviv beach scene from decades past, and a washed-out image from the Israel Museum, featuring the turnip roof of the Shrine of the Book. A fluorescent light flickered, a sign that it was a bad idea to attempt a heart-to-heart with one as hysterical and irrational as Tager. I imagined the twenty chairs populated with twenty serious people, shaking their heads in disbelief that someone so rooted in the Jewish community, someone so well-positioned to understand and participate in our story, could get Israel so wrong. Sorehead.

"Hi, Sarah. Hope I didn't keep you waiting too long," Tager said, entering the room and grabbing a chair.

He wore no jacket, the tails of his white oxford shirt sticking out at the bottom of his threadbare acrylic sweater that was the gross color of imaginary eggplant. His salt-and-pepper mustache and goatee did not suit him even if he had shaved the remainder of his face in the last week. Bald men are always tempted to grow bad facial hair.

I know because I married one. Lucky for me, my husband, Stan Gutman, finally accepted my advice, forgoing the look of an academic Grizzly Adams.

Tager could be as slovenly as he wanted because he didn't work in an office, and he was not part of the local network of companies, stores, and facilities that produced tangible goods and services. He worked, if you could call it that, online. Managed consumer perceptions, social media, marketing data—calling himself a "brand manager." Oh, please.

"How's the wife and kids?" I said, doing my best to force the corners of my mouth upward.

"All good, Sarah. I ran into Stan—he mentioned a new grandchild. Mazel tov."

A flash hit me that Stan might have influenced this meeting to my disadvantage, but I needed to forge ahead. We met a half hour before the convening of the federation's community committee, of which I'm the chair. Tager attended meetings as an observer but chaffed at being forever a fly on the wall, wanting official status. Over the past few months, he had been badgering us about how he could become an at-large member. He sent a ridiculous email claiming that the committee withheld information about his joining because of his political views: more precisely, his misunderstanding of the nature and needs of the modern state of Israel. This meeting was my idea—I hoped to clear the air and put an end to his misbegotten belief that he could contribute to the committee.

Tager sat down and leaned forward with his elbows on the table. "Sarah, I know we have our differences, but keep an open mind. I love Israel just as much as you do ..." He stated the usual: he lived in Israel, schlepped in the Israeli Defense

Forces, but came to a different conclusion than the rest of us. His views were supposedly more nuanced. According to him, he was the one with a monopoly on the truth about Israel, the US Congress, and how we ran things here. The way he made it sound, those of us on the committee spent our lives in a rosy mist of Israeli folk dancing and paddleball.

"Yoni, please." I started off slow. "I want you to know that all my life I've been a liberal. I'm old enough to remember the Freedom Riders in the sixties—what a great thing that was. How Rabbi Abraham Joshua Heschel marched with Dr. King at Selma. I cheered for that. The Voting Rights Act. Yes. But you can't write about the situation in the West Bank the way you did and expect to be welcome at the community committee." His letter to the editor of *The Oregonian* had been published two weeks previously. In it, he criticized a local man, a real anti-Semite, who had sponsored hateful slogans, such as "Stop Israel War Crimes," on TriMet buses. Tager told the man to focus his energies on ending the occupation, rather than pointless public incitement. This use of "the O word" was a real no-no for the community committee.

"Sarah, I don't know about you personally, but the federation officially supports the two-state solution—an independent Palestine next to Israel. This is what I mean by ending the occupation."

"We do support two states." I kept to myself the thought that the Palestinians already had a state—Jordan. "We will actively support a peace process only when there is a real Palestinian partner. Mahmood Abbas is not credible."

"To be on the committee, I have to give up my First Amendment rights?"

"We're a consensus organization. To participate, you must honor the consensus, even if that means not writing as many letters to the editors as you would like."

"How you arrive at consensus is another mystery. All you do in meetings is report about the efforts to do the stuff

Sidney says you should do." Sidney Weinbach was the federation staffer in charge of administrating the community committee—the guy whose job it was to deal with this kind of troublemaker. Tonight's meeting would be Tager's last. Weinbach was famous for his bureaucratic maneuvering and rule changes that kept out those who would hold us back. Weinbach would find a way to stonewall this putz. The federation was a community organization, but not *so* much of a community organization that people could say just anything.

"There are a number of subcommittees that convene periodically to discuss different issues," I said, being intentionally vague. He had brought up a topic that rubbed me the wrong way. Tager was right that Weinbach handled just about everything, set the agenda, selected the participants on the subcommittees, and prevented me, the chair, from making the most basic of decisions. I had asked Weinbach why things functioned as they did on so many topics, only to be disrespected with the idiotic *Fiddler on the Roof* answer: "Tradition."

"So how *do* I join as a member at large?" Tager's voice was sharp. "I don't see any applications at the reception desk."

"We'll let you know." Lucky for me, Al Slovik came in, nodding, before taking his usual seat next to the crudité plate with hummus. "We can talk more later."

Tager glowered and stood up before taking a seat against the far wall.

Soon the others filed in, and I said my hellos, the embers from my discussion with Tager smoldering. He didn't get it. We were good people. I had been helping people all my life as a CPA. In my retirement, I contributed time and effort to many groups to make the world a better place. We of the community committee were the elite, the movers and shakers, the girls and guys who showed up at meetings and got things done. We were unsung heroes. We weighed in on public policy issues, including Oregon legislation about the minimum wage, sex trafficking, gun safety, you name it. Most of us voted Democrat, and we were staunch supporters of Israel—and I mean *staunch*. No shades of gray, and no equivocation or questioning—I had a nose for bullshit and, unfortunately, I smelled it too often when we talked about Palestinians and the situation in Judea and Samaria. Support for Israel meant following the plan one hundred percent lest we allowed those who would harm Israel a chance to get in the door. Tager could have all the deep thinking and nuance he wanted; we were the ones doing the real work, telling the anti-Semites that they wouldn't be tolerated.

Last week, Stan had become exasperated when I complained (perhaps a bit too much) about Tager's obnoxiousness. He asked why I bothered with this committee. I replied to his question with a question. "What's being Jewish all about?" Stan didn't pick up that this was rhetorical, and started telling me about this guy who wanted to convert as he stood on one foot. I had to interrupt, as we all know this story—the great sage Hillel saying do not do unto others, blah, blah, blah. Finally, I said it plain and simple: "Standing up for what's right. That's why I donate my time and energy. That's what good Jewish people do."

The meeting started with a *drash*—the interpretation of the weekly Torah portion. As Slovik droned on in a monotone, I wrote my daughter Leah an email on my phone asking if she, her husband Bruce, and the kids would come to the house for dinner. You always need to schedule in advance with the younger generation.

Slovik, who worked in financial services, must have thought this was his meeting to pitch every one of his theories of Parshat Bamidbar. He plodded on for twenty minutes in that extra-loud voice of his. His son, Oded, went to our Jewish school and public high school, then to Whitman College in Walla Walla— the town so boring they tried to gussy it up by naming it twice.

Oded now wore dreadlocks and was making artisanal cheese in Silverton. *A good kid finding himself,* Slovik said.

My phone beeped, and I looked at Leah's text: emojis of celery, pizza, and a drumstick. Why couldn't she hit the "reply" button and write something in English like a normal person? I put down the phone and pretended to pay attention to Slovik's conclusion. I said my *yasher koach* with everybody else, mainly to celebrate that Slovik had stopped talking.

After calling the meeting to order, I began our agenda. State Senator Roselyn Ward sat in attendance and gave us an update on the budget being worked on in Salem along with her anti-smoking initiative. Next was intergroup outreach, where we heard about Jewish-Catholic dialogue. I noticed Tager scribbling notes, no doubt gleaning information to share with his bolshevik friends, and I tried to figure out how his knowing about the upcoming Nostra Aetate commemoration would trip us up.

Then came Israel. Max Levy, the head of the Israel Advocacy Subcommittee, explained how the federation was funding an Israel emissary to visit high schools to give presentations about Israeli history and culture—even serving falafel to kids who stuck around after class. Levy paused. "Pita, falafel, all the trimmings, and cherry tomatoes," he said, looking intently at our faces, as if hoping to catch a perplexed look. "Israeli scientists invented the modern cherry tomato. The other similar varieties spoiled too quickly for mass distribution." Levy looked up expectantly, perhaps hoping for a round of applause or an acknowledgement of the tomato miracle, but received nothing. He returned to the topic, explaining that the mission of the emissary was to immunize young people from becoming hateful critics of Israel. When kids went to college, they would have a lesser chance of supporting the boycott, divest, and sanction movement against Israel if they had met an Israeli and knew of the many positive contributions Israel made in science, technology, healthcare, and agriculture.

Tager extended his hand in the air and looked intently at Levy, waiting to be recognized. Everyone stared at him, then me, to see if I would let the one with only observer status comment. Eyes burned. I looked at Weinbach, who appeared dour and bored. If I didn't recognize Tager, Weinbach wouldn't blink. Weinbach has been successfully ignoring these types for years. But Tager was acquainted with everyone in the room, retired or not—synagogue, favorite charities, policy issues— and he maintained friendships with a few. Not to let him ask a question might reflect poorly. Recognizing him to speak, if only to prove to him and all in attendance that we weren't the know-nothing ogres he accused us of being, struck me as the right choice. I took a deep breath, letting it out slow as I pointed to him. "Yes, Yoni?"

"When you talk about your mission to stop the hate," Tager said, slouching in his chair, "consider not using the words 'critics of Israel.' A person can support Israel and still have legitimate criticisms. A different word. Disparagers, maybe?"

Silence.

"Moving on," I said, my anger igniting. Levy's face twisted into tight scorn. Something would have to be done. I made a note to contact Weinbach later. I reminded everyone that the committee strove for respectful dialogue. I shot Tager a sharp look and hoped he took the hint and would never come back.

The next day, rain fell hard, and I decided to forego my water aerobics class at the community center and focus on cleaning out my email inbox. If there was one thing about being a community leader, it was the endless amounts of email one was forced to wade through. When Stan and I became emp-ty-nesters nine years ago, we devoted ourselves to bettering our community.

I read the latest email from Weinbach:

From: Sidney Weinbach <SidW@PDXfed.org>
To: Sarah Gutman <progjew36@linkpdx.com>
Sent: Wednesday, May 13, 2015 8:34 AM
Subject: Community Committee

Hi Sarah,

Tell Yoni Tager he will not be able to attend the next community committee meeting next week. We will be having a special closed session. We can explain this by saying we need the privacy for members to ask questions about the committee's budget.

Don't worry about Tager. We will be making some rule changes ASAP to keep him out. Things are currently unacceptable.

Best,
Sid

I felt satisfied that others shared my anger and suspicion about Tager—or at least that Weinbach did. Weinbach was not popular with those who cry and moan about Palestinians, and this might in part have been because Weinbach was challenged with people skills, often resembling a more petulant Richard Nixon with furtive looks and a scowling demeanor. What the soreheads didn't understand was the spirit of community we represented, as collectively we were stronger than by ourselves. I wrote a particularly emphatic email to Tager, telling him he was forbidden from attending our next meeting due to the executive committee's need to have a high-level, confidential discussion.

When the next meeting came, I walked into the conference room and took my seat next to Weinbach, who was playing Angry Birds on his phone. (I'm not that out of touch!) Happily, Tager was nowhere to be seen. The guy had the common sense to realize that when I laid down the rules, I meant business.

We listened to the *drash*—this one by the bearded guy from the Reconstructionist temple. He was one of the sore-heads, but his attendance was sporadic and he represented an actual congregation, even if all they did was beat bongo drums and sing Leonard Cohen songs. He had to be tolerated. Tager represented nobody, just bad thinking.

"We have a full agenda," Weinbach said, "so let's start the meeting and get going. A few quick announcements. As we're pressed for time, we'll be taking no questions. If you need clarification, send Sarah or me an email." He paused, looked down. "The executive committee decided that the policy of allowing observers is unacceptable. Therefore, anyone who wishes to attend the community committee meetings as an observer now needs to get permission from me."

I should've been happy, but I was miffed that Weinbach wouldn't even let me, the chair, decide who got to attend. Weinbach could let me do *something.* I told myself that I should be grateful that the annoying Tager was gone for good, as there was no way in hell that Weinbach would ever allow Tager to attend a meeting.

"Because of Yoni Tager?" Harold Levin asked, incredulously. "Because of him, we need to change the rules?" A semi-retired attorney, Levin mainly defended people accused of low-level drug crimes, so I could cut him some slack because of his challenged work environment. "Okay, he's got his own way of thinking, but that he shouldn't even be allowed in here? Sure, we disagree, but isn't that always the case in the Jewish community?"

"He spoke bad about Israel," Vanessa Glover said. Vanessa, now supposedly employed by the federation, spent many weekdays doing what she called "maintaining relationship," which meant long, gossipy lunches with the big, small, and everything-in-between donors. Her second home, the community center gym, was where I saw her helmet of dyed-black hair on a preternaturally smooth face bobbing away on a treadmill. Partial to low-cut blouses even though she was pushing sixty-five, she had been a business development officer and fundraiser at several non-profits, all of which fared poorly as a result.

"I overheard him at Interfaith Advocacy Day in Salem," Glover continued, referring to when we met with our state legislators to discuss issues we advocated for in common with Christian congregations. "He told people how he supports an independent Palestinian state, based on the '67 borders, next to Israel."

"Big whoop," I said, tested by her obtuse reasoning. "So do we. It's even on the brochure." The difference between our imagined Israel and Tager's was that he would have the prime minister negotiate with terrorists. That doesn't sit well with us.

"I heard Tager talking about the occupation," Glover said. "Settlements being awful. How it's against his morals, ethics, or something, to control a population, even if they're all murderers." She tried not to look too smug that she had caught Tager using the "O word." "He told stories about the stuff he did in the army on the West Bank."

We all nodded, knowing no one would now question Weinbach's decision. Despite Tager sending his kids to the Jewish day school, being a member of the Reform congregation, and taking all sorts of highly urbanized Jewish people camping, his stance on Israel made him not one of us. Not even close. I remembered seeing Weinbach's report about Interfaith Advocacy Day, and how only eleven people participated, four riding with Tager. My mind jumped to who we could ask to make up the difference for next year. Ten years ago, we would get fifty or sixty people, joining with the Presbyterians, Catholics, and Baptists. Nowadays the local Christian congregations were rife with hateful people supporting the boycott, divest, and sanction Israel movement. These groups were where the anti-Semites resided. Who could feel comfortable around such people?

"Tager said we need to get beyond the shallow *hasbara* and talk about the *real* Israel, not the Jews-made-the-desert-bloom nonsense," Glover said.

"Moving on," Weinbach said, clearing his throat.

Tager says we need an update? He should reboot his own operating system. If he opened his eyes, he would see the startup nation, with a robust technology sector and a three-hundred-billion-dollar economy. If I had heard half of what Glover reported, I would have let him have it, telling him in no uncertain terms that Israel was the only democracy in the Middle East, respectful of its minorities, supportive of all peace efforts. And if he loved his West Bank pals so much, he could go live with them in their hovels and have no rights whatsoever.

My temper ran hot, so it was probably best that the cold fish Glover had done the eavesdropping.

The next day, the sun shone and brought reassurance that the negativity had passed, spurring me to get out of the house and return with a beautiful bouquet of white-and-yellow narcissus. After sorting mail and sitting at the computer for a moment,

I got up to find Stan. We had a plan to go to REI, as Stan wanted to buy new hiking shoes. I had no shopping list, but I liked the store and felt challenged to go outside and do brave things just by looking at all those nifty gadgets.

I walked into the family room to find Stan relaxing in the yellow wingback chair in the sitting area off the kitchen. He liked the wingback chair, as he could read, nap, or keep an eye on the birdfeeder. The wings of the chair caught his head from flopping too far to one side. Today, his Kindle sat closed on his lap, his beloved red quarter-zip fleece haphazardly draped over the ottoman, the material pilled and faded to a dull pink from multiple outings and washings. He sat gently petting our cat, Eve—named for the Barry McGuire song, "Eve of Destruction." He had given Eve to me as a gift, saying she was a "therapy animal," so when I was upset I could pet her and, presumably, more easily let the anger drift away—that was the theory, anyway. He initially suggested that we call her Trip, short for the triple *A* of "anger-absorbing animal." But when we saw her insatiable antipathy to rolls of toilet paper, I remarked that Destruction-Causing Animal was more appropriate. That sparked him to suggest "Eve of Destruction," one of his favorite songs, and the name stuck.

Stan stood up and dropped Eve to the floor, walking to the kitchen counter where he took a sip from his teacup. Today, as most days, he wore the Oregon standard of a flannel shirt and blue jeans, the gray tufts on the sides of his head subdued into a reasonable proximity of a hairstyle. I had to concede that his fashion sense was better than that of many men of his generation and profession, as he dutifully ordered new shirts and pants each year, both from the same catalog, ensuring the vibrancy of newness critical for a gentleman over sixty.

"Ready to go?"

"With a doll like you?" he said, moving to get his shoes on by the bench by the door. "You bet."

He was a cornball and could say things like that and get away with it. I admit that I was an unabashedly sentimental person too, but I didn't wear my heart on my sleeve.

Stan had been a science and environmental educator. He grew up in Ventura before going to UC Berkeley in 1966, a year after the free speech movement protests. He liked to tell of how he was a straight arrow when he entered Berkeley—not looking for conflict, political or otherwise. When he graduated with a degree in botany, his professors assumed he was off to a redwood forest to live in a commune and grow pot. Back then he wore his dark hair in a ponytail, parted down the middle and usually corralled in a beaded headband purchased on Haight-Ashbury. Stan liked to tell the grandkids he had been a hippie with hair down to his butt.

I grew up not so far away, in Pasadena. My school years were somewhat less fashionable, and I took accounting courses at Pasadena City College. My father was a florist and shade-tree mechanic, always tinkering with a stream of jalopies he hoped to string along for a few more months of flower delivery. On weekends, I was conscripted to help prepare centerpieces for banquets or ride with him as he made deliveries, the experience allowing me to understand the demands of business and how to manage in the world. He had an easygoing nature and got on well with the few Hispanic employees he hired in the later part of the 1960s. He spoke with the Yiddish-German accent of one born on the Jewish side of Bremen in 1913 and came to America with his parents in the mid-1920s. He couldn't care less about prayer but liked going to synagogue to see his friends and talk baseball and wrestling. He was known around town—by the rougher elements in the banquet halls and catering kitchens—as "the Flower Jew," as his face, voice, and demeanor spoke of centuries of Europe's *shtetls*. He met my mother, who had been born in Odessa, while growing up in the same neighborhood of Brooklyn. Why they had set out together as a young married couple to the wilderness of California in the late 1930s, and how they had survived the Great Depression years was lost to time.

When I got sentimental, I wished for one more family dinner, all of us bringing the dry irony to bear on the small insults of the day. I knew memory played tricks on us, but I couldn't remember one dinner when my father wouldn't utter *"Af ale yidishe kinder gezogt"* (All the Jews should be so lucky) even if the main topic of conversation was how difficult it was to make a living. Father, always the optimist. From my mother, I learned the curses.

As a family, we cheered and prayed for Israel, like all the other Jewish people, sending the coins collected in our *pushke* to Keren Kayemet for tree planning, of course. Israel's wars, the euphoria, the existential threats, my parents' dire reminders of how awful the world could be to the Jews, made me ripe for becoming a starry-eyed Zionist. One night in 1975 at Temple Beth David, a *schnorrer* told the story of a kibbutz re-established a year before by people like me—North Americans and Europeans who spoke English and had skill sets that didn't include munitions expertise or advanced swamp draining. By the end of the pitch, I could stand it no longer, and planned to rise to become an *olah* to the Jewish homeland.

I had been helping with the books at my father's business and at a local clothing shop, and became more depressed by the day about my prospects, vocational as well as social. The local boys who I could get a date with were about as inspiring as loaves of two-week-old challah. I admit I was a late bloomer, not all that adventurous, but I couldn't help but be moved by the spirit of the times, the changes in race relations, the cynicism toward the government, and the declaration that women not be discriminated against in the workplace and society. Israel shone on the horizon as a new beginning, a young country without the hang-ups, rigid social hierarchies, and sexism of the rest of the world. Golda Meir, an excellent example of how a girl could remake herself in a new land and achieve greatness, had resigned as prime minister the year before. For all her accomplishments, Meir spent time on Kibbutz Merhavia picking almonds, tending chickens, and working in the kitchen, and it spoke volumes. If that work was good enough for her, it was good enough for me.

I filled my old footlocker from summers at Camp Ramah with pioneering clothes and work boots, as well as Chaim Potok books. I bought *My Name Is Asher Lev* to take with me. I'm still not sure what the big Jewish lesson with that story was. Sure, there was the family conflict of a New York Hasidic boy who drew a picture of Jesus—I would have told the kid to draw something else and been done with it. The point was that no serious Jewish person was to be caught without that book, and I wasn't.

The kibbutz was called Gezer, which was the name of a Canaanite city-state mentioned in the Torah. In Modern Hebrew, it means "carrot," which worked fine given the unremarkable buildings and general squalor. The fields and barns looked much like they did in other places, with irrigation pipes, tractors, and other machinery lying around in various stages of disrepair, but with one distinct and wonderful difference. The kibbutz had an actual tell, an ancient mound comprising the remnants of the biblical city of Gezer. The big grassy hill with a few hewn rocks jutting out of the earth in clumps made a perfect spot for reflection after a long day. When I arrived, I climbed it, filled with the sense of prophecy about how this Jew had been reunited with her homeland. I was smitten. Seeing the boy and girl soldiers hitchhiking and at the bus stops, the religious Jews from other countries in their garb, the land itself brought back to life—who could resist these things?

Walking out of Ben Gurion Airport on a humid night, not knowing anyone, was the high-water mark of drama and excitement. I met up with my ride, a young man about my age with a full, blond beard and twinkling eyes, who introduced himself as Avi. I kvelled, happy to meet a real *sabra* in his native environment. Avi turned out to have been born and raised in Denmark and spent only a few years in Israel, but he came to embody my experience in Gezer. He wore sandals on every work detail no matter how filthy his feet became, and he seemed to own only two shirts and one pair of khaki shorts, reveling in being a devil-may-care "natural" person. This was the fashion of the time. I tried hard to get into the kibbutz swing of things, but I guess I was too bourgeoisie, too soft from my pampered upbringing. I enjoyed clean clothes and a lack of bug bites.

Perhaps the enormity of developing a viable agricultural settlement, the new culture, and the rebellious spirit of the times encouraged us to relax other areas of our deportment. Before becoming cognizant of his hygiene, I saw Avi as a handsome man, and my mother's voice rang in my head about how it couldn't hurt to join his work unit. In that respect, early Gezer was like JDate, the promised land of love. Most of us were single or with casual associations, and only a few residents of the kibbutz were married. Situations changed almost every night with all the flirting, trysts, betrayals, and drama that follow affairs of the heart. If ever I had a few wild oats, they were sowed then. Stan and I met on a stinking hot day—literally, as we were both covered in flies and filth from working in the cow barn. How's that for romance?

Given that Tager was a sorehead who sat quietly through meetings, looking absently at his phone and doodling in a notebook, I was surprised that the rule change got him all riled up. The day after the community committee meeting, when the rule change debuted, my email inbox was jammed with different members recounting their phone calls with him.

Weinbach called an emergency meeting of the executive committee, and the six of us met in the office of the federation CEO, Jeff Goldschmidt.

"Thanks for coming on quick notice," Goldschmidt said when we took our seats. Quite the dandy, he wore a turquoise bow tie and striped vest, looking more like a fanciful weatherman on the local television station than a steady-hand-on-the-tiller federation CEO. He rarely paid attention to the community committee; he was the big gun for fundraising. The way he sighed deeply when asked about the committee, you got the impression it wasn't his favorite part of the job. He had his hackneyed verbiage, repeating that as the committee was a community organization, the community could decide for itself how best to conduct its affairs. He politely overlooked Weinbach's ongoing micromanagement.

"Like many of you, Yoni called me, very displeased," Goldschmidt said. "He thinks he's banned from the community committee."

"He is," Weinbach said. "He will not be granted observer status by me or anyone else here."

We all nodded.

"Yoni wasn't aware this is a private organization, which gives us greater leeway in how we conduct our affairs. It's important we frame this the right way," Goldschmidt said slowly. "I told Yoni—and feel free to use this among yourselves—that his departure is necessary. I told him he made people nervous to the point that the members of the committee couldn't focus. Members have a right not to be made nervous." His voice had become peppy and smooth.

Goldschmidt believed that if he said things with enough smile in his voice, he could tell the truth. I saw the direction he was coming from, but it was not the right strategy. Tager didn't have one drop of smile in his voice, ever. He was the humorless comrade haranguing the masses. When Goldschmidt had told Tager that he needed to adjust to not attending meetings because his presence made people nervous, Tager did not react well. By all reports, he became infuriated that the CEO of the federation told him to buzz off because of his manifold nervousness-inducing qualities. I would have told Tager that his credentials had been revoked without explaining what said credentials were in the first place. (I was the permissive parent, Stan the strict one.)

Tager had called the different members of the committee to protest the rule change.

"He called me up at work, real pleasant and chatty," Slovik said. "Then he asked me straight out if he made me nervous to the point I couldn't focus. I said to the guy that I'm okay with it, but the others ... It's like you're in a restaurant, and you don't like the food. Go to another restaurant. Tager says, 'A restaurant? What the hell you talking about? I'm being thrown out for my political opinion, and you make it sound like I'd prefer pickles on my hamburger.' I told him we're not political, just a community organization."

"I just hung up on him," Barbara Levy said, "ended the whole thing, *chik-chok.*" Before the meeting, she had told me that after the call with Tager, she was so upset that she needed to take a Xanax and spend an hour on the phone with Weinbach talking about legal repercussions.

Tager also called Avi Mendez, Carol Goldman, Lisa Wasserman, and Lou Carr. Most of them put on a good face, saying it wasn't them necessarily who had complained, but others might be more sensitive, and this was for the best.

"Don't engage with him," Weinbach said. "If he calls, put down the phone. If he emails, forward it to me."

I figured that Tager left me off his call list because he knew

I was not one to be trifled with. Still, despite his transgressions, I was a forgiving sort, having raised two children and survived their phases. I needed to explore whether common ground existed between us.

When I got home, I ignored Weinbach's blackout on communication and called Tager's cell. "Yoni, listen, you've got to let this thing go. Stop pestering people."

"Sarah, glad you called. How can the committee represent the community in any real capacity if you refuse to let anyone participate who doesn't agree with you?"

"People don't want to hear from you. They don't like you, your ideas. You want to be Che Guevara, go live in the jungle. At federation, we are positive, good people, doing things we all agree are good."

"That's really weird, the way you keep using the word 'good.'"

"Our policies are set by our parent organization. There's no room for discussion or feedback."

"Then why bother pretending to have a deliberative body?"

"It's a working committee. We need to discuss who will be doing what. That's why we meet," I said, hopeful for an opening. "We should have coffee and talk this out more. I want you to know how upset I am about this whole thing. If you let me tell you what's in my heart, you might be more reasonable."

"You're talking about undoing the rule change that all observers must be approved by Sidney, right? Maybe reach some sort of compromise?"

"I'm talking about a frank exchange of feelings. This would do us both good." I meant it. If I could tell him about my voter-registration activities, how I ate a Ramadan plate of saffron rice and chicken last year with Abdul Hakam from the Portland Mosque, or how I donated handsomely to a Jewish-Arab school in Israel, he would understand. He would know I was not anti this or that but an informed, good person trying to do the right thing. Communication was the tool of better understanding.

Unfortunately, the sorehead hung up.

Even when up to his knees in manure, Stan cracked jokes about whatever thoughts drifted across his mind. His favorite topic of ridicule was the Kibbutz schnitzel, which would make good shoe soles in a crisis or could be ignited and flung at an advancing enemy. His jokes were predictable, but after delivery, he'd smile wide and hover, like you had to laugh. He hung on your response. Laughing with him felt like good times from high school, even after we had just met.

Before Israel, he worked for several years at a firm near Monterey Bay that harvested seaweed, threw it in giant vats, and extracted different chemicals. He found it a soul-killing job incommensurate with his having taken the trouble to graduate from college.

He told me this while shoveling manure, but I knew what he meant. Our simplest actions were heroic in the context of building the Jewish State.

I don't believe in love at first sight, but I immediately noticed Stan. When the *hafsaka* came during our work, he was one of the few men who didn't take out a pack of awful Israeli cigarettes and bathe himself in rancid smoke. For the record, plenty of women smoked, too, but less. Back then, every meeting meant sitting for hours in a room with uncomfortable chairs, drinking weak instant coffee, and breathing stale smoke that never seemed to go away, no matter how many fans or open windows. Avi was one of the worst, as he had grown up in a depressing, unpronounceable factory town in nihilistic

Europe, where disregard for health was entry to the club. I laughed at the thought that we might have been better friends.

The first few weeks on the kibbutz, I worked in the dining hall, washing dishes and cutting up cucumbers and tomatoes from bottomless bins. The work was boring, repetitive, and hot. I stuck it out there three weeks before the supervisor, Galit, told me that dining hall work shifts were temporary and I could request a new assignment. That's how I came to work in the cow barn with Stan. After a few months, he became a prominent figure. His degree in botany allowed him to visualize what needed to be done to, say, grow sweet corn. First, he would draft a shopping list, then a calendared water and fertilizer budget. Eventually these abstractions became a plowed furrow, and then a field of robust plants with commercial value.

The two of us connected easily, as we were both Californians, new on the kibbutz. Both of us had come to Gezer with dreamy visions of Israel. At the end of the workday, he often picked up his battered classical guitar, singing the songs of summer camp: Bob Dylan, Neil Diamond, and Cat Stevens. On hot nights, he took his shirt off. His smooth, tan skin and long hair were favorite memories.

Despite our easy camaraderie, my relationship with Stan took a while to deepen. Stan was overjoyed to toil away in a field all day for the basic pleasure of being outside. He could note different birds and weather patterns with the earnestness of a scientist. With the others, I only had to indicate I was open to life's possibilities. With Stan, I needed my wiles to get into his field of vision. On weekends, he'd forego all social events and disappear, going "walkabout," as he called it, wandering around the neighboring roads and fields. Someone would stop to ask what he was doing or who he was, and he'd have a new friend, an invitation to dinner, a political diatribe, advice on crop rotation, or a lecture on European history. On

Gezer, anybody could ask him for help, and he'd walk off his assignment to do someone else's.

Stan's ability with seeds, fertilizer, tractors, and shiftless, idiot volunteers contrasted with his dysfunctional social life. After the first year, he continued to hope he would win the undiluted affections of Galit (formerly Gloria), who had grown up in Paramus, New Jersey, and liked to say that she was from New York, implying Manhattan. When pressed, she would sigh and act like she had to explain the obvious, saying, "New York vicinity." With this level of equivocation, Pasadena might have been a suburb of Manhattan. She had Stan wrapped around her finger, with her pixy hairdo and pouty lips. She discarded him the minute she sensed somebody better, different, or more skilled at navigating the convoluted network of alliances and interests that passed for democratic leadership.

I arrived with the best of intentions to bring my skills to bear on a new country, a new entity—but unfortunately, things aren't always as advertised. The kibbutz was supposed to be composed of egalitarian, noncompetitive, serious-minded people. I had never encountered such an assembly of back-stabbing, low-minded opportunists looking for a free ride off the sweat of everybody else. People came to Kibbutz Gezer for a life easier than wherever they had been. Avi, Matt, Mordechai, Galit, Reynor, Jordan, and Rivka were types that wouldn't be able to cut it anywhere else, so they latched onto the kibbutz movement with a death grip.

From the telling, it probably sounds like I wouldn't last five minutes at Gezer. Yet I stuck it out for three years, in part because I saw the potential for what might be—the shadows of greatness in the collective energy of a restless diaspora. These visions came late at night when darkness and a stillness of spirit put me in a philosophical mood. In the light of day, the impossible personalities, limited resources, inertia, and bad luck made me doubtful of the smallest of victories—yet the adventure continued.

After a year of working like a medieval serf, I applied to be a full member of the kibbutz. The deliberation took longer than it should have, and it wasn't like there was a steady stream of recruits. True, I had a few disagreements now and then, but if the leaders wanted a vital, intelligent, ambitious worker to make Gezer thrive, I was a shoo-in. What made me even madder was that Stan didn't understand what advantage full membership in Gezer meant (until I explained it) but received approval almost instantly. He was a good-natured worker bee, but there were few like him—versed in the science and technology of agriculture—who could launch new crops with any likelihood of success. This was still back in the day when the kibbutz was supposed to be an agricultural entity— not like now, where all the land is rented out and the money comes from hotels and light industry.

I finally received notice of full membership. At the first opportunity, I set up a meeting with the central adminis- tration, sending them my resume with my business college education in large type, with the intention of becoming office staff. Nothing doing. The bookkeeping was fine the way it was, thank you.

My time on Gezer taught me that if you wanted something badly enough, you had to go get it yourself. Waiting around for clear thinking from those in management would only get you another three-week shift washing dishes in the dining hall. As my father had been a florist, I have always been a great appreciator of flowers. I lobbied for a beautification program to plant flowers and ornamental shrubs around the kibbutz to enhance the minimal landscaping. For several weeks, the leadership adamantly refused even to hear my plan. They eventually agreed to it, probably just to move on to another topic, as if the money I had asked for was too small a sum to take up their precious mental energy.

Although I grew up cutting and arranging flowers, I didn't know how to plant them. Starting this project turned out to be the best decision of my life, as I needed to consult with Stan frequently and have him help or assign volunteers. Once the first blooms came up, the notion that the beautification plan had been a hard sell was absurd. Even better, once I was seeing Stan daily, Galit faded from his thoughts for good. Many a long day of landscaping in the heat ended with Stan and me on the tell or in the eucalyptus grove, sharing a glass of wine and talking about nothing—merely enjoying each other's company, the cessation of labor exquisite. Within a few months, we registered ourselves as an official couple (an actual designation—this was 1976), which meant that we could cohabitate, and we did.

Slowly the kibbutz and the country became less foreign, and we met more Israelis from neighboring communities. Most men our age had been called up to fight during the Yom Kippur war of 1973. The country was still in shock, grieving for war dead, traumatized by contemplating annihilation yet again. The euphoria of a resounding military victory snatched from the jaws of defeat still gives me shivers. Stan felt that fighting to a stalemate and with several thousand Israeli dead underscored the fragility of Israeli military superiority. Many battles hinged on small tactical advantages likely to be bridged by Arab armies in a few years.

I began to drop hints about our future, asking Stan about what natural materials he might choose to construct a *chuppa*, or if it was better to do his initial military service now, before other responsibilities came into his life. He answered like a typical man, not reading anything into the questions. The second question led him to reveal that he had come to Israel on a temporary resident visa, not as an immigrant like myself, because he didn't feel he was the soldiering type—he would have been quickly drafted into the IDF had he entered Israel as a new immigrant. The taint of Vietnam hung heavy in his mind, giving him an antiwar perspective even for righteous wars of defense like ours. He liked wearing his hair long, talking to his anemones, and pretending he didn't understand all the back-stabbing and maneuvering in the swirl of personalities at Gezer.

I fell in love with Stan for all the right reasons—he was a kind and generous man—even if his political and social naiveté put him at a sharp disadvantage. I knew from the outset that we could be a great team—a whole greater than the sum of our parts. I wanted him to be my husband, my project, for I knew that with my subtle direction we could rise even higher. The big plan I came up with was to commercially raise lavender, jasmine, and rose, selling them locally for decoration, and to industry for cosmetic scents. He handled the technical projections of acreage, labor, and expected return, while marketing was my forte.

I again went to the leadership meetings and tried my best to convince those dullards of our key entrepreneurial excellence. After many long and tedious discussions, gallons of instant coffee, and enough second-hand smoke to give all of Pittsburgh cancer, I was allowed use of a rust-bucket powder-blue Ford with a ripped bench seat and trick clutch and half the seed money I requested. Those days weren't like the email blasts of today. There were only a few phones on the kibbutz, so all business had to be conducted in person.

Each morning, I optimistically drove off to raise awareness of Kibbutz Gezer flowers. Initially, I found some opportunity. But mostly I found that without the vitamin P of *proteksia*—connections—none of the big buyers would let me in the door. Still, I doggedly kept at it, thinking of what Golda might have done.

The rain fell hard across Portland's west hills, the weather conducive to working at the computer. Time got away from me and before I knew it I realized I had no energy to shop or cook. I called my daughter Leah and told her we would meet her and her family at the Captain's Table, a seafood place near the community center. When I called to inform them, my oldest grandkid, Devin, who was six going on sixteen, answered the phone. I had only to put the vision of chicken tenders in his head to get compliance from the adults.

As Stan parked the car, Leah and her husband Bruce pulled up in their red Nissan, allowing us to lend a hand with getting Devin and his sister, Tamara—my little *bubbala*—into the requisite booster and high chair. Stan remembered to get crayons from the staff so that he could color for the grandkids.

As we settled in, I scanned my mind for a good conversation topic with Leah and Bruce, as they didn't follow politics and world affairs the way I did. They were millennials, and subject to the powers of Facebook and Twitter. Issues didn't set them off—more like waves of social forces. They would ask if I had seen this viral video, or they read me something important that, say, a Black Lives Matter activist had written on social media. I read about these things when they got written about in the *Times*, but they usually passed me by the first time around. Leah and Bruce mostly grasped the issues I want to talk about, but when Israel came up, Bruce appeared perplexed and might hesitantly ask questions until Leah gave him a look or poked him under the table. I didn't let this put me off. Bruce had grown up in Colorado, in a home that used Passover as an excuse to go skiing. At least he was Jew-*ish*.

The server came and introduced the specials of razor clams and paella, Bruce ordering a bottle of pinot grigio while I asked for two whiskey sours for Stan and me. "Too much trouble in the world," I said, letting the words fall out in a sigh.

"Let me guess," Leah said. "Someone's getting in your grill at the federation on the Israel thing."

"*Yes!*" I said, excited and worried that news had spread more rapidly than I anticipated. "Tager didn't call you, did he?"

"Who?" Leah said before recognition hit and her face brightened. "I know Yoni. We went camping with his group before Tam was born." Her face grew stern. "No, he didn't call, but you know, we go through this every few months. Someone says something about Israel, Palestinians, US politics, foreign policy, or *something,* and you have a meltdown."

"I don't have meltdowns." I lowered my voice to a near-hiss.

"Hissy fits, rage riots, angerpaloozas, whatever," Leah said, making Bruce snort and look up from his phone. "We've been through this a few times before."

"You don't know what this guy says about Israel." I realized I might have to start at the beginning and spell out the odiousness of Tager's transgression.

"Sarah, please—we don't have to go into all that here," Stan said, patting my hand. "Look, here's a grandchild." He turned to make a face and tickle Devin. "People have a right to be wrong. Life's too short to get bent out of shape this way."

"He used the word 'occupation,' I bet," Bruce said, "and regards the Palestinians in a less-than-absolute manner."

"He most certainly did." I was happy that finally someone understood what I was up against.

"Let's not go down the Israel rabbit hole just yet," Stan said. "We're all here now. Other people might have something to contribute on another topic. Let's relax." He raised his drink, clinking the glasses. "*L'chaim.*"

Leah and Bruce shared a look. A gal doesn't live sixty-seven years on this planet and not recognize what a look between husband and wife signified. This one no doubt originated in ancient Mesopotamia and had been with us ever since, signaling that a conversation had taken place, a full discussion concluded, a decision reached, signed, sealed, and now, finally, delivered. Leah and Bruce, earnest and sitting more upright, glanced at each other one more time. This did not bode well.

"Look, Mom, there's something I want you to know," Leah said. "We're taking Devin out of Hillel Day. We want him to go to the Spanish immersion program at Ainsworth."

"*El espanol es el lenguaje del amor,*" Stan said. I wanted to kick him under the table.

I forced myself to remain silent and sip my drink. The pellet of anger I righteously nurtured all day, the spark burning slowly underneath a thick wool blanket, suddenly had been doused with gasoline. I wanted to scream at the top of my lungs, "WHAT THE HELL IS WRONG WITH YOU!" But I had to sit and marinate in that awful feeling that the plane would soon collide with the mountain. In the cockpit, the radar alerts and altimeters were squawking, beeping, buzzing, the warning lights were flashing, but the pilots were bound and gagged, forced to witness the horror of the impending catastrophe.

I looked at Stan, who patted my hand again, his creased face flushed from the cocktail. He already knew! My own family conspired against me. Had I made the final transformation into my own hysterical mother?

"And Tamara?" I asked, awakening from my reverie. The kid took her cue, slapped her fist on the highchair tray, and looked up at the ceiling.

"We'll see about Tamara," Leah said. But I knew Leah. She liked things neat and easy—she often called herself "eco-conscious" to get out of extra driving. I knew both kids would go to Ainsworth, as it was close and free.

"More money now available for the 529 plans," I heard myself say.

"Devin should learn a second language relevant to our life here," Bruce said. "A trip to Israel in the eighth grade is nice, but what happens in ninth grade?" He refilled his glass. "If

Devin wants to study for a bar mitzvah, he'll get the religion from that direction."

"Spanish, huh?" I said, feeling that I'd been punched in the gut. "Leah, how is it you don't want all that good stuff you received from the school, all that great *naches,* for Devin? Public schools have classes with forty-five kids in them, unknown curriculum, learning styles. You'd be putting the kid on a bad course."

"Leah spoke to Sandra, the counselor at Hillel," Stan said, "and I know this from teaching for forty years. Some kids do better in richer social environments. They need more kids to interact with."

"What richer?"

"There are sixteen kids in his grade, only three other boys," Leah said. "Devin needs to be happy. He's not happy at Hillel."

"How can you know what happiness is when you're six?"

"You know more about it when you're six than sixty," Bruce said.

"Public school?" I said. "They'll fill his head with all sorts of rubbish. You need a Jewish education so the kids know what's going on."

"Sarah, please," Stan said in his unflinchingly direct tone, which warned that I needed to cool it. "You'll still be their *bubbie.* You'll have the opportunity to let them know the important things."

"Mom, this is Israel again," Leah said. "Every day Israel is in the news feed. Not the Israel you'd recognize—one of billionaires and technology companies, not kibbutz communal dining halls. It's about what to do with two million Palestinians in the West Bank. Sure, there's terrorism, but the Israel you inhabit doesn't exist anymore—or if it does, it's only with your cronies in the federation."

I took a big swallow from my drink. Leah was wrong and impertinent. I sacrificed to get her through Hillel Day and then to Lewis & Clark College. All that liberality. All it did was fuel her willful nature. How could she say these things? I had done everything right. Leah had gone to Israel for two weeks in the eighth grade and a gap-year program in Jerusalem. She, if anyone, should know what needed to be done. If only she could see the video footage from StandWithUs that Weinbach had screened six months ago, showing the awful anti-Semitism on the Berkeley campus, or the video of the aftermath of the Dizengoff bombing in 1994.

"You're wrong. It's the same Israel," I said, my voice staccato from excessive self-control. "The issues look slightly different. Modern, yes, but it's always the same—the Jewish people need a refuge, a sanctuary from all the anti-Semitism of this world. In my day, the KKK. Now it's the boycott people. You think you know something about the world? You'll see."

"Remember those nutty Muslim Portlanders who wanted to blow up a synagogue, among other things?" Bruce said. "They were pissed as hell about how Israel and the world treat Palestinians. If Israel had more compassionate policies, we might all be safer."

I heard Bruce loud and clear, but I pretended I didn't. I forced myself to stare down at my fried calamari appetizer and started eating mechanically. I heard Stan trying to change the subject or crack a joke, but I was numb. A flash of recognition that we had been here before, the ending preordained. I was naïve to think that I could convince Leah and Bruce of the urgency of the Jewish condition. At those moments, I wished I could verbalize the images in my head, the suffering of the Holocaust as I understood it through friends who told of anguished, remote survivor parents, the way my father was humiliated by the gentile business community in the forties and fifties. But I sat in silence. If I could bring just one of these thoughts to life, let Leah and Bruce feel only one percent of their poignancy, the talk of taking Devin out of Hillel Day would cease, as would giving him a choice about having a bar mitzvah—*as if he were trying on shoes!* They would be of one mind, *Am Yisrael Chai*, and all this other bullshit would vanish.

I turned to Devin, who looked sad that the adults were silently yelling at each other, dutifully playing with a small race car on the corner of the table. I asked him about the "creepers" in his favorite game, Minecraft. He gave me a wan smile. Another question about what he was building in the game, and he brightened, signaling to me, Leah, Bruce, and Stan that the episode of bad feeling had passed, and we were once again a family.

Driving the Ford back from Beit Shemesh, just west of Jerusalem, after an unsuccessful meeting with a flower retailer, I pulled into Kibbutz Tzora on a whim. I figured I would walk the grounds until I found someone who would hear me out. My thinking that day was that if Gezer found a partner to produce flowers in greater quantity, a buyer would be more interested—share the wealth, grow the market, all that good stuff. Walking around Tzora, my first impression was that here people got things done instead of smoking and arguing all the time. The place had beautiful, modern buildings, all the lush grass you could ever walk on, trimmed hibiscus everywhere, plum and apricot trees, even a petting zoo next to the childcare facilities—the well-groomed goats and sheep were part of the advertising.

I walked into the first business office I came across to find several women at new desks, each with their own phone, briskly moving through stacks of receipts, a pace foreign to the administrative flow at Gezer. A middle-aged man with a shaggy pompadour leaned back in his modern office chair and read the paper at a slightly bigger, messier desk. Before I said anything, he stood up and smiled. "Sweetheart! What can I do for you today?"

"I'm from Gezer and ..."

"Coffee. Vered," he said to the woman nearest. "Milk and cream?"

That was my first encounter with Zalman Paz. In that meeting, I learned that he only listened to the Beatles' *White Album*, as it contained all the music one needed; that his four children were all safely out of the army; that he had driven across the United States twice and noticed no difference in geography or climate ... and why hadn't I stopped in to introduce myself earlier? I don't remember his title or what exactly he did on Kibbutz Tzora, but when I told him about the flowers he said, "Come!" in his raspy baritone. And off we went to walk around the fields and barns, talking to cynical men in dusty work clothes, who asked endless questions, to most of which they already knew the answer. Always Zalman flirted with me, daring me to react, but still the business discussions continued.

The next week, I came back with Stan. He talked to the men who knew about the tractors and irrigation, then with Mordechai and Reynor, who drafted the terms, then with Galit who did whatever she was supposed to do, and the agreement took shape. Zalman, besides being an expert on all things, grew up on Tzora and knew everyone in the country— and I'm exaggerating only a bit. He made a show of calling cosmetic manufacturers in front of me to illustrate how well he knew the people and how easy it was for him to set the appointments. The magic of Kibbutz Tzora was wonderful, but I realized Zalman was still an old-world kibbutznik when I stopped by and found him in the machinery shed or out in the fields, wearing filthy coveralls and taking his shift at whatever drudge work had come his way. He never looked embarrassed or put out when I found him laboring, and he always greeted me with good cheer and his overly solicitous manner.

Gezer and Tzora put together two substantial orders for rose and lavender for Ahava cosmetics. Our gross earnings totaled more than $34,000, which was significant in those days. My luck had changed, and I felt the other members of Gezer had to acknowledge my contribution, my success, as opportunities to expand presented themselves.

The day I learned that Zalman died, I was driving back from Holon, where I had tried to find more outlets for our cut flowers. An ordinary day, dusty roads and falafel stands, listening to Hebrew radio in the truck to pass the time. In those days, a radio played constantly in almost every building and home—a typical background for work or a meal. Until I had to be on the road, I gave it little mind. From the radio I learned the word *pigua* (terror attack) and took note that it wasn't an infrequent occurrence in Israel or the rest of the world. That day I heard a *pigua* had occurred on Kibbutz Tzora. By the time I arrived, the ambulance had departed, and people milled around outside the dining hall with stunned expressions.

The police forensics team crawled around on hands and knees to collect the bomb fragments, concluding that the terrorist dug up an activated landmine or found an unexploded artillery shell from the northern border. He had jury-rigged a crude detonator and disguised the bomb under rocks and garbage in the plowed furrow of a cucumber field. The obstacle forced the tractor driver, Zalman, to get down to move it, detonating the bomb.

I went to Zalman's office and hugged his coworkers, incoherent and overwhelmed with sorrow, loss, anger.

That night, the images haunted me. An activated landmine. Artillery shell. A mustached Arab walking around with a suitcase or maybe a package, riding buses, drinking coffee in town, while he, his family, and everyone around him continued to live only because of the unknown forces keeping the bomb in check—some fuse defunct, a wire separated from its post. The terrorist had transported the bomb tens, if not hundreds, of kilometers. Maybe he gave the package to his wife, girlfriend, or child—all ignorant of the terrible contents— telling them where to take it. All that effort to kill just one of us. Not a marketplace attack, bus station, airport, hotel. Only the dusty fields of Kibbutz Tzora.

In the morning, I acknowledged that terror attacks were impossible to prevent with a determined foe. In my heart, I knew that the members of Kibbutz Tzora were the winners, the heart and soul of the country, the ones who did everything right and succeeded. If they couldn't prevent the attack, nobody could. At night when I struggled to sleep, moments where logic is often absent and other forces weigh in, part of me blamed Kibbutz Gezer for the bomb. Had we been more unified, had the country been more cohesive, this tragedy never would have happened. I saw clearly how the Palestinians would kill us one by one, over the years, having the patience and hatred to figure out, slowly and methodically, how and where to plant their bombs.

Before we could recover from Zalman's death, emotionally or with the flower venture, Mordechai from Cedar Rapids pulled the plug on our Zionist enterprise, convincing the leadership with pseudoscience and invented financials of the impracticality of farming flowers. Of course, nowadays Israel exports tens of millions of dollars of flowers to Europe—probably tulips to Holland even—but that's the way the cookie crumbles.

With the collapse of the flower partnership, I felt stymied and frustrated by leadership at Kibbutz Gezer. The main group—Mordechai, Galit, Rivka, Ira, and David—had no plans for advancing the kibbutz beyond an endlessly debated screwdriver factory, and continuing a mix of fruit and vegetable crops that were profitable only by the slimmest of margins. Despite a dearth of new ideas, nobody had any compunction about raining on ours. Gezer could have been a major supplier of florist shops, as we were strategically positioned between Jerusalem and Tel Aviv. The money needed to keep things going was modest, but the shekels went to Ira so he could make ugly sculpture in his studio space tucked away in the corner of a machinery shed. The pieces of metal he randomly twisted and then gave lofty names like "Icarus" or "Soul Reborn" never achieved a single sale despite appearing in an art fair and a gallery showcasing kibbutz works.

For all I know, Mordechai and the lot thought the squalor and dilapidation of Kibbutz Gezer were the culmination of their Zionist dreams. No question the place was authentic, with the ancient tell, the government subsidies, the soldiers hitchhiking on the roads with their rifles and kitbags, the fruit orchards, and the volunteers and kibbutz members wearing the *kova tembel* (fool's hat)—a minimal floppy cone of fabric now a national symbol. For them, the kibbutz needed to be imperfect and chaotic, designed to remain the opposite of shiny, material comfort.

In the weeks after Zalman's death, I continued with my work assignments, but I became a clock-watcher, restless to be far away from the others at Gezer. Stan tried his best to pull me out of this funk by doing more around the apartment and taking me to the movies in Tel Aviv. His ministrations troubled me, for he understood nothing about what I was going through. I was acting more distant and secretive than ever. I worried that I had started the relationship out of necessity and needed to confront him on several issues if we were to have a future. I wanted him to understand the reality of the world we lived in, why I had come to Israel, why he should change his visa status and serve in the IDF. Every day these thoughts were forefront. Under the weight of sadness and inertia, they faded as the hours dragged on.

Fridays on Gezer meant a half day of work and a dinner more elaborate than other days. The nice meal wasn't because we wanted to honor Shabbat—we were proudly secular on Gezer—rather, this was the local custom. I entered the apartment around ten in the morning, feeling ambivalent that the weekend had arrived. I stripped off my work clothes and took a shower. I heard Stan enter the apartment and then leave. Later I found him in the main room, looking nervous.

"Sarah, you once asked a question that I didn't really answer. Take a look at what I got here."

Grinning with a jittery energy, he opened the door to our small backyard where he had set four eucalyptus branches in the earth in the shape of a rectangle with an old *tallit* held aloft and flapping in the breeze. The branches, still with bark and leaves, had been wrapped with purple wisteria for added effect—his version of what a *chuppa* should look like. The proposal speech meandered, but he eventually got the point across, saying he couldn't imagine living without me and how awful these last few weeks had been.

With all the unburdening of emotions that went along with the proposal, he told me he wanted to go back to the States and work on a master's degree. He fretted for days over that, worrying that it would kill the relationship. When I said "let's go" without blinking, he whooped with joy. All of those burning questions turned to ashes with the plan to move back. Part of me still wanted to prove to myself and everyone that I had what it took to make it in Israel—but other voices called.

I went to the front hall, and on the entryway table the blown-glass flower Leah had purchased at the Portland Saturday Market brought me back to recent disappointments. I looked out at the wet foliage and put on my puffy coat to go to the market with Stan, who wanted to purchase fish after again failing to catch any. I told him the latest update about Tager and how his ilk had to be kept out of the federation at all costs. He took it all in, nodding. "People have different opinions," he said slowly, measuring his words. "The natural condition for the Jewish people: at odds with one another. No joke."

After parking, we found a cart and started shopping when a young man in office attire called out, "Stan? Stan Gutman!"

"Chuck! Nice to see you," Stan said, extending his hand. "Sarah, you remember Carol Goldman's son, Chuck? One of my best students. It's a *shanda* he studied political science instead of biology. What, you're still working for the city?"

"Policy advisor for Commissioner Fowler," Chuck said, his face spreading into a big grin.

I saw Chuck's mom regularly at our Reform synagogue and at the federation. City hall took the heat from the boycott and divestment people, so it was a surprise when Chuck said, "Stan, I remember you were big into Israel, talking about your time there, bringing speakers to campus. What's going on with the students today?"

"I'll tell you straight," Stan said. "The average Jewish college kid doesn't want anything to do with Israel, either to defend or criticize. The debate is confusing and vicious, always the name-calling. The probability someone gets called a Nazi is, well, a hundred percent, give or take. The Jewish kids, when asked about Israel, just say no time for that, I've got to study for the LSATs."

"Sounds right," Chuck said. "I was hoping for some good news here."

We said our goodbyes. Stan gave me a look that I interpreted as an exhortation to bite the bullet and give in, let the soreheads crash the party. I shook my head. We had covered this ground so often; we were like performers reciting lines.

I clenched my teeth and thought about how at his core Stan just wasn't a serious person. At the drop of a hat he could run off to pursue pleasure at the cost of relationships, social and professional. He missed the point, seeing student participation as a harbinger of what was to come. I struggled to get to Israel after my student years; now there were trips with Birthright Israel, which provided a free ticket and so much opportunity.

On the drive home, he said, "We're all Americanized. Jews have become whites. The kids don't see themselves as a persecuted minority. If the only choice available to them is to call anyone critical of Israel an anti-Semite, they'll just turn away."

"Tager isn't coming to the federation to contribute anything, or to be a team player," I said. "He just wants to tear down what we're building. We're positive people, doing constructive, positive things for our community." My heart wasn't in it. I had begun to ruminate, and once a thought appeared in my head, it was hackneyed and trite, hanging there, static, endlessly repeating. Stan always wanted to make friends—to bring new people into our home, and outsiders into the Jewish community. He wanted to try and see the world through the other's eyes. He was a true child of the sixties—all this peace, love, and understanding. My head ached with the possibility that he approved of Tager and his antics.

When we got home, I busied myself preparing dinner, feeling belittled by Stan's refusal to condemn Tager. We ate mostly in silence, making small talk about the grandkids, the weather.

That night, I revisited, again and again, how Weinbach and myself had tried delicately, then with growing directness, to tell Tager how things operated at the federation, hoping that he would fit in or not be a nuisance. The insult of having to answer his rude questions, and deal with his disrespect for Weinbach's authority and my own, piqued my anger. In my mind, the conversations I had with Barbara Levy, Al Slovik, and Jeff Goldschmidt repeated like a broken record, all because of Tager's insistence that we bend to his deluded will. My pulse beat faster. Before I knew it, it was two in the morning, and Stan snored beside me, Eve on top of the covers between us. I stroked her, figuring I would have a partner in insomnia. She awoke, stood up, and stretched. She walked up on Stan's chest, sniffed his breath, and bedded down on the other side.

I needed to do something. My head roiling, I went to the den where I have my office and tapped the keyboard to wake the computer. I didn't know what I wanted to say, but I was certain that I needed to send Tager an email to put to rest the notion that he had gotten to me, made a difference, caused any disruption. He would not be coming by the federation, calling our members, asking for permission to attend. If he hadn't understood, he would now. But despite all the fire in my mind, all I could come up with was one sentence.

> From: Sarah Gutman <progjew36@linkpdx.com>
> To: Yoni Tager <yonster@willamnet.com>
> Sent: Thursday, May 28, 2015 2:07 AM
> Subject: RE: Talk
>
> Bridges have been burned!

I hit *Send*. Telling the sorehead that there would be no more games, no more discussion, and that those most qualified were taking charge and leading in the appropriate direction, made me feel better. I knew these late-night verdicts rarely panned out in the light of day, but the simple act of emailing brought relief. I still could be decisive, if not find the right path. I took a deep breath, and walked back upstairs to wake Stan and set the record straight.

BATSHEVA ON THE ROOF

MARCH 1996, JORDAN VALLEY, WEST BANK

DAVID OSTROV

I SAT IN the patrol truck's front seat, pleased we had pulled into the shade of a eucalyptus grove and escaped the blunt trauma of the sun, if only for a moment. Rippling waves came off the Jordan valley floor, the heat paralyzing in its intensity. The driver and soldier behind me were asleep—or so knackered by the heat that they had been rendered all but unconscious. I kept watch, listening to the radio's irregular hissing chatter.

Our patrol sat half a kilometer west of the Jordan River, the earth pockmarked with clumps of scrub. An occasional tree broke the flat, dry landscape, which was framed on either side by the rocky valley walls. It was my great honor to be the non-commissioned officer on the patrol, which meant that everybody could give a toss except me. Someone had to remain in the land of the living to pay attention to the radio if all hell broke loose. It wouldn't, because it was daytime, and nothing ever happened here during the day.

Yesterday, my American mate from the beginning of my army service, Yoni Tager, had fallen asleep while driving slowly along the fence. We crept along, letting the tracker look for footprints, when Tager's head fell to the side. I caught the wheel with time to spare before we drove into the fence. I rapped him hard in the face with the back of my hand, and yelled at him, but my heart wasn't in it. The heat made everything feel so far away, and the words sounded theatrical and irrelevant. Instead of expressing remorse for endangering all our lives, Tager wondered idly if the wire fence would have stopped the vehicle from going into the minefield. We talked about it until we got back to the base, but never reached a conclusion.

I took a long drink from my canteen, acknowledging that the deprivations were far below those of Lebanon. The many months since had dulled the sharper points, but Lebanon had been real soldiering. In contrast, our present assignment felt like a child's game. None of us wanted to go back north. We had served our time. Let some other blokes deal with the nervous gut rot, roadside bombs, bunker living, and no showers for months.

I thought about Lebanon and reflected on my experience in the Israeli Defense Forces. Despite doing my duty with vim and vigor, part of me felt like a fraud. I fired my rifle and brought my training and expertise to bear on several combat situations, yet I couldn't claim to be a combatant in any profound sense. Several times I concentrated fire at shapes and shadows but had nothing to show for it. This was the nature of soldiering at the low level. A grind, a slow slog, the individual fighter not expected to know the score, the strategy, or the result—we followed orders and figured out our contribution when we were old men. In Hebron, too, we all hung tight and toed the line, keeping the lid on the pressure cooker.

My thoughts drifted to my sometimes girlfriend, Nurit. We had met for drinks on a weekend furlough a year ago. She looked hot in bicycle shorts and a low-cut orange blouse, with large silver hoop earrings peeking out from her loose mane of black hair. Lipstick and eye makeup, recently refreshed from a red vinyl bag, gave me hope. In Cape Town, Mother might have called her look "tacky" or "cheap," but here things were different.

"Are you enjoying yourself, my warrior Rambo?" Nurit had asked. "Like the calls to attention at three in the morning? Has anyone stolen your wallet yet? And the kitchen work, now that's really the stuff of fighters. Is this what you wanted?" She had turned to look me in the face, and although her mouth appeared taught and stern, her hazel eyes were playful.

"Learning plenty."

"For me, the army was having to deal with a bunch of spoiled kids who'd never been away from home."

"Good times," I said, thinking of her stories of partying and having her own apartment in Arad. She had fired a gun during basic training but mostly helped with an educational program for wayward youth. Her stint in the IDF was less than eight months. "Still going to study for a BA degree?"

"Maybe," she said. "I want to go to the US or the UK for it. I know it'll cost more, take more time, but it would be good. Israel is so ..."

"Small?"

"No. Everyone is out to fuck each other here. I get the feeling it's different abroad, like there's enough for everybody."

I shrugged, not wanting to say anything. I had opinions about foreign study, but I had no inspired thinking about what I could say that would make a difference. She could tell me nothing about the IDF, and likewise I had no clue what she wanted out of life. Our distance, the impossibility of transcending it, spurred me to impulsively take her in my arms, planting a deep kiss on her lips. She squeaked in an inviting manner, kissing me back with equal fury.

In an instant, all negativity vanished.

I looked at my sleeping mates now, hating to see all our

hard work, the tight discipline established in Lebanon, pissed away. Our unit had unconsciously undergone a transformation from no-nonsense soldiers to a bunch of blokes who were cutting corners every chance away from base. Once the pressure slackened, we unraveled. On our last patrol, Tager had particularly irritated me with his dodgy philosophical musings.

"It's a piss-poor assignment," I had said, complaining about our posting, which was basically driving north and south along the border fence all day and night, waiting for a terrorist to appear. "We trained hard and can do more. Let the border guards or *milooimniks* do this."

"Israel Border Police, Golani, paratroopers, doesn't matter," Tager had said. "All the same. Hezbollah, Syrians, Palestinians, Jordanians. Same players, same conflict, same idea. The names aren't important."

"Bollocks. Subtle differences, political considerations, nature of conflict and engagement. Every briefing you can see how screwed up the officers are about open-fire procedures. Every kilometer on the border has subtlety."

"That's the point. The border. Today the border is so fucking hazy you need a philosophy to define it."

"And what might that be?"

"Protect your ass and your buddies at all costs. Everything else can go to hell."

"Even if it means going against orders?"

"Especially if it means going against orders. The will of the army, the government, Israel, is unknowable, abstract, and subject to change any day the Knesset is in session. All stupid reasons to get shot. Ideology, too. The reality of the present. Danger and bullets. These are the enemy."

I had blinked, wondering if the Yank was joking. Tager sat there, cool as cancer, forcing me to remind myself what in fact we were discussing. If a transcendental love of Zion and Eretz

Yisrael had once been the rationale for fighting hard, now, per Tager, the stakes had been drastically lowered.

"Goldfinch B, Goldfinch B." A voice a crackled over the radio now, jolting me alert with our code name. "Go to post ninety-four for line check."

I picked up the handset. "On our way." I shook Yehuda Alkana, who slowly straightened up, stretched, and spat. "Fire it up. You heard the girl. Yallah, post ninety-four."

Mother must have noticed this growing cynicism and frustration when I had seen her on my last furlough, I thought as we prepared to move out. On my second day I had lounged in front of the telly and watched a sevens tournament on Eurosport. She came to speak to me with an earnest expression, abruptly changed her mind and turned to go, and then became teary-eyed—for what, I haven't a clue. A motherly realization of my final loss of innocence? My growing callousness to my surroundings? My reluctance to be articulate about anything? But she's the one who might benefit from psychotherapy, for she berated me like a tot for leaving dishes in the sink and clothes on the floor and then clung to me weeping, asking me not to return to the army, pleading with me not to be so distant.

I had tried to snap out of my dullard's holiday and told her I was fine—the same as always, just beaten down by tough living and the usual idiocy of army life. She wouldn't be comforted. Maybe she was alone too much. She went back to Cape Town, ostensibly to visit relatives. Her parents were long dead, and she had one sister with whom she didn't get along. Last time I spoke to her on the phone she evaded all inquiries and didn't know when she would return. Father, of course, said nothing.

Our squad's official posting was to conduct a variety of security operations around a twenty-kilometer section of the Israel border north of the Dead Sea. There was a dusty Arab town nearby, and a few Israeli settlements growing grapes, melons, and tomatoes. But things were quiet. A few times each month, things got going when there was an infiltration, but it was not clear these were linked to terror or even crime—just Palestinians wanting to visit their relatives on the other side of the fence. Today we were on a daylight patrol, and our sole responsibility, assuming complete and total war failed to break out, was to check the effectiveness of the electronic fence. It was an electronic marvel that could send HQ a signal indicating where the wire was touched. Trucks dragged steel mesh near it, grooming the powdery dust to a smooth surface which would reveal all tracks by man or beast. Listening devices and motion detectors picked up a spectrum of noises and shapes. The area was liberally garnished with minefields sealed in barbed wire, making our contribution to the security scenario excruciatingly boring and routine. The border fence was actually a few kilometers west of the Jordan River, which was the official border, as the creek twisted and turned through low, swampy land, resetting its course each spring. We spent scores of hours between the fence and the river, which meant a jihadnik from Iran could walk virtually undeterred right up to us—but still it was a rare day that our pulse rate lifted off the baseline.

Alkana turned the vehicle around, and we headed off in the new direction. This would be the last task of the day. We had started the patrol at 4:45 a.m. when I slowly walked the road near the river on foot, followed by a tracker and the patrol vehicle. Despite the possibility of terrorists concealing themselves under every bush, in the early mornings I just enjoyed the great panoply of birds, the misty swamp, the tall grasses, and the stately trees, believing that I could snap into focus should the situation require it. In my reverie, I had managed to say the right words into the radio and let everyone know the good guys hadn't been overrun. Today after the first sweep, we parked in a shady nook and ate breakfast from the box we had filled from the mess hall with hardboiled eggs, cucumbers, tomatoes, yogurt, and halva. The pure silence and stillness, the unobscured view in all directions, and the complete lack of motion made even the pretense of vigilance hard to muster.

"Check it out!" Alkana shouted now over the engine noise and wind.

I turned to see an ibex running in the mined corridor between the security fence and the low barbed-wire fence to the east. Erosion by winter rains had exposed many of the small boxes of the anti-personnel mines, and the ibex twitched and jumped among them alongside the truck. Alkana sped up, maybe thinking that if he pulled ahead of the ibex it would veer off from the mines. I looked appreciatively at the lithe animal, wondering if we were about to witness the death of something beautiful. The situation felt miles away and the outcome merely a footnote. Finally, the animal turned left, glided over the barbed wire with an effortless hop, and headed for Jordan without looking back.

We arrived at our coordinates. Alkana shut off the engine and got out to press on the wires while I radioed the mission sergeant that we had started testing the fence's sensitivity to touch, as well as the motion-detection capabilities. Alkana waved the vehicle's long whip antenna to create movement, and the three of us stared at the radio. The voice of the mission sergeant crackled over it. "Okay, boys—all reads right. Return to base."

I climbed back into the patrol vehicle and Alkana started the engine. I thought of the endless silences of our apartment without Mother's presence. Father usually worked late, kept a taciturn demeanor as a rule, and would ignore me completely if I didn't wish his company. He eagerly anticipated his firm's IPO and maintained a tight-lipped confidence that he would become a certifiable success. He purchased two new suits for this anticipated ascension—even a silver Rolex in the duty-free store at Ben Gurion. But most surprisingly, he started working

out at a fitness club. On my last visit, I had seen him twice in
the kitchen in shorts and vest, putting a bag of ice on his leg
above the knee. He said he was trying to rehab his leg again,
although I couldn't remember any previous attempts. The leg
had always been an excuse why we never enjoyed much rec-
reation as a family. When I was a boy and wanted Father to
take me to climb Table Mountain, he set me on his lap, saying,
"Worst things and best can be one and the same. See here, I
broke my leg. Terrible thing, for it ended my rugger days. But
because of it, I met your mum."

Growing up, my sister, Edna, and I had cataloged all the
irrelevant, cluttering details we could glean about our parents'
courtship, proving to ourselves that Mother and Father had
once been young and in love. Mother worked as a nurse in
a Johannesburg hospital, and Father relocated to the city to
avoid conscription in Rhodesia. Father played outside center
for a local club and fractured his femur above the knee on
a dry windy Saturday. The way Mother told it, "Just twenty
and new to the hospital, so I had to work weekends. Usually pretty quiet. Then all of a sudden I hear all this cheering
and singing—coming from the admitting room—half a rugby
squad. Filthy jerseys, all of them. A few drinking beer—*in the
hospital,* mind you. This mountain of a man sang a blue song
about a camel in the highest of pitches, all the while your
father moanin' on the gurney."

A few times during high emotion, Father had been per-
suaded to sing the ditty about the camel who tried to bugger
the sphinx. "Of course, when the head matron heard the
racket, she didn't stand for any of it," Mother said. "She shooed
those rugger hoons out of there like they were nippers."

Father's version of events centered on how pretty Mother
looked in her uniform and how attentive she was to him.

"After his leg was set in plaster," Mother said, "he sat in

the solarium wearing a red bathrobe and sunglasses, looking like a movie star, reading the *Financial Times*."

After Father's leg healed, the courtship had become the usual dinners and walks in the park. Mother was so impressed that at only twenty-six, Father had set up a procurement office in Johannesburg for the family textile venture in Bulawayo, and conducted himself like a real *macher* for anything that could be bought or sold. This is where Father as boyhood hero comes in. Although the textile factory eventually failed, we never lacked for money. Father always found a way to work things out. He even got into nefarious business dealings with the headmaster at the posh school Edna and I attended, which made tuition cheap or nonexistent. I never learned what that might have been—gambling debt, most likely. When I want to be like Father, this is what I think about: never being over-whelmed, never being paralyzed by circumstances, keeping the compass guided by a hard-edged logic that's like a cable pulling you through the gray morass.

I bounced in the front seat as Alkana sped toward the main gate of the base. Why he hurried was a mystery as the tedium inside the base was not so different than that experienced on patrol. I had my rifle next to me and absentmindedly picked at the electrical tape around the magazine. In Lebanon, I had wanted to learn how to best prepare for ambushes and firefights, and carefully noted how the veterans configured their kits. In careful imitation, I taped two magazines together offset—one sticking further out than the next and separated by a spacer so when things got hot I could reload in the blink of an eye.

"For my parents," Tager said, almost yelling to be heard from the back seat over the engine and wind, "being Jewish is prayer and abstraction. For us, it's real. Don't get any more real than this."

"Yaw, some bloody reality," I said. I looked around at nearby Highway 90, the few cars on it headed south to

Jerusalem, the landscape barren and desolate. "You said your dad was a chemist?"

"Pharmaceuticals, but he won't share the pills."

"Where you stay, with your uncle? What does he do again?"

"The only davening shellfish salesman in the Jewish home-land. That's the guy."

"He'd get on with my old man. Not one to be bothered by contradictions." I leaned back and remembered how Father had made the big announcement four years ago at a Sabbath dinner, after all the blessings had been recited, the candles lit, and the wine poured, saying he was eager to rekindle youthful ideologies and make *aliyah*. He could've said he wanted a go at a new business. Pompous bastard. I hadn't seen it coming. Always a stalwart assimilationist, Father enjoying drinking and gambling, sunshine at the club, swimming pools, houses with gardeners and housekeepers, and big German sedans. I admit the status quo had been sweet. For years Father told us that majority rule wouldn't be the ultimate evil or the end of our world. Yet suddenly Zionism popped into the mix. To be fair, the elections didn't have anything to do with it. If the deal hadn't come along, or had come along in Texas, he might have claimed to have always wanted to be a cowboy.

Father was old school, and the best characterization of his style and outlook could be discerned from a cherished black-and-white photo he hung in a prominent place in his office. In the picture, Father and his three mates posed wearing matching dark suits with narrow neckties and derbies tilted at rakish angles in front of a gaudy Sun City casino—looking slightly tipsy and arrogant, like a fearless band of financial marauders. This must have marked Father's arrival as a person of sub-stance and means, for the proprietor gave them all free meals and board to stay at his establishment, and cemented their reputation as big-time card players. Coming a few years past a disastrous textile venture, the photo was proof positive that

Father was not a failure. The photo might have provided inspiration, for the other three became wealthy beyond wealth, and served on boards for universities and charities, with multiple trophy homes and wives. But Father still had to hustle. Larry Cohen, one gambler, had introduced him to the Israeli deal.

"Always Israel in the back of our heads," Father said at the table after the initial surprise of his announcement had sunk in. He held his wine glass loosely and leaned back, crafting his words in the tone of well-established fact. "The time was never right. The time now is auspicious indeed. Economy's strong there, good capital markets. And can you believe it? Rabin shook that *mamzer* Arafat's hand. On the White House lawn of all places, too." Father shook his head. "Maybe he knows better than me and good things will come. If there is peace with the Palestinians, then the region could really develop quickly."

I wasn't going to say no. Cape Town meant good times, rugby, surfing, and friends, but the deterioration of the government and a divided society kept pressing in on us with rising crime rates, urban decay, and the unshakable feeling these problems would get a hell of a lot worse before they improved. That year Father bought a Glock, his second pistol, and carried it to work every day in a shoulder holster. Edna and I welcomed a move to Israel as an acceptable, if not ideological, change—each of us could name twenty families who had decamped for Sydney, Los Angeles, or Israel.

Mother, the only clearheaded one among us, adopted a grumpy pragmatism in paring down our possessions to trade a two-story villa with garden and pool for a five-room apartment in a nondescript middle-class Tel Aviv suburb. She looked away when Father talked about Zionism, never giving the sacred notion of Israel as our homeland any credence. "Nothing's ever good enough for your father," she liked to say when exasperated with some new headache of living in Israel. When she set up shop, her life wasn't so radically different than before. A new group of friends, including women she already knew from Cape Town, another country club, fashions showing a bit more skin, and a scrawny Nigerian named Elvis who came twice a week to clean. With stony resolve, she went to *ulpan* three times a week to learn Hebrew but had resigned herself to never speak the language. She learned to curse from an Odessan babushka—not just in Hebrew but also in Arabic. Father, of course, was appalled. I clapped and hooted the first time she let an Arabic hot pepper fly when a driver cut her off.

Edna, who in university proclaimed her loyalty to a new South Africa, couldn't resist the pull of the Mediterranean, Tel Aviv nightlife, and a chance to put all that dutiful Hebrew school attendance to good use. As a family we became insufferable optimists—like Americans—when we first arrived, delighted with any scrap of garbage in Hebrew, thinking how beautiful and ancient the land, the language. After a few months, we gradually emerged from our stupor and resumed our regular behavior.

"When you think you'll see the old man next?" I asked Tager.

"Couple of months. June maybe. He's starting to warm to the idea of me being a soldier. He's always been a right-winger on Israel. He's hoping I'll personally expand the border with my own invasion. Maybe blow up a bunch of terrorists with a crate of C-4. Better yet, start a new hilltop settlement. That would make him happier than all get-out."

"First on my father's mind is to sell Europe expensive tech. Business first."

"He's more Israeli than all of us! We're just a bunch of nutty Americans waiting for the Messiah."

"Let me guess—a fighter like you started your own local Betar group, right?"

"Naw, a local *yeshiva*," Tager said. Both of us had been active with Betar youth groups in our respective countries. "Despite being a bunch of bookish dweebs, even the old Hasids agree that debate and learning only go so far. Before Betar, I practiced locked-down arguments for use against neo-Nazi groups—not that there were many in my neighborhood. I practiced statements with a logic so crystal clear that I believed all who heard them would gnash their teeth at the discovery of their complete wrongness. I learned the hard way." He took a deep breath and rubbed a spot on his leg. "Now I don't have much to say to a neo-Nazi except at the end of a two-by-four. Some guys just aren't the thoughtful types."

Tager said it true. Israel is practical reality, vivid and resplendent, life or death, and everything else a pale shadow. First time walking down Shenkin Street in Tel Aviv, I felt the hyper-reality of the place—the striving, hustling, hive-like feeling, on streets crammed with stylish restaurants and bars, coffee houses, and hummus joints. I felt it acutely when I first arrived, desperately wanting to know where to go, who to be with, where best to watch the sun set over the Mediterranean—all of it pushed me to look for the quintessential Israeli experience. I volunteered for the army, choosing on my own volition all the disappointment, sweat, dust, pain, aggravation, and bureaucratic insanity. Father drilled it into me that that the military would be "crucial for my absorption into Israeli society" and all that rubbish, making it sound like the reward could only be found decades later and under a microscope. I saw things differently. I needed to do this for the here and now. The country was a living, breathing place, impossible to discover within classrooms or offices, and I set my sights on finding it in the field, carrying a gun under a burning sky. Mother wasn't thrilled, but sensed the inevitability of the decision.

Since I had arrived, it occurred to me more than once that I wasn't going to achieve my initial cosmopolitan daydream. I admit that I was naïve. Trying to attain "Israeliness" is like trying to become black. You aren't—so no matter how vivid your imagination, meticulous your attention to fashion, timely your opinions, well-simulated your reactions or gestures, you'll never really know.

Basic training, as per its design, cured me of whatever boyhood fantasies I harbored about the martial life. No cutting-edge weaponry in secret state-of-the-art facilities. There was nothing grand about Israeli army bases—they were just seas of dirt, sand, mud, and razor wire, with a few rough cement structures, warehouses, and tents, all sprinkled liberally with trash. The plastic bags got blown into the razor wire, where they stayed for eternity. Everything that wasn't broken, stained, or substantially rank was destined to become that way soon. Only during twilight did the eye find relief, for then the garbage disappeared, and the land looked smooth and whole as the first stars came out.

I wasn't the typical recruit, as I immigrated after I finished university. I was on average five years older than my comrades, and able to run faster and lift heavier loads—for me, the big tests were sleep deprivation and attitude maintenance. I never had doubts about how I would get along with my squad, as I'd always been an affable bloke, but during the first week, some idiot thought he could interrupt our five hours of sleep with a loud conversation on his cell phone, the wanker too lazy to get up and walk away from the tent. I told him to shut up and then to shut his bloody mouth. Then I overturned his cot and put my knee on his chest and cocked my fist, ready to fire my knuckles into his teeth should any further discussion be needed. It wasn't. From then on, things flowed easier. Most Israelis in the squad were all piss and wind.

I never considered myself an intellectual, but I would be lying if I told you my university years were a waste. Even though I couldn't become Israeli, I still craved a deeper understanding of the concept. I was not a simpleton. I understood that Israeli society could offer prototypes in every shade and color to support your base assumptions. And I had my opinions, which had to be verified just like every other foreign-born tosser who had washed up here: opinions bred through Hebrew

school, Betar, an orthodox synagogue full of cranky Lithu-
anians, watching news coverage of yet another bomb blast,
taunts on the rugby pitch, faded black-and-white photos from
Europe, and a familiarity with Jewish history stretching back
to the destruction of the Second Temple. The hype told me
that modern Israel as a collective body, a metaphor, was hitting back extremely hard. Everything else was commentary.

I woke up to Eitan, the sergeant keeping the duty roster,
kicking my cot and grunting. The roster hadn't been posted
when I crawled into my sleeping bag, so I knew Eitan's lumpy
face could well be my alarm clock. I rolled from my side to my
back and opened my eyes.

"Kitchen duty," Eitan said and ambled out the door.

I dressed and lumbered to the mess hall, the sun hot and
high in the sky, the muted colors of the green and gray buildings looking additionally dusty and wilted through my haze of
lingering sleep. I walked into the kitchen and put my rifle on
the metal table in the storeroom. Even though we were inside
the wire, theoretically we had to be ready to stop peeling potatoes and grab our guns.

"Gideon, you bastard."

"David, you whore," he said, slapping my hand. Gideon
was one of the original blokes from my induction group, and I
liked his easygoing manner. The cook in charge of the kitchen,
a soldier named Pasternak, was rumored to have worked at
food production in civilian life. I didn't notice any contribution of excellence on his part—the nosh never changes. Music
from Galgalatz, the IDF radio station, played loud while the
other soldiers laughed and arranged serving platters with a
variety of salads.

Pasternak had Gideon and me opening and peeling avocados. The task was pleasing in that we could work at a good clip without too much concentration; soon we had filled a large plastic bin with avocado quarters.

"Hah, what's become of us, *habibi*. Two failed commandos!" Gideon smiled. He furthered the joke by flipping the paring knife into his opposite hand, letting a few deft air punches fly to simulate slitting the throat of an attacker.

I smiled but didn't want to go that route and be reminded of my failure.

Back when Father had been all about my absorption into Israel, he gave me a long talk about how the CEO of his company had been a fighter pilot—one of the most revered military roles in the country. Father boasted that based on this alone, the venture would never lack for investment. The R&D vice president was a missile boat captain, while another important bloke had been a helicopter pilot. All this was to let me know that what I did in the army would determine whether I would drive a bus or be a future prime minister. Apparently, no one got venerated for being a Golani schlepper, so I tried out for the select unit: the *sayeret* (commando squad).

"The tryout burned me to cinders," Gideon said, lamenting how the blisters on his feet took six weeks to heal.

I nodded. "Those stretcher drills were brutal." I recalled how we ran for hours with one soldier on a stretcher, rotating each corner every ninety seconds.

Gideon meant well, but wanting to talk about the *sayeret* left me cold. Last year when I had called Father to tell him I hadn't made the selection, I felt like a nipper with a bad report card. I stood in the dust and heat to use the pay phone by the commissary. Father's voice boomed when he picked up. "Good of you to call, boy. Howzit? Soldier's life treating you right?"

"No worries."

"You made it, right? Got selected?"

"They didn't want me."

"Did you try hard? Tell me you gave your all."

"I tried hard, but it's not about ..."

"Want something bad enough, you've got to go get it, or just make excuses sucking on soup." He took a deep breath, not bothering to filter his utter disappointment. "The plan now is to try for officer training. Don't muck this one up. It'll be your last chance to distinguish yourself."

I hung up, my thoughts scalding him for being too much of an arrogant sod to hear me out. Not long after I felt good, he felt bad. Truly, I wanted to be part of the *sayeret* more than anything, but my reasons and his were different. Father thought years in the future, imagining boardroom presentations and potential investors. I wanted something I could believe in right now—something uncontestably genuine and untainted.

We finished with the avocados and began putting the quarters on orange plastic plates before dousing them with lemon juice, salt, and pepper. Before we came to the end, Pasternak told us to start on the dishes, which were stacked to overflowing in an industrial steel sink. The radio played good music, and somebody broke out a giant Toblerone chocolate bar a relative had recently purchased in duty-free. I felt a bit lighter.

"Crazy you didn't make the *sayeret*," Gideon said. "No one could touch you—guys fell, you picked them up. Volunteers were needed, you said 'I'm here.' The army is so fucked up, don't recognize star talent."

"Cheers, mate," I said, embarrassed I had once placed so much emotional capital on being a commando. Now, with the end in sight, I was certain that the army was far from being a meritocracy and that I was not a particularly good soldier.

Only twelve of us from the platoon had elected to brave the tryout. On the day, we boarded a bus that took us from our base in the north to one in the dunes on the coastal area between Tel Aviv and Haifa. There, we marched all night. We were allowed to nap on the ground for a few minutes before being roused and given a new exercise. We sprinted up and down baking dunes, lugging ammunition crates and full jerrycans to imaginary fight positions, and dashed back to take another load. We ran to the firing range to shoot our rifles, out of breath and deprived of sleep. We gobbled field rations wherever we found ourselves, savoring any moment that didn't inflict searing pain.

And despite what I may think now of the army, the potential for transformation loomed large. I was resplendent, pure, knowing what the goal was and why I suffered. I volunteered to carry the heaviest loads and took the longest turns at carrying the stretcher. When we all lay on the ground drenched in sweat with our tongues lolling out and the officer called for a volunteer, I jumped to my feet and staggered to the next assignment. Sometimes the call-ups were just to mess with our heads, seeing who would rise to the task even if it was only to move a hundred meters. Blokes cried when the call came to move, knowing they had to get up but unable to do so. Hamburger feet, guts cramped and constipated from field rations, crotch chaffed raw. Soldiers walked into stationary objects asleep on their feet—or sank to their knees, fell over, and didn't get up.

For a bloke like me, all these things came easy. My mind kicked out a soundtrack, and the animal took over. But as with everything, tricks were built into the system. You couldn't just do the drill. You had to lend a helping hand to others and show leadership by organizing the tasks. But my Waterloo was the psychiatric test. Some things you couldn't fake.

The officers chose the third day of the five-day tryouts as the one for the psychiatric evaluation, most likely because we were fatigued enough to have lowered our defenses but not so tired that we'd be incomprehensible. The officer running the show called us off the firing range to lounge around outside an administration building, kicking us back to consciousness for our turn with Sigmund Freud himself.

Inside the air-conditioned office, a gaunt man in his thirties sat at a steel desk, looking like a Swiss schoolteacher. He had a narrow face and frameless glasses, a three-ring binder and notepad in front of him. He looked ill at ease in uniform, and sat with his legs crossed, shoulders caving in on a pigeon chest, his voice an uneven murmur. As I answered his questions about my parents, childhood, and reasons for volunteering, he put his finger to his lips in a quick, silent response before jotting down a few notes.

I discounted this man as easily fooled—and as a result I am not a commando. I should have spoken freely and honestly and unburdened myself. The result would have been the same, but I could have had the bonus of revealing myself to a member of the mental health community. In my mind, I framed the interviewer's questions as if I was a robust kibbutznik youth, tanned from agricultural work, feet tough from wearing simple leather sandals, mind fit from a healthy thirst for academic knowledge, and a sincere belief in Zionistic causes. I spun all my answers from this perspective. The Zionist lad would admit a particular vulnerability, and reveal a thoughtful intelligence in a nonaggressive or boastful manner, yet exhibit enough rage to show he would fight to the bitter end, whatever the cost.

The bloody question was so simple. Who had the greatest influence on my growing up? I could have said Menachem Begin, Theodore Hertzl, Zeev Jabotinsky, our black gardener Titus, anyone. But no, I spoke of the man I had told myself before the *sayeret* tryout that I could not mention under any circumstances. "Chris Pretorius," I said, feeling extremely clever. I recited cock-and-bull tales of how Chris had been an outstanding role model of honor and commitment to his family and comrades.

The truth was more complicated and disturbing. Chris had been a surrogate older brother, a mentor who ushered me into the rugby, beer, and *boerewors* culture of South African manhood. After my bar mitzvah, I strove to break out of the ghetto of Cape Town Jewry, and spent all my free time on the rugby pitch, where I got on well with my teammate Bushie Pretorius, Chris's younger brother. Chris had recently finished mandatory army service. He enchanted Bushie and me with crazy tales from his stint in Angola. Chris's stories emphasized the daftness and complete lack of spine our allies, the UNITA forces, showed on the battlefield. Yet in the telling, he maintained that the South African Defense Forces' undertaking was a hero's job.

What I had wanted to convey to the IDF shrink was that Chris tried to the end to understand his circumstances and do good work. In hindsight, though, it's a black mark on Chris to say he never doubted his mission after all the failed invasions, the lost battles, and the comical notion that the UNITA forces were backed by covert US aid while fighting Soviet-backed Marxist forces protecting American oil interests. After Angola, Chris joined the security forces, where he became an enthusiastic participant in all sorts of dodgy crackdowns. In recent years, Chris had been summoned to face the Truth and Reconciliation Commission.

Chris took a keen interest in Bushie and me and wanted us to understand the tools and machinery, as well as the values, of his world. On Sundays during the school year, Bushie came over, and we lifted weights in the garage. We'd go for a run and finish up with a swim before planting ourselves in front of the telly. Chris knocked on the door, solicitously greeted Mother or Father, and then asked if we wanted to go on a "field trip." We always jumped at the chance, as these excursions indulged our curiosity about military hardware and weapons. Chris took us for a ride in a Vickers armored car, and to a firing range where we shot pistols and rifles. He let us sit in the driver's seat of a parked water cannon, carefully explaining the controls and gauges. But Chris also had a cruel streak. Once at the firing range, he called "clear," telling us to go downrange to change out our paper targets. On the way back, he yelled, "ANC *attack!*" making the dust around us jump with bullets until we cowered on the ground. Bushie pissed his pants. It was ten minutes before I stopped shaking.

After the firing range incident, I hesitated to go with Chris when he showed up. On these occasions, Father glared at me until I changed my mind. Bushie assumed that he had to do what Chris said. When Chris knocked on our door, if Father answered, he inquired what Chris intended to do with us. Chris never hesitated in gleefully telling his plans with the excitable tones of the truly inspired. I saw that Father regarded Chris with a calculated admiration, as a path untaken, and a cheerful bloke who grabbed life by the balls and gave fuck-all about polite society. Sometimes the two shared a bottle before Chris took us out, and Father became animated and chatty, a rarity on most weekends.

I told the IDF shrink about Chris's friendship in later years and how he looked out for me on the rugby pitch, defended me from abuse by teammates, and helped equalize any slights. My interviewer was lost in his own world, tapping his face and jotting comments on a form. Exploring Chris's role in my life brought to light that Chris had been a policeman and a member of a squad that enforced the Indecency and Immorality Act, making the interviewer's eyebrows twitch. By this time, I knew I had made a mistake bringing Chris into the equation. I told myself that there was a difference between Chris and me, but in the scrutiny of the interview, doubt had risen. Fears that I was the brute who loved mayhem and suffering for the sheer freedom of expression danced in my head as I tried to tell the shrink about Chris's positive aspects. The more I spoke about Chris, the more the memory of our last field trip crept into my mind, making me trip over my words.

Bushie had called me on the phone, as it was past nine in the evening, saying that Chris wanted to "show us something." Enough time had passed from the firing range incident that I again held Chris in good esteem. I arrived at the Pretorius car park to find Bushie and Chris waiting beside a police vehicle. Chris wore his uniform. That wasn't unusual, but he had already strapped on his weapons belt, containing a billy club and pistol. A shotgun leaning against the squad car hinted that we were going to do something out of the ordinary. We drove for an hour through winding canyons and wind-scrubbed bush before we arrived at a town I knew of vaguely—a squalid place where coloreds and blacks who worked menial jobs in Cape Town lived. A few tidy houses, countless shacks cobbled together, and lots of junked, burned cars. There was no greenery, and everything was covered in a patina of red dust from the dirt road.

We arrived in front of a small *shebeen*—a rough structure of scrap wood and corrugated tin—and through the open door, I saw mismatched tables and chairs and the bar. The place was empty, but the inhabitants of the town, a crowd of dark faces, eyed us warily from a distance on the street. We parked next to a dented and scratched gunmetal paddy wagon, with all its glass covered by wire caging. We got out. Chris greeted the other security officers with a nod. He had resolutely refused to comment on our undertaking in the car, but now that the cast had assembled, it was time to lift the curtain.

"What's the story?" Bushie asked.

"This place, selling white puss to the *kaffirs*," Chris said.

I snorted, believing we would watch as the *shebeen* was soaked in petrol and burned to the ground. As the information sank in, I took care of my bearing, not wanting to be a quivering tit like on the firing range. Enough humanity still coursed through my veins that I prayed not to witness anything too extreme. Stories circulating at school about mutilations and killings haunted my sleep.

The scene appeared under control, if not exactly calm. Four handcuffed blacks, their clothes bloody and torn, were led to the paddy wagon, heads bowed, saying, "Yes *baas*, no *baas*." Chris conferred with his mates and left Bushie and me to wonder what would come next.

"Bloody shit storm," Bushie whispered. "White whores. A fucking bomb going to blow. These blokes going to turn the whole *kraal* inside out."

We nervously glanced at Chris, who carried on in the light way he always did, not reflecting the anxious tension ricocheting around the assembled. Looking like he was having a relaxing picnic, Chris smiled and opened the boot of his car, took out four cricket bats, and handed one each to me, Bushie, and two young officers. I took hold of the bat and instinctively ran my hands over its edges and noted it wasn't up to match standard. The face was mauled with jagged indents and stained an ocher color. It felt impossibly heavy in the cool air as I looked at Bushie, who gritted his teeth.

"In you go, lads," Chris said, giving us a push into the *shebeen*. The dank interior smelled of stale sweat and piss, and in the far corner sat a bar made of rough lumber with several beer vats behind it. "These *tsotsis* are guilty of bad business judgment. As members of the constabulary, our job is to confiscate the means by which they practice an illegal trade." Eyes twinkling, Chris moved his head broadly from side to side as if addressing a large audience.

We looked at him, not comprehending.

"You, my young friends, are the demolition crew. To put these *moffies* out of business, we're going to turn this shack into nails and dust."

One of the older officers came in from outside and set a

large silver stereo on a chair. "Hear you've got the score to this here opera," he said to Bushie, winking.

Bushie fished around in his pockets and dropped a cassette in the machine. He pushed the play button, and as the music came up, we looked at each other, knowing what was expected but not sure how to start. The impending violence combined with the music produced an odd sensation, knocking us down a peg. We looked at our shoes, and then at the ceiling. Chris scowled at us, and I closed my eyes, searching for the spark. In a flash, the punchy guitar riffs of Motörhead's *Ace of Spades* exploded in the back of my brain, and my eyes flipped open. I bounded across the room and sprang off a chair, whipping the bat down over my head and onto the bar, exhaling an earnest shriek. The bat busted through the top of the bar in a crash of splintered wood. This sparked the others to life, and they hacked at the objects in their vicinity with a workman-like seriousness.

Had I carried out mere destruction, I might not have felt so conflicted. I reveled in the pure delight of mayhem. Sweat streamed down my face as I tried to work the bat as fast as I could, destroying the most valuable items in the shortest amount of time. Beer vats gushed to the ground, glasses became fragments. All the while I rode a wave of teenage adrenaline, screaming the words to heavy metal songs, celebrating rage as ecstasy.

As I swung the bat, I saw the others pick up their pace, probably tasting a fraction of my fever pitch. Within minutes, everything of size and value had been reduced to wreckage. We walked around kicking the debris, looking for undiscovered treasures to smash, randomly swinging the bats just to see where they would land. Chris, who had stood outside with the shotgun, came back in and turned off the tape player, and said in a low voice, "Well done, lads, really well done."

I believed I had won a great honor, achieved secret knowledge, observed life from the new perspective of the initiated.

I thought of telling Father and letting him know I was now a full participant in the landscape of men. But I thought better of it, figuring on any workday he would object for all the sundry reasons—I might have gotten hurt, good boys don't run around busting up *shebeens*, they study hard and become lawyers and doctors—yaw, yaw, all the usual. Never did it occur to me that this wasn't a legitimate police action. Given the state of the Apartheid government, I supposed this was just a day at the office. Only when I told Edna a few days later that I had stuck up for the pride of South African womanhood did things clarify.

"You stupid shit," she said. "Those blacks and coloreds out there probably didn't do anything wrong other than fail to give the coppers the proper amount of payoff. Whores are everywhere—look around! White and black. Did you see any white women out there?" I hadn't. Edna said the blacks were harassed enough by the comprehensive tenets of the disgusting Apartheid laws without having a team of "hopped-up little deros" enthusiastically doing the dirty work.

I felt ashamed, angry that I had been so easily manipulated. I couldn't shake the feeling that Chris knew me better than I knew myself, and this dance of destruction was food for the dark, chaotic regions of my soul. Edna's chastisement that I was a tool of Apartheid nailed down my feelings of transgression, for Father and Mother made a point to *tsk-tsk* and *tut-tut* the Afrikaners' futile struggle to maintain any consistency and decency in their government. During these discussions, Father would mention that the average Afrikaner sympathized with the Nazis, as both pursued similar ideals of racial purity. Despite her usual cheerfulness, Mother grimly maintained that every country on earth had its dirty laundry, and plenty of places were worse than Cape Town. Where exactly, she never specified, but she said these words with the conviction of the converted. Despite our staunch rejection of minority rule,

I can't say any of us did anything to show our political stripes except Edna. At university, she organized bus trips for white students out to the "Homelands," or Bantustans, making it a point to have an active social life with both blacks and whites.

Whatever inner turmoil I had over demolishing the *shebeen*, Bushie appeared to suffer no self-recrimination. While I started university, he went straight into the army, choosing the intelligence branch after boot camp. That first year when I saw him on furlough, he was eager to share stories of intrigue and torture, explaining how a common method to get a man to divulge information was to lock him all night in a mortuary, or in a tiny wire cage with a snake. I felt that old pressure to keep composure and not flinch when I listened to my old friend, and hoped he wouldn't lose himself to such inhumanity. As it turned out, Bushie went to London to study engineering after his mandatory service. Chris even quit the security forces in the early 1990s as he saw the inevitability of majority rule. He told me, "No stability. No right. No wrong. We're fighting for the *kaffirs* now."

As my Israeli interviewer continued to probe about what Chris Pretorius meant to me, all the apparent signals must have been flashing neon. Through fatigue and inexperience, I lost sight of the appropriate answers—becoming confused by the circular questioning, and forgetting what my original stance had been and what answer I had given to similarly phrased questions just minutes before. Obviously, I said nothing about the *shebeen*, as I realized the impossibility of convincing anybody I was fit to maintain honor and purity of arms if the truth came out.

The interviewer grew agitated, rubbed the back of his neck, and looked at me with growing frustration, as if he knew I was holding back. He kept at me, asking about the Apartheid government, how I reacted to social slights, and what I liked about rugby. Did I view Chris as a violent person? Eventually my dogged circumvention forced him to give up. When finally it was all over, I got up, numbly disbelieving I could have gotten everything so wrong. Walking outside into the heat, I blithely tried to maintain the hope that I had a chance, but I returned to the field with the sole desire to disappear forever.

The radio in the base's kitchen switched from music to news and ended my conversation with Gideon as we wanted to learn the latest developments. We worked through the stack of dishes in silence as others flung jokes across the room. I stared into the suds and swirled the water into patterns, and let my mind drift. If I had told the shrink that I liked fighting and winning, causing hurt where I could, because it was fun and I was good at it, what would have been the result? Same as before. A psychiatric test isn't like O levels, where a bloke can cram and goose the outcome. The evaluation revealed a condition, one that didn't need to be given expression in the army or anyplace else. I cleaned another cooking pot, almost mollified that I was where I needed to be. I knew that once out of the army I would make sure never to return.

The next day I had nothing until the evening hours, so I spent the afternoon reading newspapers and napping. As the sun started to set, I got up off my rack, picked up my rifle and ammo harness, and went outside the barracks. I rechecked the duty roster and then headed down to the motor pool to go on night patrol with Mr. Chaos himself: Tager. Lately I had come to appreciate his antics as each day dragged on like the last one. Even better, Tager was NCO on this mission, so he could worry about all the usual details and try and stop Alkana and me from falling asleep.

In the twilight, we loaded the Humvee with all the required supplies and set out. True to form, Tager had his own ideas of what we needed to bring on patrol. The first order he gave was to instruct me to drive to the edge of a settlement that grew table grapes. He hopped down and cut several bunches, throwing them into a cooler packed with ice. Further down the road, we stopped at a site where a farmer had dismantled a shed and collected several pieces of wood. Tager said tonight was Lag B'Omer, even though it wasn't. We passed through the gateway and crossed over to the Jordan side of the fence. We drove a few circuits on both the low and high roads before setting up camp on a bluff overlooking the tomato fields of Jewish settlers who took advantage of the fertile floodplain. Alkana built a fire, and Tager threw his rifle and ammo into the back of the truck. I followed his example and settled into the timeless stupor of burning through stacks of nighttime hours.

At midnight, I poked through the tall grasses with a flashlight, looking for scorpions. Finding one, I luxuriated in its arachnid otherworldliness and provoked it into striking the end of a stick before I slowly ground it into the dirt under the heel of my boot. Tager sat staring at the lights of Jordan on the other side of the valley, and Alkana listened to wailing souk music on his Walkman.

I began to poke the fire when the radio came alive. "Turkish horseman, post eighty-four," the mission sergeant called out. We all stood up and walked briskly to the Humvee to stare at the radio. This was code for an infiltration. We took out the mission book and waited for our coded orders, which the book would translate. Seconds later, it became evident that the infiltration was far away, and we wouldn't be needed. We were further redundant as "the terrorist" had run from Israel to Jordan, getting caught on the Israel side of the fence, putting us far from the operation. Ever the optimist, Tager radioed the commander, asking for instructions—but of course we were ordered to stay put.

"Long night, doing shit nothing," Alkana said.

"We're on the bench for this one," Tager said. His voice wavered and he cracked a crooked smile. "Time to spark a jay, help keep panic in check during these moments of high stress," he said, taking out a hand-rolled cigarette. His face illuminated by the lighter, he pulled on the joint, finishing his breath with a hiss.

"Prison if we get caught," Alkana said, taking the joint from Tager's hand and inhaling.

In the dark, Tager pointed the joint in my direction. I shook my head. Sitting quietly in the night, I divided my attention between the heavens and the twinkling lights of the Jordanian village a few kilometers away.

During the week, our commanding officer, Alon Carmeli, called me into his office. "Go home," he said, handing me a bus pass.

I grabbed the slip, not waiting a second to analyze my luck at starting my furlough early. I figured the reservists had given the base extra hands, and my number had come up.

I jogged back to the barracks, padlocked my kitbag, and jammed it under my rack. I grabbed my backpack with my dirty laundry and half-walked, half-jogged to the front gate. The guard smiled and waved at my good fortune. Off the base, I set off for the highway at a good clip, occasionally breaking into a run, out of my nut to be leaving. A patrol moving along the fence saw me and picked me up, driving me the rest of the way to the Egged bus stop on the highway.

I stood on the side of the road and squinted each time a car approached through the rippling waves of heat, but then stepped back in case the vehicle had Palestinian plates. Soon I saw the red and white of the bus in the distance, the driver slowing down when he saw me. Plenty of empty seats with most of the men and women in uniform. The other passengers looked like settlers headed to Jerusalem for shopping or a night out on the town. I took my seat and appreciated the upholstery, the air conditioning, the ambiance of civilian life. I wanted to swim in the sea, stroll around Tel Aviv in only a T-shirt—just exist without an endless pile of gear hanging off my body. I had to travel home with my M-16 and one loaded magazine, the gun bouncing and chafing when I jogged. Now it sat between my legs, a constant reminder of the inconvenience of the army. Not carrying a gun for a good long time would be restorative. The army bored the hell out of me, but all I wanted to do at home was be twice as bored—lounge in a bed until I couldn't stand it, eat beyond being full while watching the telly, and sit in a café for hours for the modest pleasure of witnessing the flow of a non-militarized humanity.

I flipped open my cell phone— a birthday gift from Mother before she departed—and dialed Nurit, the only person I unequivocally wanted to see. I hadn't called in a while, and found it maddeningly difficult to think of anything to say, as my life was dull as dishwater. Nurit was out in the world, listening to new music, seeing the latest movies, getting on with her life in every way. I didn't know what I intended to say as I heard the electronic pulses of her ringing phone and imagined the hair that swirled around her head in rich abundance, her plumpness, her responsive twenty-two-year-old body, the way she bit her lower lip when she climaxed. Her answering machine kicked on. I said, "This is David ... call me," and winced when I closed the phone—I had intended to say something playful or witty.

We had met at a friend's birthday party on the beach soon after I arrived in Israel. She wore a tight black dress and sat on the sand with her legs folded beneath her, a sultry daughter of the desert. That night, she drank wine with nonchalance and teased me for looking so out of place. Her mother had come from Iran, her father from Bulgaria. Her dark looks and unrestrained manner were a testament to the salad of ethnicities, attitudes, and history that shaped modern Israel. She was a whiff of the Orient, an explainer of all Israeli culture, and exactly what I needed. Most of my people were lily-white Ashkenazic yutzes from Vilnius—the city of pickled herring.

Finding Nurit and trying to figure out what made her smile goaded me to any number of foolish behaviors. I thrilled to learn she worked as an elementary school physical education teacher in Rishon Letzion. She had no interest in big-boy sports and found my rugby playing a bore, yet always sounded happy to hear from me and grudgingly agreed to watch me play. The third time at a match, I lost my temper at this bloke who stiff-armed me in the face during a side run. I teed off on him proper with fists of fury, and got sent off by the referee, a real wanker. Nurit positively glowed from the excitement, full of humorous chastisement, and hung on my arm as if I wore an Olympic medal. As we walked away from the pitch, she kissed me sloppily, tasting the sweat and blood. She liked my parents way too much, and said that dinner at our house was like being in a BBC broadcast, as Mother used teapots and Father pontificated like he was Lord High Chancellor.

I enjoyed her parents—warm, expressive people who welcomed me into their cramped apartment for lamb stew and full-volume, detailed commentary on everything under the sun. Nurit was politically left, a die-hard Labor Party supporter, and I was mockingly labeled "Mr. Security" when I told her I didn't support the Oslo Accords. At dinner I repeated Father's pronouncements about the peace process. "The way I see it," I said, trying to sound respectful, "Rabin is the bloke who starts the business. No matter how poorly things are going, how many suicide bombers, he always tries to raise more capital. Can't believe his baby won't grow or

thrive. Someone from the outside needs to manage the store."
Nurit hotly defended territory concessions for peace, while I
resolutely maintained that Palestinians and Arab neighbors
couldn't be trusted.

When I informed her that I was volunteering for the
army, she laughed and assumed I was joking. As my induction
loomed, our time together became strained, to say the least.
We had been going out long enough for all those beautiful differences and anthropologic explorations to turn into burning
oil drums of conflict.

Even if I had parted with us screaming at each other, the
next time I called, all was forgiven. Maybe it was all charity
for the soldier in the field, but I'd take what I could get.

I hadn't seen her for almost three months. A few upbeat
and friendly voicemails encouraged me to call when in town.
The last time we met, we shared a cup of coffee at a café.
With a weary sadness in her face she insisted we talk about
our relationship—never the thing a bloke wants to hear. She
had something specific in mind, but I was too daft to figure
it out. She didn't want a clean break or an engagement ring
but something more confusing and rarified: a memorandum of
understanding for things forever unsaid or, perhaps, a pardon
for situations she insisted that I had no right to know about.

As a way of ending the conversation, I suggested that we
would be friends, really good mates—meaning that phone calls
and coffee were allowed. If the moon was full and all planets
aligned, full-on, grind-the-night-away shagging was allowed as
well. She was always generous in this regard. She dressed the
part, wearing see-through shirts with lacy black bras underneath, tight skirts or jeans, or tube tops—all in seductive
purples and blacks.

I scanned the low hills now as the bus labored up the road
to Jerusalem. I tapped the phone to make sure it was working
properly and wished it would light up. I forced myself to resist

the urge to call again. As the craggy dun hills rolled past and the engine noise became a security blanket, weariness overtook me. I leaned back and shut my eyes, feeling the cool air bring pinpricks to my sweaty skin. I drifted to sleep as I juggled a list of the pleasures I would enjoy first.

Back in the barracks after my four-day holiday, I wearily pulled out my kitbag, undid the padlock, and removed my helmet, ammo vest, field jacket—all items that screamed how repetitive, dull, and awful my life had become. I wore civilian clothes, and as I stripped and numbly put the uniform back on, a feeling came like I had received a life sentence.

If you're in a bad way, there's no better place than the military—dull routine with endless expanses of time for crushing self-analysis and brutal recrimination, and plenty of guns and dangerous machines to animate your imagination if you start to hurt. A Humvee headed out the front gate on patrol, and I looked at the .50 caliber on the roof, thought about the grenades and the mortar, and went through a series of what-ifs. I continued to get ready, hoping for a reprieve of a cataclysmic nature—lightning strike, earthquake, all-out war. Any of an assortment of destructive, random elements would suffice. Tager had been insisting we travel together to an exotic locale once we finished army service. The notion had left the realm of the theoretical and now animated my thoughts like no other—Thailand, India, Nepal, Costa Rica, Argentina. Sun, beaches, sporting adventures, and excitement of the will-she-won't-she variety.

I pulled my boots on—carefully tensioning the laces—took a deep breath, and headed down to the motor pool. I mumbled a greeting to Tager and Alkana and with little discussion got on loading the required equipment into our patrol vehicle. All the ordnance and supplies—night-vision goggles, starlight scope, flares, extra ammo, spare radio batteries—were a stupid joke to the unbroken nothingness that awaited us. I checked the oil and water of the engine—all under the watchful eye of Carmeli, who peered out from the radio room with an unusually sour expression. He'd gotten wind of the shit going on and looked for a way to turn back the tide. We knew he was watching, so until we left the base and were a kilometer down the road, everything was by the book.

I drove straight to the vineyard, and we loaded up on grapes. Carmeli had unequivocally told us to stop doing this, as the farmer had repeatedly complained—but this meant little. We drove through the gate to do a cursory patrol on the Jordan side of the fence before settling down on a hill to fritter the night away. We had stashed a ratty foam mattress by an abandoned guard shack, and we set up a rotation to take turns laying down on it, not saying explicitly that those not on the mattress had to stay awake. Alkana got the first crack at the mattress, which left Tager and me to pace around the Humvee before we sat down on an outcropping of flat rocks. I stared at the twinkling lights of Jordan while Tager noisily ate the grapes.

"What? You and Nurit have a spat?" Tager cocked his head. I took a deep breath; there was no way I could make this sound any less sordid. I'd had enough simmering in my own misanthropy and decided to lay it out even if it left me feeling exposed and betrayed. "I went home a few days early. I open the door, and Nurit and Father are in the living room."

"Whoa, dude—like, you know, doing it?"

"No, nothing like that."

Tager caught the emotion in my voice and shook his head. "I'm missing something here."

"She went to the apartment to get help with an application for some university in California."

"Okay." He drew out the word, leaning forward to focus. "What's the sin in that? This a Westsiders versus Eastsiders thing?" Irritation crept into his voice. "Was she fighting him off?"

"They acted so weird, so embarrassed. Something happened or was going to. In the air, thick as molasses." I didn't expect compassion but figured that after running my troubles through Tager's bizarre thought mill, I would gain a new perspective. "I know Nurit has other boyfriends, and Father's been acting strangely. Something's afoot."

"Weird," Tager said flatly. He walked around the Humvee, as if not understanding what I had told him. He walked out into the grass before returning to lean against the vehicle. "I feel for you, bro. In this case, I can offer you something beyond googly-eyed sympathy. I can offer you rabbinical wisdom, putting to use my wasted years in Jewish day school."

"Smashing. Let's get to it then." I already regretted my decision to confide in him.

He took out a joint and a lighter. "You know who Uriah the Hittite was?"

"Yaw, Batsheva's husband."

He lit the joint and inhaled. "He was the most kickass soldier in King David's army. A commander with the most luscious babe of a wife. The bod that seduced a king and launched a thousand hard-ons."

"I know the story. Cut to the chase."

"King David gets drunk at breakfast, sleeps the afternoon away, then goes out to his balcony at sundown and scratches his balls. He sees Batsheva washing her booty on her roof and goes nuts. Bring her to me, he screams. When she arrives, he freaks her doggy style. In his post-coital clarity, he can see the problem. When he learns she's pregnant, the problem looms larger. Old Uriah has been off at the front, fighting, winning the battles, winning the war, carrying out orders. So King David figures if he can get Uriah to *shtup* his wife then nobody will be the wiser about his itchy little muscle twitch. He summons Uriah to come home from battle, telling the dude to stop at his home and bathe and relax before seeing him."

Tager pulled on the joint, shaking it at me before exhaling. "You see, right here you've a fundamental conundrum of life. If Uriah had just slipped it in, played a little loose, he would've kept everything. *But no.* Because he is the most ass-kicking soldier of the brigade, his duty, loyalty, is to his men in the field. How can he in good faith dine on sumptuous food, bathe, wear fine clothes while his men are dying on the battlefield, sleeping on the hard ground, not getting enough to eat? Duty, honor, loyalty—this is the Hittite. If he slipped it in, he would've been fine." Tager seemed to be warming up to some invisible crowd. "The war would carry on as planned. Uriah would come home to a beautiful wife. But he walks into court with the dust of battle on his cloak, loyal to his men, the army. King David greets him, says keep up the good work and, before returning to the front, why not say hello to that cute little wife of yours? You could use a rest. Super stud just goes back to the front, thinking the king is going to reward him for his piety. Hold him up as an example. Bestow riches and honor on his house. What does he get for his awesome devotion?"

"Skewered on a spear," I said, wondering what exactly Tager's point was.

"Damn right. He could've just slipped it in. Fast and hard. Slipped it in on the side, on route to the palace while his horse drank water. *Slipped it in,* and he would've had a great life. For his loyalty and honor he's betrayed by his king and the very men for whom he labored to set such a high standard." He continued, slower, "The king told Joab, a general, that during the attack everyone should fall back except Uriah. Thus, true honor and loyalty were rewarded."

"Totally fucking beautiful," I said, "but what the bloody

hell does it have to do with me? What, I should've said `Excuse me, you're having a private moment,' and turned and left?"

"You played it right. Go and sit down, pretend everything's as it should be. Technically, nothing's happened, as far as we know. There's nothing to do." Tager climbed back into the Humvee, struggling to return to the place of departure. "The issue isn't what the fuck happened, if Nurit or your dad's thoughts are impure. Now you're wondering how you're going to manage this ugly *thing* that may or may not have happened, and this is where the story becomes da shit. I choose to live with a certain amount of falsehood in my life. Rather the falsehood than to die a pointless death like Uriah's. We're modern people and must embrace complexity. Otherwise, the contradictions of this world overwhelm us. We must accept a bit of falsehood in our lives, the gap between ideology and reality, between what we want and how things are. Two fields of opposing power can exist side by side, one not canceling or interfering with the other. Both equally true. Love and hate. Nurturing and destruction."

I grabbed the joint out of his hand and inhaled, coughing as the acrid smoke hit my lungs. "I'll show you complexity, motherfucker."

As I stared across the valley, I wondered if Tager had delivered that long-winded spiel just for entertainment's sake, or if somewhere a pearl was buried. Mother had been gone four months already. Father had thrown it all away a while back, and I was the last to know.

THE MOUNT

OCTOBER 2015, NORTHWEST PORTLAND

AARON SLOVITZ

"AARON, CRAZY THINGS happening that shouldn't," Rabbi Ben said.

I nodded and composed a concerned look. I focused on pressing my lips together and squinting for a few beats as I sat calmly in the rabbi's office.

"Linda Haber—who's not so old, by the way, nor is she young—says she's not buying Israel products. Like she did with South African lobster. She needs to tell me this? Doesn't think the settlements a good idea?" Rabbi Ben paused and shook his head. "She's been corrupted by a bad influence. Ignorance. Partial information." Looking grave, he set elbows on his desk and leaned forward, lifting his glasses as he rubbed the bridge of his nose in a quick meditation. He wore a rumpled oxford, a tie of vivid yellow and orange swirls, and beige slacks. His scowl was deep-set and foreboding.

"We'll find an expert," I said. "Show a movie." In my role as the synagogue's executive director, I tried to contribute hard-headedness, business sense, to the rabbi's musings, but when Israel came up, I was the silent factotum, merely an enabler to the streams of rabbinic thought.

"We'll do an event," the rabbi said. "Use the Rosenburg Chapel. Explain the boycott, divestment, and sanction Israel movement. Why it's bad for Israel. Why it's anti-Semitism, plain and simple." He looked directly at me and lowered his chin, as if expecting an argument. Maybe I stared back too intently. I reminded myself what I learned in my master's degree program: if you're executive director, your job is to execute. Only congregants and the rabbi got to vent on opinions—political, theological, emotional—that came to a head.

"We'll need a screen and projector for the videos. I'm thinking of a panel. Invite Sidney Weinbach. I'll speak as well. Who else?"

"Maybe someone who opposes boycott, divestment, and sanctions but with a different perspective," I said. "Maybe Rabbi Feingold could speak." Feingold was a local educator.

"Don't want to overwhelm. This should be anti-BDS 101. Different speakers should illustrate the same, basic points."

"How the BDS movement is anti-Semitic?" I already knew the answer. This was how our metropolitan synagogue, stuffed to overflowing with higher degrees and all kinds of professional achievements, handled Israel—one size fit all.

Rabbi Ben, fifty-four years old this year, stood five foot eight inches in socks and sported a substantial gut which spilled over the front of his pants and expanded to even larger dimensions given the rhetorical needs of the moment. No one would say he didn't have a good set of pipes, yet he rarely raised his voice. He liked to start discussions and sermons in the tenor range and finish in staccato contralto, his left hand punctuating the central and final point with a restrained animation. On his fleshy face he wore Oakley frames, a purchase he had been most proud of a few months previous. I observed the rabbi gently rubbing his finger over the "O" on the frames, pleased with the prominent trademark and perhaps the lifestyle it suggested.

Two weeks ago, on a perfect weather day when religious observance was far from the minds of congregants, the rabbi took his family to picnic on the beach at Oswald West State Park. Back in the office, he commented how his fifteen-minute walk from the parking lot to the sandy cove was a refreshing commune with nature, an adventure, a lift of the spirits, an epic journey. Gretchen, an office admin, later told me that every time someone in Portland says "epic," an angel dies.

Although the previous rabbi did not wear a *kipa* outside of the sanctuary, Rabbi Ben wore one in his daily life and enjoyed the whimsical nature of a few of them, placed in the middle of his bald head, where they were ringed with tufts of salt-and-pepper hair. He had the expected ones, with concentric rings in somber earth tones, but also *kippot* with the knitted Hebrew letters of the abbreviation for the Israel Defense Forces, with flags of Israel and the US, and with the logo and lettering of the Boston Red Sox, his hometown team. He spoke of having one with Bart Simpson on it but had never deigned to wear it at Congregation Mount Zion, known affectionately to all as "the Mount."

I could imagine the event: the concerned, nodding faces, the older generation telling tales of anti-Semitism in the fifties and sixties, likening current times to 1930s Germany. The hard proof that society was spinning down the drain could be seen in the highlight videos of campus BDS supporters— for these activists were the most vocal and radical. Forget the retired schoolteachers and social workers and people of faith who calmly supported BDS out of concern to lead ethical lives. The videos showed a wave of radicalized youth, many Jewish, who burned Israeli flags and hated all things sacred, and turned the Holocaust into a word to describe the destruction of Palestinians by Israelis. The tsunami of anti-Semitism that stood on the cusp of washing everything decent and righteous away never materialized. When an Israeli newspaper sent a team of reporters to investigate hotbeds of anti-Semitism and BDS in California universities, they found that at the most notorious campuses, only a handful of activists showed up regularly to protests or meetings.

"We need the screaming girl. You know, the StandWithUS die-in video," the rabbi said. A "die-in" occurred when students in sympathy for Palestinian dead pretended to die on a campus quadrangle. At a given command, the students dramatically fell down, and then gently propped up their cardboard signs to keep the spectators in the information loop. Rabbi Ben liked this video, as the young woman it prominently featured displayed raw, animalistic anger and screamed insults at her perceived Israeli tormentors. He found the video, a montage of rage and noisy, jumbled images useful in putting the audience into a receptive mood for his soothing voice and cogent perspective. He also liked videos of abuse screamed by Palestinian students, mock West Bank checkpoints on campuses, and fake house demolitions—all which underscored the irrational hatred of those in opposition to our better viewpoint. The videos shocked people out of their complacency, that much could be said.

I looked out the rabbi's office window and saw a homeless guy in a stained parka take an interest in the backseat of a car, and I wondered if he saw something he wanted, admired his reflection, or just randomly stared in his stupor.

Rabbi Ben finished his thought, cueing me to make a sound that I was listening. He bounced his fingertips together. "We need respectful discussion. We need coherence. Bringing in different points of view won't be helpful."

No surprise here. The Mount's leadership, the board of trustees, reflexively maintained the notion that Israel needed to be supported unconditionally. The videos of the BDS protests showed nothing but outrage, and gave me a headache. There was little to mitigate the ugliness, the slander, the vile calumny pictured. Israel was called a "Nazi state" by hateful people openly saying hateful things hatefully. The cherry-picked footage became a kind of propagandist heroin— irresistible, bringing forth righteous anger and loathing, distilled a hundred times. It felt good to be so angry when the evil of the world was so expertly delineated. But when the adrenaline ebbed, when the next day a person soberly reflected on the material presented, no one felt any smarter, and no nuance had been added to the layers of complexity surrounding the issue. All that remained was the thought: "Those people are wrong, and we're right."

We had trodden this ground before, when the Mount presented a speaker series that had required "coherence," which meant that speakers needed to confine themselves to an Israel-right-or-wrong-we-support-you perspective.

"I know who'll be good—Rabbi Hersh," Rabbi Ben said, referring to the Orthodox rabbi who worked at an organization for Jewish outreach and education. Hersh, in his thirties, energetic, with a full brown beard uncontaminated by gray, wore the black suit of the acutely religious. He defied a common belief held by many Reform Jews that all Orthodox rabbis were aged. He looked good, spoke with brio and eloquence, did Facebook, sent tweets, and even Instagrammed his wife's holiday food specialties. His views on Israel didn't educate our congregation, but merely highlighted the polemics of the debate. When asked about realities on the West Bank, Rabbi Hersh shook his head. "What? I've been there. Plenty of land for everyone."

Why did I choose a career in Jewish community? What madness had I suffered? Was my father a rabbi and this the family business? Hardly. My parents were Jewish lawyers in San Diego. My mother handled estate issues in her own office while my father did contract law at a large firm. We visited synagogue a few times a year, and I had a bar mitzvah, but religion was much less important to me than Led Zeppelin and the Padres.

In my early years, I always tried to set myself apart from my Jewishness and reserve it for when it would not be burdensome or put me in an awkward light with my peers. I felt embarrassed for my lack of knowledge, lack of observance, lack of *Yiddishkeit*. As the years went on, I asked myself what lay at the core. What was the touchstone experience? Was it my father telling me again and again which members of *Star Trek* were Jewish? Leonard Nimoy's subtle infusion of Jewish culture into science fiction? Was it the picture of Rabbi Heschel with Reverend King at the Selma March in '65? Lenny Bruce's take-no-prisoners comedy?

The Judaism I am proudest of, that inspired me to get a master's degree in Jewish communal services, was the Judaism that bred and sustained nutjobs like Joe Rozman, the Mount's own radicalized leftist. Joe got a kick explaining at poker that BDS made perfect sense. He worked at Intel, rode an electrified recumbent trike to work, and sported Hawaiian shirts most days of the year. He enjoyed telling anecdotes which stood traditional wisdom of any kind on its head, and he celebrated abrasive debate.

Joe trolled us heavy at poker and refuted with a hearty sangfroid the idea that BDS was unfair. He put all the responsibility on Israel and ignored Palestinian terrorism. The nervous trepidation at the mention of the BDS movement, the hand-wringing and forlorn looks—Joe wouldn't have it. At the last game, he squinted and turned his palms to the sky. "BDS is a response to a problem, not the problem itself. The problem is the occupation. You want to talk morality, start with fifty years of martial law for almost three million Palestinians in the West Bank."

I started my master's program out of frustration and my failure to find resonance with other pursuits. I enrolled, primarily, because of a weird compulsion to want to feel Jewish all the time but not to have to pray so much or eat bland food. Every academic pursuit that might have led to a different career resulted in late-night self-loathing as I stared at my textbooks and wondered what torture had been thrust upon me. My early jobs in finance left me with the inkling that some inherent nature, central to my conception of self, was being poisoned. It never occurred to me that this might be the natural transition from an irresponsible young person, who recklessly searched for fulfillment, to a consistent adult. Only later did I understand contentment comes from suffering and hard work. With the melodramatic seriousness only youth can muster, I understood that I needed to search harder to find my direction. Had I known that others suffered from this same confusion, I might not have taken everything so seriously.

When pushed by my parents to articulate the reasons for enrolling in the master's program, I could only come up with "one could do worse." That appeared legitimate in their eyes, as odd as it sounds now. With my enrollment, I felt relieved that I never consciously had to be Jewish again if I submerged myself in a wholly Jewish environment—the *Yiddishkeit* was automatic. I was twenty-five years old, so sue me if I sounded like a moron.

An influential professor from my master's program, Efraim Brom, resembled Joe Rozman, with his rotting Birkenstock clogs and heavy rag wool socks to keep out the Philadelphia cold. The first class I had with him, New Directions in the American Jewish Community, started with Brom placing a box of Manischewitz matzo ball soup mix on one end of the long table at the front of the room. To the right of the box, he set two silver filigree candlesticks. He continued arranging objects symbolic of Jewish experience on the table: a *mezuzah*, an anthology of Jewish humor, a miniature flag of Israel, a Seder plate, a DVD of *Schindler's List*, an IDF sticker, a photo of Menachem Begin, Herman Wouk's *This Is My God*, and so forth, ending with a Bible on the far side of the table.

The task Brom laid out for us was to use the objects as a starting point for students to summarize their orientation to Judaism. This was the first day of class, and I didn't know many students—most looked like me, devoid of *kipa* or other visible signs of observance. How I would start my career as a Jewish professional appeared to hang in the balance of what objects I would pick. I didn't keep kosher or the Sabbath, and my post-bar mitzvah years and young adulthood had seen me spinning elaborate plans to escape the crushing tedium of synagogue attendance.

A young woman, Miri, started the exercise. She picked up the filigree candlesticks and confidently talked about lighting the Shabbat candles as the perfume of freshly baked challah brought back childhood memories and remembrances of relatives who had been born in Europe. She continued to recite a maudlin gloss of every Sholem Aleichem story ever written with the slow cadences of weighty emotional proclamation. I expected Brom to become as teary eyed as I thought I should become, dance a Hasidic jig, sing a *nigun,* and recite a pithy phrase in Yiddish, praising to the high heavens this fine example of Jewish womanhood.

To my surprise, Brom offered no validation of Miri's deep connection to the rosy *shtetl* of her fevered imagination. "You've watched *Fiddler* a hundred times too many," he said derisively.

As a movie buff, I had seen the big films where the tough drill sergeant beats down on the recruits to establish order. To see this happen in a class meant to instill a professional attitude about how to interface with Jewish community was weird, to say the least. The course showed that the new direction apparently was to be an asshole. I became convinced that Brom had no specific plan but was hacking his way through a poorly conceived class with no practical application.

Brom continued in a bombastic manner about the need not to over-sentimentalize as a Jewish professional before calling on the next student to offer his connection to these amorphous concepts of personal identification. A guy from Newark, Marc, stood up and walked toward the table. Sensing Brom's sour demeanor, Marc cut it short and quickly picked up the Bible.

"Since my bar mitzvah, the source of wisdom."

"Wonderful. Next!"

Down the line it went, the other students presenting mixtures of piety and tradition, the Talmud and chicken soup, to varying degrees of success, hoping for the "right" answer, which was an impossible balance of textual reverence and old-world schmaltz. Brom clarified with a sneering cynicism that if I had warm associations with Birkenstock clogs, I needed to update my thinking.

My turn arrived, and I felt like the convict hauled before the warden. I picked up the book of Jewish humor, not positioning it with any other objects.

"You want this degree to tell jokes?"

"Not jokes. This is the wisdom of the Jewish faith." I tried to sound grounded in conviction, but my voice wavered, as if I was struggling not to be a smart-ass.

"Think about it. A thousand years in Europe. North Africa. Middle East. Always the Jewish people keep existing. Why? Because the essential nature of Judaism is to assert the right to be different. Logically there should be no Jews at all in the world, given the history. This insistence on the power of the independent mind is the core of Jewish humor, even the basis of what it's like to have the Jewish head, the *Yiddisher kopf*. A bold assertion of the right to be an outsider, to see things differently. This is who we are as a people, a bunch of goddamned comedians."

"Good," Brom said, nodding, "There's hope for this one."

Finding street parking close to The Mount felt lucky, and I flexed my head to stop any internal discussion comparing luck and intelligence, *mazel* and *sykhl*. I paralleled my dented gray Kia into the spot and frowned as heavy rain fell—I had forgotten a jacket. It was early fall, but it could have been late November with the gray skies, cold, and thick rain.

I hustled into the front of the four-story red brick office building next to our ornate sanctuary with a representative artwork of the Ten Commandments proudly covering the front of the modernist structure. Passing Reuven Rubin's *Sea of Galilee* in the hallway, I entered the central office space of the Mount, wishing Gretchen and Amy good morning with a brisk nod as I made my way to my office.

I sat down at my computer and read an email from Bret at Badger Robotics—the tone professional and cool, informing me that another applicant had been hired for the marketing manager position. I tried to find a thought to mitigate the rejection, but anger burned. I had journeyed to the Badger offices in Hillsboro four times, met everyone in the department, and gone out to lunch with Bret and the department staff twice. I was more than ready to ditch Jewish community and get on with my life.

I told myself that working at Badger wouldn't have made my existence substantially different—every situation had its own unique attractions and annoyances. Earlier in life, I had been insecure, and needed the provincial shelter of the Jewish community. But that time had passed. My last meeting with

Rabbi Ben highlighted my weariness with how a theology of Israel worship increasingly precluded the acceptance of the stranger and multiple points of view. Walking (or running!) away from the inner workings of the Mount had been my solution for the stagnation I felt.

I put on headphones, turned up a Spotify playlist, and threw myself into the paperwork for Israel's Ministry of the Interior about the conversion to Judaism of two newborn babies. Portland, known in Tel Aviv as "the womb of Israel," had become a mecca for gays to find a surrogate mother to bear their children. This occurred as the egg donors, surrogates, and in vitro fertilization clinicians were all in one state and Oregon's flexible laws allowed two men to be listed as parents on the birth certificate. The clinic that ran the show even had two staff in Israel, helping people through the process. Oregon had clear surrogacy laws, the kids had US citizenship, and most surrogate mothers felt an urge to help nontraditional families as well as get some *kesef.* It never hurt that so many of the surrogate mothers did yoga, consumed lots of funky vegetables and kombucha, and referenced nature in a way that sounded like the rapture—all this played well on Shenkin Street.

I carefully filled out the forms, my Hebrew limited to the questions on the documents and little else. Rabbi Ben would say the blessings, the parents would dunk the kids in the *mikvah*, and all would be mostly kosher in Eretz Yisrael. I looked at the clock and stood up, happy that the weather had cleared for my lunch appointment with my friends from the congregation, Yoni Tager and Jacob Hect. We started out playing poker but now got together to talk politics and life. As Tager liked to tell it, after high school he had come down with a bad case of Zionism and enlisted in the Israel Defense Forces. And as a result, any discussion of politics, local or national, would always include Israel, part and parcel of any Jewish-American political vocabulary. I was glad for the distraction, as my failure at Badger continued to simmer. I set out toward Chen's Noodle Bar, Tager's restaurant of choice.

While I was crossing the red brick of Pioneer Courthouse Square, my eye zeroed in on a placard with a blue six-pointed star of Israel over a white background. "Today They Control US Congress, Federal Reserve, US Media. Tomorrow? The World? I$RAEL."

The man holding the placard looked about seventy and had wisps of gray hair falling out of a faded yellow cap. He wore a long, dirty parka, which suggested that he slept outside. It was open in front, and around his neck hung a black-and-white *keffiyeh*. He saw me checking him out, smiled, and handed me a flyer.

When I got to the restaurant, Tager and Hect were already seated. A foregone conclusion was that someone would joke about our becoming *alte kakers*—fussy old men complaining about everything under the sun.

The solidarity of Tager and Hect was based on a lifestyle I aspired to but couldn't achieve. I kept being invited to these lunches perhaps because they enjoyed the civic engagement the synagogue provided, and my position cemented this feeling—I was the color commentator as the two sparred over issues of the day. Our kids were friends through the religious school, which meant our bond sustained itself through family activities where we could drink beer and crack wise.

Each exhibiting something similar to an old-world religious perspective, Tager and Hect emphasized knowledge achieved through direct, participatory experience. During the winter, both obsessively watched the approaching storms roll down from the Gulf of Alaska. The swirling masses of low pressure were like bowling balls aimed to smack the pins of the Cascades hard with precipitation. When flurries of email circulated through the men's club list with screenshots of temperature gradients and forecasts, the die was cast, and a group would head up to Mt. Hood. This willingness to sacrifice a day of productivity for fresh ski tracks on heavy, wet Northwest snow was a singular act of devotion.

A similar desire spurred both men to take fanciful trips to far-flung destinations to show their young kids life's opportunities. For Tager, that had been ten days in Bogota in 2013; Hect had impulsively taken up an offer for a week at a beach house in Hossegor, France, last October.

One can't live in Portland and not know a bunch of guys like these. Marketing people even have a nifty term, LOHAS—lifestyle of health and sustainability—to describe a devotion to a range of products, values, activities, philosophies. This is what I wanted: to exist freely in the liberal realms of Portland, to think and feel without the constant need to bite my tongue. Badger Robotics would have represented a step in the right direction. Bret had let me know that the office cultivated a come-as-you-are culture, where each month the team watched a film or heard a speaker—the point being that new ideas were welcome, if not required. The first time I met Bret, he unapologetically met me in his office wearing garish Lycra cycling clothes, having just come in from a "short" training ride of close to two hours.

We're all Jewish in Portland, all reasonably progressive, but the complicated algorithm of LOHAS better explained why Hect and Tager skied with a manic ferocity unseemly for two desk-jockey dads in their forties. An independent marketing manager of a few boutique apparel brands, Tager had the flexibility to exist anywhere at any time, as long as one of his devices had a signal. Hect found and funded real-estate investments for his father's firm, which meant his schedule was his own.

Two Aprils ago, the Mount's men's club staged a fundraiser

where sponsors pledged money for the most vertical feet skied at the Mt. Hood Meadows Ski Resort. Joe Rozman organized the event, the funds going to the Amyotrophic Lateral Sclerosis Association. He awarded prizes to those who logged the highest numbers. Hect won the congregation's contest, skiing fifty-two thousand vertical feet, which pissed off Tager more than Hect's support of Israeli West Bank settlement.

Tager rationalized his loss, saying that he needed to return to the lodge for food and water in the late afternoon, while Hect stuffed his pockets with energy bars and wore a hydration pack. Hect boasted righteous living, legs of steel, and an avoidance of gluten allowed him to best Tager by two thousand feet.

After the drinks arrived and our orders were placed, I asked Tager how it was that he had gotten his start digitally managing different brands. I hoped he would remember that I was networking to find new employment. "I did it before anyone knew what it was," he said, distracted and fidgeting. "You brokenhearted about the Iran Deal?" he said to Hect.

"Get serious. No point in making deals with Iran if they're sending missiles to Hezbollah," Hect said, leaning back.

I was glad this issue had concluded, as it consumed office chatter for most of the summer. The staff in the Mount's office cheered the passage of the deal, all the while being on the lookout for Rabbi Ben, who we didn't want to offend.

"So what's to talk about, anyway?" I said. "With a deal, there's something. Without, Iran gets to do whatever the hell it wants, sanctions falling apart as our partners France and Britain rush in to sell telecom and Peugeots."

"The Republicans used the wrong playbook, helping to get the deal passed through Congress," Tager said.

"How so?" Hect asked.

"Dermer, the supposed Israeli Ambassador, colluded with Boehner to get Netanyahu a chance to address Congress to talk about Iran, completely bypassing the White House and Obama. Israel is supposed to be a bipartisan issue. That's Washington since time immemorial. Now Israel is a right-wing, militaristic Republican thing. Rationality and diplomacy are Democratic. Netanyahu might have played it better with an approach less over the top."

"Dermer's not a diplomat," I said. "He's a political operative. Dermer scored his political points and went home. A diplomat might want to build a substantive relationship with a friendly power."

"Christians love Dermer," Tager said. "He's huge with the evangelicals. When he gets pushback about the occupation, breaking the bones of Palestinians, excessive force in Gaza, he delivers his line—the IDF deserves a couple of Nobel Peace Prizes. He never tires of that one."

"If Dermer's the guy strengthening the US-Israel relationship, we're all fucked," I said.

Walking back to the office, I again passed the square. The man with the placard and *keffiyah* was gone. I wasn't a materialist, but I saw Hect and Tager as having enviable lives. Time for career, family, sport. The Jewish community felt like a bucket of crabs, members fighting each other in petty disagreements, and gossiping incessantly. I knew this was how it was supposed to be, but I held in my heart hope for better.

"Stop posting selfies," Rabbi Ben said, poking his head into my office and smiling broadly. He grew concerned when he smoothed out and examined the flyer I had picked up from the square the day before, staring at the word "I$RAEL" spelled out in thirty-six-point font.

"There's going to be a demonstration in front of city hall," Rabbi Ben said. "People are going to be calling for Portland to divest from stock holdings of Motorola, Caterpillar, Hewlett-Packard, and G4S, as these companies are absurdly cited for selling to Israel. I found out about it at the Oregon Board of Rabbis meeting." He frowned. "I want you to put it out there on our email blast, website, and Facebook. See who can show up. We'll counter-protest, drown out the anti-Semites with our own people."

I wrote this down on a pad, but my face gave way and drifted into a slightly negative look. Earlier in the year, I had made several suggestions concerning the Mount's programming about Israel. The rabbi had rejected them outright. Since then he scrutinized my face and posture whenever the subject came up, looking for any hint of dissent.

"I understand, Aaron, I do," the rabbi said, seeing my unease now, and sitting down in a chair. "There's always a few misguided souls stirring up trouble in Samaria and Judea. Two months ago, as you know, I was invited to participate in a select group of progressive rabbis to go to Israel, to learn what members of the Knesset, the security apparatus, felt about the deal with Iran. What a *shanda!*" he said, taking a deep breath.

"'Mankind faces a crossroads,' declared Allen Konigsberg," I said, knowing the rabbi was a huge fan of Woody Allen. "'One path leads to despair and utter hopelessness. The other, to total extinction. Let us pray we have the wisdom to choose correctly.'"

He smiled, leaning back in his seat. "The reason I mention the trip is that I wanted to tell you about this Palestinian man the group spoke with. While we were in Jerusalem, we met with Science Minister Danny Danon and Education Minister Naftali Bennet. Thoughtful men both, but here it is. After we left the offices of the Knesset, we returned to our hotel, the Waldorf Astoria." He happily told me about the fine dining and pool.

"We go to the conference room for the last meeting of the day. The mayor of Jerusalem, Nir Barkat, was there, with others from his office. A nice guy! Also in the room, an older gentleman, a Palestinian. He's wearing a gray pinstripe suit with a vest, very old-fashioned style. And, of course, the *keffiyeh*. The guy is close to ninety years old. He tells us about his life. Born in Aleppo, lived in Damascus—this all before Israel statehood in '48. Then he became a merchant in Ramallah before moving to East Jerusalem to go into business with a relative.

"These trips aren't propaganda, Aaron. All sorts of people and opinions. We can ask any question. The answers aren't scripted. This was Mr. Walid. He begins by telling stories about the corruption of Arab society, how there was always an official, whether at the post office or birth registry, with his hand out asking for *baksheesh*. Mr. Walid's story was about Arab society, even if the big topic of conversation on this trip was Iran—which isn't Arab, it's Persian. This was the local flavor, something to set the tone for other, far-reaching discussions. What really burned me up was when Mr. Walid went into detail how the Jordanian officers would routinely go to his furniture store—all of them cut from the same cloth, with aviator sunglasses, peaked cap, shiny black boots, polished leather holster with a pistol. They sauntered around, inquiring about Mrs. Walid or the children, in a soft voice, then asking for 'contributions' for security. These officers lived nearby. They lived well, flaunting their wealth, living opulent lives. And if anyone complained, they'd be arrested and tortured.

"Aaron, do you think the IDF behaves like that in the West Bank? I'd have Mr. Walid tell those among us who have doubts that he has no interest in living under the Palestinian Authority. And Mr. Walid didn't say it, but the guy from Nir Barkat's office did, that when an Arab family finds out that a son is gay, a family member might even kill that child. Who can allow such barbarism? Google Tel Aviv Pride Parade, you'll see people from all over the world coming to celebrate being gay in Israel. What a land of contrasts! What a country! I can find a *minyan*, eat a *glatt* kosher meal, then watch a crazy pride parade, all within a few hundred yards of each other. What other country on earth can you find such riches, such tolerance, such compassion for the conquered?"

I gave Rabbi Ben my face of grave concern and agreement, and nodded sporadically. Over the past year, I had heard Tager pontificate on this same subject. His central theme was that few in the American Jewish establishment knew anything about Palestinian life under Israeli control. Mr. Walid could tell all the tales he wanted about how bad the old days were when Jordan ruled East Jerusalem and the West Bank, but where were Mr. Walid's grandchildren, telling the visiting rabbis how it is today?

The next day the rabbi burst into my office and shouted, "Why didn't you publicize our 'support Israel' rally at city hall? Only two days away! We need to get the word out. Nothing in the email blast or social media."

"Sorry, slipped my mind."

Rabbi Ben looked like he wanted to vent more, or browbeat additional contrition out of me, but the blankness on my face and my relaxed position must have tipped him off that the energy might be better spent elsewhere. Exasperated, he flipped a thumb drive on my desk. "Make sure these get printed and mounted on sticks."

I set the thumb drive down next to the I$RAEL flyer on my desk. In this job, Israel would be where the rubber meets the road: morals and history, personal identity, Jewishness, the Holocaust—it was all-encompassing, like Brom's long table of Jewish totems and artifacts. I looked at the computer screen and then out the window at the gray sky. I remembered the yearly fishing trip for fall Chinook with the rabbi and a few board members—it had crystalized my thinking.

Theo Hect, Jacob's father, sat as the Mount's fisher-man-in-chief. A hale and hearty seventy-five-year-old, he made his money with large-scale home development on the coast, and his success meant he paid for the boat. Gregarious and opinionated, he had grown up in the Northwest, and would not take no for an answer to his fishing invitation—this was his truth, as much as skiing was for his son.

This year's fishing trip occurred on a Wednesday in the first week of September. I picked up the rabbi in Portland, and we met up with Theo, Stan Gutman, and Bob Hiram at the boat launch just west of the Bonneville Dam on the Columbia River. The boat Theo chartered seated five, so the six-hour outing resulted in a deeper understanding of everyone's lives. The trip was men only—partly because of tradition, and partly because there was no toilet on board, so fishermen kneeled near the bow and peed into a bucket.

Arriving, we all shook hands, grabbed our bags, and made our way to the floating dock. The sunrise over the Gorge was itself worth the journey—a flock of Canadian geese flew by as we drank in the vista. Theo had booked through Haley's Guide Service. Malcolm Haley ran a twenty-three-foot Alumaweld Intruder. The open boat sported no frippery save a scant awning that he put on at the dock should the forecast be stormy. Despite his millions, Theo enjoyed Malcolm's authenticity. The latter was a hardscrabble guy who had given up long-haul trucking and factory work to run his boat. We walked out on the dock until Malcolm came whirring out of the gloom.

"What's the fish count so far this year, Stan?" Bob asked.

"Give or take eight thousand swimming past Bonneville," Stan said. Stan had been fishing with Theo forever; both men were passionate about chasing fish. Before his retirement, Stan enjoyed an academic career at Portland State University and taught various classes on biology and conservation.

"We always time this wrong," Theo said. "If most years the count is a hundred thousand by December, we are having a fricking bad year."

"We don't know much about anything," Stan said. "Few years back, only thirty thousand came through. Not because stocks were low, but because the fish chose to pursue other interests before returning. Maybe needing more time to find themselves, explore the nature of salmon-hood. It's still just the start of September, and I feel lucky."

We climbed into the boat and sped upriver for twenty minutes, now under cloudy blue skies that looked promising through the lens of our optimism. Malcolm tied the boat off on the orange buoy about twenty yards from the southern bank, a steep rocky slope that gave way to a dense cluster of western hemlock, which concealed the highway not far beyond. The fetch of brownish-green water flowed half a mile wide, with thirty other boats sprinkled parallel to the banks for several hundred yards. Malcolm opened the tackle box and produced four orange lures with barbless hooks. He followed our glances and said, "The Columbia River is the most restrictive fishery in the nation for sportsmen. Someone should wake the hell up in Salem and stop all the commercial gill-netting assholes from taking all the fish."

"C'mon, Mal, we just got here," Theo said. "Let's not burn through our conversation topics too quickly."

Malcolm released the spool of the bait-cast reel and grabbed the steel leader on the line end, where he quickly attached the lure. He played out a good amount of line before clipping it into the downrigger release, then sinking the steel weight ten feet.

He stood straight, and surveyed the setup and set the pole into the rod holder on the gunnel before repeating the process with the other rods. We all looked intently at the rods, expecting a strike right then and there. After five minutes, we relaxed. Malcolm noted every twitch of the rod as he sat behind the wheel, occasionally texting other boats about where fish were hitting.

"You guys feeling proud?" Bob said. "You should. Twenty-two new families joined Mount Zion in August. Not bad." In his role as board member, Bob spearheaded outreach. He had worked in the shoe industry for years, in business development roles, and loved pitching the value proposition, whatever that might be.

"Great people," Rabbi Ben said. "Most of the new members are young families, not from Oregon. Recently moved up." The rabbi made a point of saying hello to all new congregation members with a phone call or a five-minute chat when they toured the facilities.

"More Californians," Theo said. "Woe to us all."

"Hey, not so bad—you can sell them housing," Bob said.

"It's the preschool," I said. "They come for that, then stay for the latkes."

"One family asked about how we talked about Israel," Rabbi Ben said. "I guess they liked what they heard and signed up."

"What did you say?"

"We enjoy a diverse community with many viewpoints," the rabbi said, looking at the rod's tip bobbing as the current tugged on the lure. He said this in the flat, cautious manner of one who recites a disquieting piece of information—like a troubling chemical in a long list of ingredients for a favorite food. His mouth pulled tight as he fidgeted on his boat cushion.

"That guy who's always talking about the occupation, he can help us get more members," Bob said, as if assuming that younger people had divergent views.

"Yoni something," Stan said. "My wife does a lot with the

federation, and Yoni is enemy number one for her. She and Sidney Weinbach have banned him from the community committee." With a broad smile, Stan leaned back against the gunnel and stuck out his feet, his face registering the expression that comedy of an irrefutable nature had struck and nothing remained but to acknowledge it. "Imagine that—the committee for community relations banning someone. I guess I always assumed the committee existed to *improve* community relations." He scanned our faces. "I'm the only one allowed to talk this way, as I'm married to Sarah."

"I write a check to the federation every year," Bob said. "I'd think twice knowing some fruitloop mucked around with how the federation handled Israel stuff."

"When you talk to someone about joining the congregation," Stan said, "do you tell them this synagogue accepts only people who support an undivided Jerusalem? How about people who are already members? Do you tell them how to think on issues important to them, until they get angry and quit? Who're we protecting? Keeping all these people out of the Jewish community. All the other organizations, a litany of woe. Numbers in decline. Donations in decline. Nobody shows up. Boo-hoo. This guy shows up, and he gets banned by my wife." Stan cracked up.

"Seriously, Stan, doesn't it bother you this guy is talking about occupation and Palestinians?" Bob said. "Human rights, and the like? You lived there in the seventies, you know about the situation."

Rabbi Ben followed the conversation carefully, his eyes shining. I imagined that he was formulating his words as he anxiously leaned on one elbow and then the other, his face taut.

"It's not that I agree or disagree with this guy," Stan said. "The point is I remember. I remember those big truths from my youth. The truth drilled into me at school. By my parents. Etched in granite and impossible to change. Like the government, the generals, the president always tells the truth. How it's unpatriotic, unfair, wrong, to criticize a wartime president. These things were the big deal in my day. I went into the world believing in them. Then the shit blew up. The Gulf of Tonkin incident was completely distorted, a rubber stamp for the Vietnam War. The Pentagon Papers, showing the government knew damn well the war was going down the toilet and was lying about the bombing of Cambodia. All of it. The shift in opinion as the nation, *everyone*, stopped supporting the war. Over my life I've been forced to accept that the government—doesn't matter which one—doesn't always tell the truth. Fighting the good fight is for fairy tales. Governments are out for narrow self-interest.

"Now we're old." Stan paused to take a breath. "The younger people are coming up and telling us things are wrong or different, and our way of thinking is out. That's the natural order. As an educator, I see this repeated time and again. Who the hell knows what's going on in the West Bank and Gaza? Someone has to figure it out."

"Stan, I know this sounds funny," Bob said evenly. He sat opposite Stan on the boat's parallel benches. Leaning forward, he tapped Stan on his knee until given the requisite attention. "If we don't draw the line, we're not going to recognize who shows up at those federation meetings."

"My wife and I disagree on who should be included in the word 'community,'" Stan said, meeting Bob's earnestness as he sat upright. "She wants a smaller definition, and I want a larger one. I love her and we're still married, so we disagree. Not like she wants to drive an armored personnel carrier called an Escalade—now *that* would be a deal-breaker." This was Theo's car.

"We need to have *shalom bayit* ... peace in the house," Rabbi Ben said. "With larger organizations, every decision that gets made someone cries foul—the price of having a vibrant community."

"This is Israel, this is who we are," Theo said. "If these people don't want to be Jewish, don't want to respect those who came before, fuck 'em. They can go play with the Christians in their BDS church or whatever."

All this was part of the fishing ritual where most of us could speak frankly.

"I'll take the whatever," Stan said without meeting Theo's agitation. "These are emotional, political points of view, and it does nobody any good to run around condemning this or that person for not seeing the world through the same eyes. Sometimes I think the purpose of Jewish education is to ensure the next generation are either ignorant, and not giving a shit about Israel, or like Yoni, fighting for some semblance of a point of view that makes sense. And don't forget, I sent my kids to the Hillel School. All this emphasis on critical thinking, problem-solving, except when Israel is concerned. Then you're supposed to read the Dersh's book on Israel, and memorize the talking points."

"How's Jewish day school working for you?" Theo asked.

"High holidays, not so good. Hanukkah, a bit better."

"Fish on!" Malcolm rasped in his smoker's voice and moved toward the jerking pole.

Theo had determined that the rabbi would grab the pole when the first Chinook struck. He stood up, and Malcolm handed him the jerking rod.

"Easy pressure, no slack," Malcolm said.

Rabbi Ben carefully worked the rod and reel, his face a grim mask of concentration. The rest of us shuffled around him as the salmon veered left and right of the boat's stern. Malcolm picked up the net, leaned over the gunnels, and scanned the water. The rabbi strained against the rod and did a yeoman's job of fighting the fish. When the fish neared the boat it thrashed mightily on the surface and ejected the lure, disappearing in a flash.

"The action starts," Bob said, moving back to take the seat he had vacated when the fish struck. "Next up, our man Theo."

Malcolm reset the poles, and we all calmed down, happy the day's promised excitement had begun.

No sooner did we all get comfy when another fish struck. Theo deftly countered its feints and dodges with a graceful handling of the rod, relaxed and confident with head held high, eyes fixed on the line, his movements controlled and precise as he danced around the stern area. I knew the salmon had no chance. When Mal hoisted a thirty-inch Chinook, angry and thrashing, we all cheered with the shouts of those whose beliefs had been justified. Theo took out his phone and snapped pictures while Malcolm struggled to free the fish from the dip net.

"Ocean fish," Malcolm said, an embarrassed smile breaking up his craggy face, as he held the fish higher for Theo to get a better shot. The fish's adipose fin, a black nub on the back toward the tail, was indisputable. Only clipped hatchery fish could be kept.

Theo sighed. "Okay." He flicked his thumb toward the river, and Malcolm slipped the fish back in. We sat in silence, contemplating life without a salmon in the cooler, as Malcolm reset the rod.

Why did we get so bent out of shape about the faraway place of Israel? Scream about who can say what, sit in what room? Claim to represent a community of people who understood little about the place? The subject felt like tyranny, an enforced doctrine that abrogated who I wanted to be as a person, a Jew. There was a moment when I relished the debate, feeling the issue made being a lay leader compelling and important. Now all points were set, and we had been here too often before.

When I picked up my phone, I noted that the rabbi had sent several text messages the night before, starting at eight in the evening—then a few more at six in the morning. Each text said ever more explicitly that my negligence was unacceptable. I wanted to feel bad that I left my phone in the car, but again I encountered an overwhelming paralysis of thought. I had tried and failed, again, to publicize Rabbi Ben's counter-protest. When the time had come to type the words into the various empty emails and browser tabs, my mind had drifted into blackness, and I gave up.

After entering the Mount's administration building, I went directly to the rabbi's office, a spacious room with four large panel windows overlooking the sanctuary. The rabbi sat at his imposing mahogany desk on a maroon Persian rug and worked on his computer. I knocked on the open door.

"Rabbi, I want to apologize. I've been having difficulties ..."

He looked up. "Gretchen had the signs made. We'll go over to city hall at ten. We can talk about your *difficulties* later."

I went to my desk, aware that I needed to do something, and turned on my computer and read email absentmindedly. Gretchen and Amy passed by, shooting severe looks in a frisson of annoyance. At ten, I assembled by the building's entrance. Rabbi Ben thrust a placard into my hand, reading "BDS = Bigoted, Demonizing, Shameful." He wore an Israeli flag draped over his shoulders, and his US-Israel flag *kipa* had been freshly donned for the occasion. Bob and Theo showed up, and along with Gretchen, we walked out onto the wet street. Bob and Theo, boisterous and jolly, were unaware of any bad feelings; Gretchen looked pleased to get a break from office work, and suggested that we all get a fancy coffee.

The front of city hall looked as I expected, with a crowd of forty people of various ages: a young man with a messenger bag wearing a Guy Fawkes mask, a granny serenely carrying a "Stop Israel Occupation" sign, a few Black Lives Matter activists, several women in hijabs, and lots of middle-aged people milling around, curious about the commotion. Two younger people unfurled a banner. "Remember Rachel Corrie—Respect Human Rights," it said, referencing an Evergreen University student who attempted to stop a home demolition in Gaza and was killed by an Israeli Caterpillar bulldozer.

Rabbi Ben waved to Sidney Weinbach, who stood with a few others around the Liberty Bell replica in the middle of the raised vegetable beds of the Better Together Garden. A Portland police officer yawned and stretched as he paced the ground between us and the larger group.

"The Human Rights Commission is voting today on a resolution to block city investment in four companies," Rabbi Ben said. "No one in the Jewish community was invited into the meeting. No one from the community was informed about this development."

"Aren't some of the people on the commission Jewish?" I asked, having read the list of members. I recognized two congregants from the Reconstructionist congregation.

The rabbi shot me a dark look. "Not by my estimation."

I gathered someone inside the meeting was live-tweeting the discussion, as the BDS leaders kept their phones in their hands and coordinated the group to chant, "Boycott racist Israel!" and "Stop occupation profiteering!" I took out my phone and found #pdxdivest within a few tries—the commission now discussed the human rights records of the companies being scrutinized. The BDS group hoped to sway any recalcitrant members of the commission by a strong show of public support for the divestment measure, confident that their chants could be heard inside city hall.

Rabbi Ben knew his meager group couldn't out-chant the opposition, but he sporadically yelled, "Only democracy in the Middle East!" or "There are two sides to this conflict!"

An older man with hearing aids and thick glasses came

over with a woman of equal age, and explained in a quiet voice that he had been a pastor, and his faith community viewed the issue solely in terms of human rights impacts, not religion or nationality. Portland needed to do its part, he said, and divest from companies profiting from the violent conflict. I hung back and listened as Rabbi Ben and Sidney buried the couple in the usual *hasbara*.

I scanned the crowd and noticed the homeless guy who had given me the I$RAEL flyer. He was standing across the street, a look of agitation and incomprehension hanging on his face—like the Israel debate had become too complicated for a meat-and-potatoes anti-Semite like him, and he was unsure of where he should stand, who his allies were, or what was going on. He carried his Jews-control-the-media sign, wore the *keffiyeh,* but stood alone, far from the demonstration, perhaps wondering how the debate had gotten away from him.

I let the sign fall from my hands. I would not be going back to the Mount. I walked toward the demonstrators, then through them, coming out onto Fourth Street, where the pedestrians, cyclists, motorists, and shopkeepers were going about their day, taking no visible note of Israel or international issues of justice. I walked on, aware that I was off course and heading in a random direction, but satisfied I would arrive at a better place.

GUARDIANS OF COOL
SEPTEMBER 1997, VICINITY OF CHIANG MAI, THAILAND
YEHUDA ALKANA

DAVID OSTROV CREPT up to Yoni Tager, grabbing him and pinning his arms to his sides. Ostrov tightened his grip, leaned back and tipped Tager off balance. I rushed in to hold his legs and complete the maneuver to suspend him off the ground. Tager hovered in the air, unaware of his predicament. He managed only a muted *fuck you*, not having much fight. Ostrov, his face sunburned and unshaven, wore an expression of cruel enjoyment as veins protruded from his muscled forearms with his exertion. Ostrov and I had initially conspired to grab Tager because of our proximity to an anthill of almost a meter high.

I had wanted something else—to see Tager show fighting spirit, pull some martial arts move that would prove we were idiots. When we were soldiers in Israel and focused on being dangerous and in shape, I had tried something similar. Back then, Tager had inhaled, stiffened his body, and in a blast of energy, busted free as if my arms were tissue paper. Next, I was falling on my ass like I was five years old. Tager planted his foot squarely on my chest in a lightening roundhouse kick. I never saw it coming.

Now, Ostrov stumbled toward the anthill and slowly lowered Tager's head closer to the reddish-brown swarm. Tager began to flail, which forced me to tighten my grip. We were all hung over. It was worse for Tager and Ostrov, as they were the ones who could really put it away.

"Eat 'em up, bumsucker," Ostrov said. "What you get. Calling the army a gap-year program."

"Assholes!"

Ostrov stiffened his grip further as Tager came alive, struggling harder. I locked my arms and glanced around the village at the edge of the jungle, taking inventory of who might be enjoying the spectacle: the girls studiously looked bored but kept shooting their eyes our way, not protesting or saying anything; the guys fidgeted in discomfort.

"You think ants bite?" I called out, laughing. "I don't think so." I expected a drop of encouragement, someone to share the joke, but no. *Yeledim tovim Yerushalayim*—bunch of bedwetting mommas' boys. These New Age hippies clearly didn't approve of our rough play and nervously stood there gawking and grimacing, worried they'd be next if they said too much. The ants, the size of small paperclips, were quick and vicious, and accelerated their pace as Tager's shadow fell on them. As Tager's head approached, his hat fell off and a lock of greasy hair fell into the swarm. Ants grabbed the rope and shinned up, signaling we had done enough. I dropped Tager's feet; Ostrov heaved him into a standing position.

Tager grunted while he swatted the ants off his head and gingerly picked up his faded New York Yankees cap. Ostrov folded his arms across his chest and smirked at Tager who flicked the ants off the hat. Tager lunged forward as if to punch Ostrov in the face, forcing him to pull up his hands. Tager abruptly stopped. *Psych!*

He ambled over to me and roughly put his hands on my shoulders, as if to engage in a pushing contest. "You piss me off," he said, stepping back and pulling his sweat-stained T-shirt into place and squaring his shoulders. "I should've gotten laid last night, not you." I felt glances shoot our way. I didn't care, as we didn't know the others yet, but if Tager wanted to embarrass me, I'd throw the *mamzer* back into the anthill. "I invited those girls to dinner," he continued. "You're a goddamned poacher."

"She liked me because I'm not you—I'm on the spiritual path," I said, not entirely in jest. Tager could be so fucking stupid half the time. I felt my initial euphoria about trekking in the jungle dissolve, and wondered how far Tager would push it.

"Yeah, right, Mr. Jew-bu."

Ostrov's face returned to the slack expression he habitually wore, and I knew any comment from him would not be forthcoming.

Tager had started up with the girls last night, but he had enraged Ostrov, the custodian of IDF honor, with his joke about us having been on an Israeli educational program, not mentioning the army. Tager made the remark and let us ponder the meaning, his mouth twitching as if to suppress a laugh. When he made no correction and began asking the girls about their lives, Ostrov saw red; this was a high crime in his estimation. The girls caught on that something was amiss, and regarded us with reserve and suspicion until Ostrov saved the day and filled them in. He did this with a few words and a grumpy silence, some Anglo-telepathy broadcasting on a different frequency.

A Welsh office worker, Kelsey spoke with a musical lilt and had come on holiday to study Thai massage. Tager had spotted her and her friends at the bustling Kad Suan Kaew night market in Chiang Mai, where they brusquely deflected all solicitations by vendors until they arrived at a stall selling silk scarves. Tager then proceeded to be a flat-footed Casanova with his obnoxious patter. At home, I usually had no compunction about starting up a conversation with a girl, as it was only a few seconds before we found common ground or she told me to fuck off.

Tager hit like a *shirav* and quickly asked the girls about their travel plans, if they planned on trekking, and what they shopped for in the market. It was clear from our paleness and oblivious behavior we had been less than a week in Thailand. I grasped Tager's intention. He didn't want to explain too much—just be a person, not a people, history, or conflict. Ostrov stepped forward and clinched the deal with a weary look that said "my friend's a fucking asshole" and explained that all of us had recently finished army service. He added with a dramatic eye roll what an ocean of undiluted tedium all of it had been. Amen.

We went to a restaurant overlooking Wat Phra Singh, a quiet spot filled with international travelers—no one was in the mood for anything too noisy or authentic. The place sported a small bar made from concrete with a scattering of low tables surrounded by stools. The few padded orange vinyl booths and chairs stuck to the skin of our legs and made a popping noise when we stood up. Four neon Sigha beer lights of different vintages, a few banks of fluorescents, and many mismatched lighting sconces gave the small place an odd brightness of a greenish-yellowish hue. When we arrived, the old Toto song "Africa" played from scratchy speakers. It turned out the entire *Toto IV* album spun on constant repeat in the CD player—it was grating at first, but more comforting as the haze of alcohol set in and the night wore on. Not ideal for starting new friendships, but we make the best of it in this life.

Kelsey introduced us to her traveling companion, Carmen, and Petra from Germany, who they had met in the hotel. Kelsey wore an expression of dreamy nonchalance with short, sandy hair and a round, gentle face. She dressed in a faded batik skirt, a baggy white men's T-shirt, and no makeup. The first inkling we would be better friends came when we sat down, Kelsey delicately touching my chest to examine the gold filigree *hamsa* I wore on a gold chain. A silver ethnic necklace from India or Cameroon, or maybe Manchester, black with corrosion, hung around her neck, but Kelsey smelled good and drank and ate with prim manners. After an hour, it was clear that she had chosen me and tilted her body towards me as we drank. She asked about my family in Bat Yam, what I thought of Thai food, why I wanted to be a math teacher or engineer. She knew Israelis and inquired why all of us, as if dutifully following a homework assignment, brought Hermann Hess's *Journey to the East* or *Siddhartha* on our travels. This last point took me off guard and embarrassed me for being so predictable, for I had brought *Journey* to Thailand. I told her the books were admired in Israel, for if you read them when you had no real place to be, nothing to do, they had the potential to awaken deep beliefs. I kept to myself that I wanted to read the book to understand why the type of person who found Hesse's work revelatory was usually an idiot.

Ostrov relaxed after a few beers and sat good-naturedly in silence with Petra, both having a low tolerance for superficial chitchat.

Tager talked calmly with Carmen, and seemed to have accepted that romance was out of the realm of possibility, as Carmen kept her arms tight against her body and almost jumped every time he reached out for a sip of beer. He shot me glances that I took as encouragement one minute, envy the next.

Kelsey and I said we were going back to the night market for squid on a stick. We strolled by the river before going to her hotel. I now had her home address in Cardiff in my wallet, a magic incantation as well as a happy memory. I kissed her goodbye in the small hours before going back to my hostel to assemble my gear, eager to start being nature boy far away from civilization.

We had disembarked from a bus whose exterior looked like an explosion at a paint store—swirls, blotches, and waves of airbrushed primary colors depicting Buddhas and temples, with the indecipherable craziness of Thai script amplifying the impact. We waited at the trailhead for our guide to arrive. The bus had stopped at several hostels and cheap hotels to pick up travelers, and I tried to chat with the other trekkers, excited about leaving the noisy city. With no good conversation to keep me up, my lack of sleep got the better of me, and I dozed until I felt the vehicle stop. There were six Americans, a couple from Belgium, two Chinese girls from Singapore, and several Germans—all of us somewhere in our twenties. Off the bus, we stood awkwardly beside the paved road, not knowing what would come next. A field of banana trees sat to one side surrounded by towering tropical hardwoods filled with shrieking birds; misty mountains in the background looked ancient and serene. Closer to us, a bunch of low shacks stood with chickens clustering off to one side around a coop. I asked one of the Chinese girls if this looked like her home. She said no in a manner that let me understand I shouldn't talk to her.

One shack had a metal cooler in front, the Coca-Cola logo bled away by corrosion. I ambled over and caught on that this was the local snack kiosk. I dropped my pack by the cooler, fished a few *baht* out of my money pouch, and purchased a bottle of water and a candy bar from a teenager who barely looked up from her book. Tager and Ostrov followed and joined me on dirty white plastic chairs as we adjusted to our surroundings. The heat and humidity brought out the musty jungle air—a mix of rotten wood, pond scum, cut grass, and chickens. From this vantage point, Ostrov spied the anthill and planned his attack.

The dramatic lighting the occasional sun breaks provided through the morning grey urged me to acknowledge the beauty of the setting despite the hangover pounding in my temples. I wiped the sweat off my forehead and celebrated the notion that for the first time since arriving in Thailand I was finally on vacation and pursuing fun that didn't involve confusing logistical details or reading lots of plaques. We had paid our money for a five-day trek, and I was happy the guide would do all the deep thinking, and let my thoughts roam free.

Walking in a circle, Tager angrily inspected his hat for ants for the fourth time before placing it on his head. He moved toward a chair only to be alerted to a smoky red Vespa buzzing into view. The rider was a rugged-looking Thai several years older than us—he wore wayfarer sunglasses and a faded collared shirt open in front which showed skin like burnished copper. His relaxed smile softened a broad nose and heavy brow. He wheeled his scooter to the back of the shop and then came out to where we still loitered around the anthill.

"Hello, hello," he said, flashing a wide grin. "We trek in jungle! Yes!" He introduced himself as Johnny and had us organize ourselves across the way at a rutted dirt track.

When we all got to the trail—our packs, hats, water bottles, and mats made us look like children off to camp—Johnny took off his sunglasses. "No touch shrine at village entrance," he said. "Keep away from ceremonies. Always ask with hands to take photo." He mimed the action, and explained that we had to respect the tribal customs of the people who lived in the jungle. "If you don't follow rule, you have big problem. I train for many years as Muay Thai fighter." He added a quick smile.

We all nodded gravely, feeling that the pages of *National Geographic* were soon to open and smiling kids and natives in brightly colored costumes would look at us with awe and wonder, not seeing us for the idiots we truly were.

Abba and Ima had no clue why I had come to Thailand. Zero. For them, foreign travel meant a hotel with fancy soaps you could take home and a chance to enjoy luxury for a few days. Their trips abroad had brought them to London and Paris, once to Madrid. Abba's family came from Rabat, Morocco, in the 1950s, while Ima's hailed from Fez. Both had vivid memories of being targets for violence by nationalists who wished to avenge the misfortunes of their Muslim brethren in Israel. The abandoned property, the indignity of two years in a transit camp in a canvas tent with vermin and the extremes of heat and cold, dust and mud, meant that Abba didn't understand why it might be of interest to sightsee in the less-developed world.

Finding a foothold in those early days was traumatic for everyone. Abba's family had owned a dry goods store in Rabat, but the threat of violence forced them to forsake all inventory and furnishings. Saba, eyes burning with indignation, repeatedly told the tale of how when the day to leave came, he carefully locked the store's front door. He knew he would never return, but old habits die hard. He told how his legs felt like lead as he slowly walked away. Upon arrival in Israel, Saba was adamant in his refusal to do agricultural work despite no other jobs being available—this was beneath his dignity. Eventually, he established himself as a house painter and general *shiputznik,* as also my father became.

I might as well have been from another planet, so alien my life appeared to Abba—the clothes I wore, the music I brought home, my thoughts about politics and war. My heart warmed at his undisguised joy when I told him I wanted to paint houses with him to save money for my trip. We worked well together—not too many arguments. He even took me to the fancy camping store in Dizengoff Center in Tel Aviv and let me pick out a backpack as a going-away present—though he was aghast at how much a sack of cloth sewed into a strange shape cost. "I could buy five of these in the Shuk Ha'carmel," he muttered at the register.

The trip I told them about, of going to the Far East for relaxation and adventure, had only been done ten thousand times by other Israeli kids fed up with the restrictions of family and army. Abba and Ima accepted my travel plans with a sadness and steely resolve that put this on the same footing as illness or other catastrophes.

Before purchasing my backpack, I visited that store several times, as the place hosted events where young people returning from exotic destinations gave reports on conditions. We all wanted to know how much every service cost; whether the diving course, elephant tour, admission to temples, and buffets were worth it; and whether something similar could be found cheaper. The first time I did this, I noticed over-earnest North Tel Aviv types carefully taking notes about the prices and best currency exchange rates and places, coordinating among themselves when and where they would rendezvous for the full-moon party. Seeing this, I resolved not to be caught as a *frier* and got busy writing the prices down.

The first presentation I attended was led by two girls from Herzliya, who wore sports sandals and baggy drawstring pants. Anat, with a pierced nose, and Hadar, with green hair, shared information about sightseeing and getting on in Thailand. They let us know they were cynical consumers, and you always had to be ready to bargain, shop elsewhere, and not be suckers for the first pitch offered. They tried to put a good face on their travel, and talked about how interested they were in everyday culture, national parks, historic temples, and the Grand Palace, covering these points in a blasé recitation. When they talked about their visit to an island in the Gulf of

Thailand, animation took over, intimating that their real focus was to live a frugal, hedonistic life for a few months.

Now actually in Thailand, Anat and Hadar didn't seem like particularly savvy travelers, their advice sounding trite and obvious. All of us obediently followed Johnny down a rutted track. Within several minutes, the road disappeared, the insect chirps and bird calls took over, and the heat diminished in the green shade. Johnny remained silent as we hiked, stopping only to point out a noisy green-tailed sunbird, a regional specialty, which flew away before I could get a good look.

After a few low hills, we came upon the first village—a handful of thatched huts and animal pens, with pungent wood smoke hanging heavy in the still, humid air. Dogs barked and pigs squealed as we approached, while old men and women gave us quick, resentful glances as they squatted, smoking cigarettes or pipes made from sections of bamboo. I noted the disappointed exhalations of a few of the Americans as they became aware of bleary speakers spitting out saccharine Thai pop tunes.

"So much for the remoteness of the place," said Bill, a graduate student from Chicago. He put his camera away after furtively snapping several pictures. Two boys about six or seven, naked and brown, danced up to us with outstretched hands, and chanted, "Can-dee, can-dee." I had never visualized what the trek would be like, beyond being out in the sticks, so I took it all in with neither wide-eyed wonder nor disappointment, and ignored the children and walked past. I couldn't see Bill's point. From my perspective, all was as advertised—the village off the electrical and transportation lines, the locals looking like they survived off the crops they grew, not having much access to education or employment. What did Bill expect? The tinny radio did little to drown out the cacophony of birds and insects, the mud was still just as muddy, the kids looked like they needed a decent meal and a dentist. The slowness of travel, the green jungle, and the lack of anything to think about or do made me content in a way I hadn't been for some time. The elders sitting in front of their huts, impassively smoking with timeless, wrinkled faces, giving the run of the dirt to the kids, pigs, chickens, and dogs, made me feel that I had not made the trip in vain. Bill probably harbored daydreams about being a modern conquistador, all for the low price of 170 USD. I was glad we were only the latest current in the stream of tourists, for I didn't want to be anything other than a gringo passing through.

Johnny waited for everyone to catch up at the far end of the village. He tapped the red-and-white Krong Thip package to fish out the last cigarette, lit it, and leaned against a tree. Tager walked toward me next to two of the American girls, Sarah and Colleen. Sarah wore a blue bandana tied around her head while Colleen had a black ball cap with an *Earth First!* patch on the front. Tager was my friend, and I respected both his enthusiasm to get out in the world and his eccentricities. But since arriving in Thailand, I had concluded that he didn't understand what people—whether Thais, Anglos, international travelers, or other Israelis—thought about him. Judging by their expressions and questions, they weren't impressed with him or his decision to volunteer for the army, likely finding him a lost soul, who was looking for belonging with whoever would take him in. I didn't want Ostrov to know, but I thought Tager was on the right track with his wanting to quickly gloss over, if not conceal, his army experience.

Tager and Sarah drew close, and I heard him ask about her major at university, and her overall impression of UC Davis. She answered with a slight tone of impatience and a few sighs—perhaps disappointed Tager had not been more fully briefed on the excellence of her academic experience. Tager paused in his questioning and let his gaze wander.

"You went to Israel on your own? I mean, your parents didn't make you, right?" Sarah shared what little she knew about the West Bank, early Zionist history, Israeli settlements, human rights conditions for Palestinians, refugees, and all sorts of other bullshit—all in an airy tone of absolute conviction. The overall reputation of Israel did not fare well, to put it mildly. Tager took off his pack and removed a water bottle, studiously unscrewing the top. "Israel is a good place," he said resolutely. "Stop there on your travels. See for yourself how awful or wonderful it is. Fuck all the ideology, security, politics. Check out all of it—Gaza, West Bank, Jerusalem, Tel Aviv. Then you'll know the humus from the tahini."

Tager's answer took me off guard and struck me as appropriate; I was sure he would start in about how the world was biased against Israel, how we must consider history, the holocaust, anti-Semitism, and the like. Initially I had taken Tager as the American equivalent of the North Tel Aviv Guy—someone who had gone to the good schools. His parents had the top jobs with the right connections, and he came to Israel to make himself a better CV. I knew he would eventually go to university, where he would meet other kids like him from wealthy families, keeping the cycle of *proteksia* going indefinitely. After a month in the army I concluded that if personal advancement and an easy life were his goals, he wouldn't have gotten off the plane at Ben Gurion. I couldn't say that I understood his motivations or what he looked for in Thailand; he was more like a hippie searching for the full moon party than like those people who did everything because it was expected and earned them more money. In basic training he and I became buddies with the tacit agreement that we would learn how to shoot straight and properly operate the equipment, as well as laughing at ourselves a bit and not becoming total assholes. Ostrov was a total asshole who let us know that he thought we were sloppy soldiers who didn't care about seeing any mission to its logical end. But before the end of the army, he underwent a change, probably realizing there was no logical completion to any IDF mission.

When I strolled over to where Tager and Sarah stood now, he said, "You're such a whore" in Hebrew, slapping my hand. This cemented the notion that the conversation with Sarah had not gone as planned. Sarah continued to hover before Colleen came and asked her to appreciate the view of the village from another angle, pulling her down the trail.

"Yehuda, you check out those flowers—poppies," Tager said when the girls departed.

"Great, maybe buy *hamentaschen* at the bakery, *habibi*."

"Don't think those dudes are growing the happy flowers for the bakery, *motek*."

Mark from New Jersey heard our conversation as he passed. "You up for smoking the black gold?" he asked tentatively. "Some holiday fun, ya know?" He tried to let his comments float, as if they were no big deal, but his expression told me our actions would determine his. He wore a pendant of quartz and agate, his shaggy hair secured in place with a burgundy strip of batik cloth. He wore the costume but couldn't pull off the look of soul traveler, spiritual pilgrim, or enlightened wanderer—his expression and tone of voice were too intense. He asked me on the bus if I'd bought a tailor-made suit yet— and, if I had, how much I'd paid. He already knew all about Israelis—how we did a good job of passing on the information about prices and merchandise.

"We're down with that, bro," Tager said.

That night we shared a meal on a hilltop ridge in a Hmong village, and gathered in the headman's teak-and-thatch longhouse. We ate rice and corn mush flavored with pork, all served off sections of banana leaves. Much like the others, the village had plenty of factory-produced goods throughout, with most inhabitants looking like they wouldn't be out of place in Bangkok. The serving women, however, wore traditional finery of indigo skirts with red trim and sported intricate embroidery in vibrant reds and pinks, with zigzags and starbursts, swirls and loops. On their heads, they wore black cloth hats vaguely reminiscent of small chef's toques, ornamented with silver and red ribbons.

Once we were seated, a murmur rippled through the group that we had unquestionably arrived at a key experience. Bill, who deemed himself the ultimate judge of these matters, pronounced it "authentic"—the highest compliment one traveling with a backpack could bestow.

After the meal, we lounged on the longhouse floor. The serving women in the courtyard scrubbed the pots.

Mark tapped Tager and gave him an expectant look. Tager scratched his head and called Ostrov and me over. "Want to spark up opium smoke?" he asked. The notion that there wasn't opium to be had never occurred to him.

"What the hell," Ostrov said. I nodded.

Tager got up to find Johnny and sort out the details. I saw Johnny speak a few words to one of the serving women, who scooted off and came back with the supplies.

The woman knelt in front of Tager, and if she felt any apprehension or enjoyment about her task, she gave no sign— her face a blank mask, eyes unwilling to meet ours. She opened a small wooden chest containing the dope wrapped in an oily cloth and loaded a glass bowl fitted to a length of bamboo. She held an oil lamp to light the pipe as Tager sat guru-like with his legs folded under him, finishing the portion of black tar in two breaths. The group looked on, expecting Tager to foam at the mouth, glow, or change shape like a Hollywood special effect. Tager exhaled slowly through his nose, the smoke lingering around him, before uttering "Righteous" in a low, breathy tone.

When my turn came, I observed as the blackness burned orange. I pulled the smoke deep into my lungs and held it as long as I could. A wave of maple syrup coated the inside of my head, my eyes catching on the minutia of the ceiling beams as they danced in the glow from the candles and lanterns. I thought of fantastic images, but the room in front of me remained unchanged. I mutely watched as the other members of the group smoked or declined—I felt I had profound thoughts to share but not the slightest hope that I could muster the energy to speak. With ultimate resolve, I unpacked my sleeping bag and climbed in.

The night passed in lucid dreams, neither pleasant nor terrifying, and when I sat up, my head felt wrapped in gauze. Most of the group was awake, and I could see them milling about the courtyard through the open flap of fabric that served as the longhouse's front door. I squinted in the hazy sunlight until I found a pump and splashed water on my face. Tager waved me over to where the others sat on low stools around a smoky cooking fire, a wizened Hmong woman serving rice porridge into plastic bowls.

We'd been with the other trekkers two days, and the excitement of meeting new people had worn off, all of us making less of an effort to strike up conversations. Sarah and Colleen, perhaps because of a commitment to remaining clearheaded, now were centers of conviviality, drifting from one group to the next. When Sarah sidled up to Tager, she said, "You know, I'm Jewish, too. Or half. My dad."

I didn't get what Tager was supposed to do with that. I gathered that at one point he had kept kosher, gone to synagogue—but those days had passed, and it didn't seem like his interest in girls depended on religious affiliation. He shrugged. "You can be Jewish and not think Israel the best place ever. It's a good place, even with all the problems."

Sarah let the discussion of Jewishness and Israel drop, and the two walked down the trail as I got out my camera to take pictures. The point of being in Thailand was to reward ourselves for all the suffering in the army, and that meant not thinking about home if I didn't want to. I frowned, scared that the whole time in the jungle I would relive my army life with no hope of enjoying the present. I wanted something else: to be far away from Israel in body and spirit.

The army had been hard, a real test of my mettle, and I was proud to have served in a respectable unit. The lasting benefit was an understanding of how things worked in the real world—all the raids, killings, accidents, fuck-ups, and mayhem that resulted from giving guns to boys contributed to a picture of reality that burned brightly. My neighborhood in Bat Yam had become a story map of who went to which IDF unit—the combat engineers, paratroopers, artillery schleppers, tankers ... each group with its aura of status or disrepute. My older brother Tzachi told me about his experience in the navy, how his sailor friends came from parts of the country I had never been to or considered: Qiryat Shemona, Ein Yahav, Netivot, Kiryat Gat. He visited his friends at these places when on leave, as an enrichment program he set out for himself.

Tzachi came back from these experiences in different corners of the country full of tales of unusual characters and good food, and encouraged me to branch out socially in my Golani unit. So I asked Tager and Ostrov about their lives, as they had been to different countries, even if they didn't precisely understand mine. After the first year, the three of us got along and jiggered the roster to get the same duty. Once guys are stuck together on a twelve-hour patrol, they become either best friends or worst enemies, with not much personal history going without comment. After we finished our stint in Lebanon, Tager invited me to celebrate our safe return with a night on the town. He told me that he wanted to smoke drugs and drink beer and was I up for it? I was. This was the army—a chance to meet new people, go new places, try new experiences. My neighborhood was considered the home of Tel Aviv's taxi drivers and whores by those from the upscale areas, and I wanted to see what went on in other places.

Tager picked me up in his uncle's truck: a vehicle equipped for the delivery of seafood, with a heavily insulated rear compartment and refrigeration unit. He told me we were off to buy dope, and I imagined gangsters with heavy gold chains and open shirts, speakeasies full of black light and op art, hardcore druggies with long hair and paisley clothing collapsed onto couches, all in a fancy Tel Aviv apartment.

"Where's our man?"

"B'nei Brak."

"C'mon, where we headed?" I asked, not believing that what we wanted could be found on the *shtetl*-like streets populated by ultra-orthodox black hats: their frumpy wives in head coverings, long skirts, and stockings; and hordes of children.

"Some of the Haredim are funky holy men from California," Tager said. "Playing rock 'n' roll until the *rebbe* says time for Torah study. Others just do drugs because they like them and don't have the excuse of being an American."

We turned onto Jabotinsky Street and followed it into B'nei Brak, noticing a decline in the repair of buildings, and piles of garbage and construction materials strewn in vacant lots. Steel utility poles draped ropes of electrical cable directly overhead, and a conspicuous lack of neon or any colorful display rendered the scene close to black and white. After the main shopping district, we made our way to an outlying area and stopped the truck. In the distance we saw the industrial lighting of the Coca-Cola bottling plant, looking eerie in the gloom.

Tager dropped a cell phone into the dashboard holster so that I could hear the conversation through speakers.

"Allo?"

"Hello sweetie, this is Rough Ranger Zebra Four, come in, over?" he said, laughing.

"Who is this?" the angry voice demanded.

"This's the Zionist Organization of America. We're here to make a contribution to the International Wildlife Fund. We're at the spot near the Coca-Cola bridge."

"Okay, be there in a few."

When the line fell silent, he grinned at me. "I'm trying to make this fun for everybody, but Moishe doesn't have a creative bone in his body."

I relished the lawlessness of the moment and found the garbage-strewn street and flickering brown streetlights an appropriate backdrop. Soon a dark-suited figure in a fedora approached, suit jacket draped around his shoulders like a cape, his hat casually askew on his head. A poorly groomed, wispy beard and large wire-framed glasses gave the impression that Moishe was a mature man, but on second look, I concluded we were all about the same age. We got out of the truck.

"Moishele! A jointele you have for me?" Tager asked in English with a ridiculous Yiddish accent.

"Fucking American *nudnik*," Moishe said in raspy Hebrew.

Tager handed over two hundred *shekels* and in return received a plastic bag. Moishe stalked away as we sat in the truck and rolled a cigarette.

Despite the promise of "anything goes," we were soon too stoned to do much of anything except return to the apartment Tager was staying at to read magazines and listen to music. Still, it was an excellent time, as I had been initiated into a sliver of the larger world.

The third night of the trek as we sat for dinner in a longhouse,

Mark must have decided we were friends, because he told me about Sandy, his Asian girlfriend back home, saying how she liked to fuck in the bathtub. As we ate, he opened up his head and let spill every last stupid question about the IDF—all his comic-book curiosity about weapons, ammo, patrol formations, vehicles, food, and the enemy.

It was Tager's turn to laugh at me with long looks of mocking silence. Mark knew all three of us served in the same unit, but in his eyes, only I, the *sabra*, was qualified to talk about the experience. I kept expecting Tager to bust into the conversation, as Eretz Yisrael was a favorite topic, but the calming vapors of the forest had invaded his brain. Tager exhibited a serenity, or indifference, to what people believed.

I gave Mark terse, rude answers to questions about Lebanon or Hebron, the spots he guessed were most exciting in a bombs-and-bullets way. But each inquiry, no matter what I said, only got him more pumped for the next. Mark pictured terrorists popping up like startled rabbits in a field, sparking a military steeplechase that ended with the bad guys dead or subdued to an audience's rousing applause. But thinking about Hebron now filled me with a self-loathing beyond anything I had experienced before. It smacked me like a gut punch. As Mark prattled on, I saw myself dragging the "suspects" into the courtyard in front of their terrified families, binding their arms behind their backs and pulling tight the zip ties, jamming the black hoods over their heads. Because I roughly understood Arabic, I always had to be inside the houses, yelling insults, threatening further destruction. I was chosen for this role time and again. All this fucking wide-eyed wonder at brutality, pain, and blood made me think Mark was ten years old, incapable of understanding one iota of what went through your head when you pointed a gun at someone.

Feeling a new level of disgust with myself and all of humanity, I caught the eye of one of the serving women and pantomimed smoking an opium pipe—and soon repeated the previous night's activity.

Leaning back on my pack, I stared, uncaring and oblivious, remote and untouchable as a lizard on a rock, observing my diminishing spikes of emotion as one on a mountain peak views lightning far away.

After a break of several days, we arrived on Ko Samui from the ferry. We loaded into a taxi and told the driver to take us to Lamai Beach. In the village, amid the souvenir stands and drink stalls, we found the hand-painted sign in Hebrew, just as Yaron—a traveling Israeli we ran into in Bangkok—had told us we would. The sign explained how to get to Uncle Fang's Hotel, about a kilometer down the road. We threw our packs on and marched with enthusiasm—for what, I hadn't a clue. Just something else. We soon came upon a low, cement house under a corrugated tin roof, with "Office" spray-painted in orange on the wall. We opened the screen door and walked in.

"*Shalom, shalom, hevre,*" said an Asian man of indiscriminate middle age, with a sparse mustache and shiny mustard silk shirt tucked loosely into blue jeans. He sat behind a counter of rough wood covered in papers, notebooks, and half-drunk cups of tea. A gold medallion of Buddha in bas-relief hung around his neck on a heavy chain. "*Barucheem habaeem,*" he added with a slight lisp.

"You must be Uncle Fang," Tager said, smiling and extending a hand.

"We no meet before, but I famous in Israel," he said. "Everybody know me in Tel Aviv and Jerusalem."

We paid in advance for a week, and followed Uncle Fang out to the bungalows. I might have laughed at his manner in other circumstances, but everything felt so alien and crazy anyway that I accepted this as ordinary. We walked up the steps to bungalow number four as the boards flexed and complained under our weight. The shack, built from cheap local wood, cursorily painted over in green and white, had the right look for what we had planned—anything too fancy would have been a setback. The purity of the blue sky, with the rolling, massive clouds, the white sand, and the turquoise sea made sleeping close to the elements a priority. I did not want to be in a cocoon of air-conditioned luxury, even if I could afford it. Our packs fell to the veranda, and we stripped off our drenched shirts before opening the door. The sun slammed down on us with searing heat, doing little to diminish our enthusiasm at being on Ko Samui, within spitting distance of the Gulf of Thailand.

The trek in the jungle had been an agreeable warmup, but by the third day, protocols of cultural sensitivity, mindfulness to the group, and a schedule to follow made me restless. After returning to Chiang Mai, we set our course south with the unspoken agreement that we weren't stopping until we sat on a beach. Now we were here, ready to enjoy unstructured blocks of time without concerning ourselves with anything at all.

When we had left Chiang Mai, we talked about drifting around, seeing what might interest us. But after the first day, if not the first hour—when we seriously looked at our map and pretended to weigh our options—we knew that the part of travel portioned for cultural exploration had passed. The last forty-eight hours we were on a telepathic beacon, riding an express train, and then hustling onto an express ferry to maintain momentum. On the boat we sat in air conditioning on jetliner seats, and drank endless Singhas, already starting our vision of beach hedonism and tropical languor.

Now I opened the door to the room, briefly inspected the four rattan beds, and returned to the veranda. Ostrov and Tager hadn't bothered to look at the interior—content to flop into chairs and stare out at the view. Tired and giddy, I searched for the answer to what all this time, space, and desire would bring.

We slept late from beer hangovers, and got up slowly and checked our watches, satisfied when we realized we had slept until the afternoon, as if dereliction was an objective goal. I planned to lay off the drinking and sightsee, but come three in the morning, I would be at the bar with the rest, saying "what the hell" for another round. When darkness came, I could think of no greater pleasure than many bottles of cold beer in an air-conditioned pub, where you had only to keep your eyes open to view intriguing scenes of foreign culture—even if just a darkened street with the usual array of *tuk-tuks*, drunk tourists, and local whores. No ancient temple, no matter how gaudy or grand, could compete with the pub atmosphere—where anything might happen after a few beers, but usually didn't.

During the hot hours, when my sweat ran thick with a rank smell, I began half-heartedly seeking religious and cultural sites, squinting in the bright light and pushing my finger over the pages of the guidebook in an attempt to muster the concentration to take in the passage. Sometimes Tager and Ostrov came to witness my forays at traditional tourism, vaguely amused at the bizarre conical stupas, ornately carved porticoes, and serenely sitting monks draped in orange—as if they had seen it all before. I told them I wasn't here just to be a drunk but also to take in the culture, the local ambiance of schools and businesses, and the ebb and flow of life. Ostrov looked more condescending than ever when I told him this. Tager nodded in agreement but had other priorities.

We sprawled into the chairs on the veranda after returning from the village, where we had eaten omelets and potatoes, and been comforted by the rough facsimile of food from home. High clouds and a stiff wind made the temperature almost pleasant, and we sat doing nothing with a serious resolve. Two weeks on Ko Samui, a full month in Thailand, our beards getting serious, our clothes taking on the drab and stained look that comes from being washed quickly in a bucket.

Between glances at the beach in the distance, I caught sight of Uncle Fang who slowly walked towards our bungalow. We had lived up to our contract, paid on time, and been respectful to the other guests, so Uncle Fang's approach appeared an unusual turn of events. It occurred to me that we had passed a certain threshold, our actions and appearances broadcasting a message that a specially tuned ear could receive.

"Everything okay in bungalow?" Uncle Fang asked when he drew close. Tager grabbed his bag, and quickly got up and walked down the stairs to greet him, perhaps worried that a form had been left unfilled.

"All good," Tager said.

Despite the heat, Uncle Fang wore a long-sleeved, blue synthetic shirt with a tropical design and blue jeans. He flashed a businessman's grin as his gold bracelet clicked against a heavy watch.

"You have good time here?"

"Sure, fine," Tager said, a calculating look coming across his face. He took his sunglasses off and pushed hair out of his eyes. Uncle Fang floated in front of us and gently shifted his weight from one foot to the next. He smiled at us again, nodding, looking as sympathetic as he could with his dark eyes and moist lips.

"Can you get some marijuana?" Tager said.

Uncle Fang's face relaxed—he was perhaps happy that he had not underestimated us. Tager gave him some *baht*, and he was gone for half an hour, the time it took to walk casually to the main village and back.

"Smoke here," he said when he had returned. "Don't go out. What you want, I bring. Others no good."

We waited until Uncle Fang walked a few meters away before getting busy rolling a fat joint. We lit it on the veranda, laughing at nothing in particular, other than that we were lucky bastards to have made it here—this was unquestionably the daydream we had spun our heads around when we had squatted in the freezing mud of Lebanon and the boredom and stupidity of everywhere else. The pot was powerful and the day hot. I slouched in the chair and leaned my head against the wall, feeling my eyes droop. In a flash of worry I stood up, paranoid that I had been drugged and a robber would approach to clean us out.

I walked down the steps, scowling at the tourists and hat and drink vendors ambling on the beach in the distance. I blinked, forgetting what exactly I was worried about. When the thought returned, I shook my head, smiling, and climbed back up the stairs to share the joke with Tager and Ostrov. But they were already snoring.

When I announced my intention to take a diving course, I expected I would do it alone, and made the statement with resignation in my voice. To my surprise, scuba diving had pull with Tager and Ostrov, and the three of us signed up for a course to gain our open-water diver certification. Every morning at ten, we went down to Lamai Scuba Diving, a rough cement building with heavy iron doors on the front. A shed behind the store housed a compressor for refilling the scuba tanks. We chose this shop because the compressor looked modern and well-maintained, with all the yellow warning stickers still attached and the gauges clean; that, and we wanted an instructor who spoke English better than our trekking guide.

Hans, a sixty-something German, became our instructor. Fit and lively, he wore crisp, light-colored beach clothes that set off his full head of silver hair and sparkling gray eyes. He was a friendly sort, and besides cheerfully teaching the specifics of the sport, asked us what books we read, and what we wanted to do with our lives. Ostrov didn't buy it, suspecting that a guy like him, who claimed to have given up significant success in business for life on the beach, was a maniac for the boys or girls, or some combination, and therefore had to live far from a judgmental society.

Our class of six scuba students had two German girls, Hedda and Carol, and a Brit named Robert. Hedda and Carol reminded me of the Welsh girl, Kelsey, with their indifference toward fashion and a serious commitment to energies unseen. On our initial dives off the beach, the girls fanned out their limbs and drifted like giant starfish in the current, holding still as possible, lost in sea-mother reverie. The rest of us darted here and there, searching for different fish and corals—the regular sightseeing, just underwater.

Robert was polite and quiet, and showed no interest in making friends after diving, while Hedda and Carol were open to camaraderie in the form of me tagging along on their outings around the island. Hedda had periodically studied design and art history at Leibniz University, while I gathered that Carol had no pressing need to work or study and had traveled extensively all over Europe and the US. For savvy travelers like them, there was never any pretense about who we were or why we were in Thailand. They had already met a broad selection of Israeli youth who were traveling the world after the IDF.

Soon after the course started, Hedda and Carol accompanied us to dinner. Tager and Ostrov's enthusiasm for drinking and bar life made them frown and bow out early. Later Hedda let me know she thought our nighttime antics childish. Ostrov reciprocated by letting it drop that he thought they were gay. I figured his comments were the result of his being raised in Cape Town—a culture with "excessive masculine posturing," to borrow a line from Hedda.

The three of us found companionship easy and went to meditation lectures, temples, and hikes in the forest. On a walk, the two girls chatted in German and then switched to English, signaling that they wanted me to comment. "War, for us, is in the distant past," Hedda said. "Something our grandparents experienced. My grandparents become silent like two art school manikins when I ask questions. Not a good sign. For many years I felt ashamed of our history—that's no good. So now I know I can't be responsible for past crimes, but I need to be vigilant about injustice."

"All the school kids in Germany learn about the Holocaust," Carol added. "They visit the camps."

"I understand your grandparents," I said. "Silence can be a good explanation."

"What did you do in the army?" Hedda asked, without indicating that this question was any different from asking if I wanted chips, hummus, or salad in my pita.

"I harassed Palestinian families, protected West Bank Israeli settlements, chased terrorists," I said, curious as to how my enlightened friends would react. Part of me wanted to shock them, as I suspected they thought me ignorant or cruel. Another part felt indignant, and that they had no right to pass judgement.

When I spoke about my army service, their faces became impassive, and the dynamic chatter silenced. A heavy moment lingered between us until the conservation moved on. I don't know if they resisted pursuing this because I had been respectful and polite and now I was angry, or if there was understanding of what it was to be a soldier. I wondered if their country's experiment with fascism, their grandparents' experiences, made them sympathetic to my situation. I didn't want to ask, knowing that whatever they said would piss me off. Better to let some things go.

In five days, we passed our final scuba exam. Hans noted each question we got wrong, ending the course only when we convinced him we understood the material. This made me feel we had chosen the dive shop wisely—I was glad that Hans wanted to prevent us from doing anything stupid in the water. Hans sent off the forms that registered us as open-water divers and gave us our laminated cards that allowed us to rent equipment and go out to reefs with the dive boats.

Scuba diving surprised me like a kick in the ass, catching me off guard with the innumerable varieties of reef fish and awesome vistas of sea and land from the deck of the dive boat slowly returning to port. After the first dive boat experience, I purchased my own mask, fins, and snorkel, and began regularly signing up for day trips out of Hans's shop. Part of me felt that I needed an activity to stop the drift the travel had brought, where nothing felt real or familiar, reliving my life like a stranger looking in a window and not liking what he saw.

After a month on the island, an ambient lethargy settled over us. The pace of our days was set by the chirp of cicadas, bird calls, and the pound of the surf. For Tager and Ostrov, nightlife continued to be the spotlight. When darkness came, we cruised the bars in the village, looking for a lively crowd, not packing it in until all options were explored. I didn't take the scene as seriously as Ostrov and Tager—I was content to sip beer and stare at the moon over the water. When things got too slow, Tager insisted on going to the next place or leaned on the bar and tried to squeeze conversation out of the staff, frustrated by their lack of English or curiosity. Ostrov always looked amused by Tager's antics, and was stubborn in his stance that no one would outlast him drinking, staying out late, or whatever weirdness they might encounter. Both logged wild nights, which included fucking vacationing women and lots of alcohol. The sloppy, drunken maneuvering I always passed up, looking for escape from other avenues.

I awoke when the beads of sweat turned in to a trickle, the heat and white light of morning coming up full force. Again, I had left "the party" early after saying that I wanted to chill on the veranda and go to bed.

Tager had given me a look indicating the wild shit was soon to start and how in God's name could I leave at a time like this? The bar was almost empty, the stereo playing a medley of AC/DC, Chicago, and Talking Heads. Tager and Ostrov were enthusiastically talking to two sleepy Danish women who looked close to forty even in the dim light—office workers on a spur-of-the-moment holiday. The two advertised what they had with loose bikini tops showing plenty of spotted skin and crow's feet around their eyes but with a flirtatious attitude that welcomed all attention. Tager's main tactic—suggesting skinny-dipping with the hope of "accidentally" bumping into one of them in the dark—lacked subtlety to say the least, but where would a guy like him, or any of us, learn anything else? I was curious to hear the details of any encounter, as it would be embellished and exaggerated to a comic degree. Tager would insist that we accept his ridiculous claims at face value. These were the times I liked the best. Ostrov would chime in, both of us chipping away at Tager's lame efforts to depict himself as a smooth man of the world.

I sat up, pulled on my T-shirt and shorts, grabbed my water bottle, and flopped into a chair on the veranda. For an hour I read the guidebook—an indication of how bored I had become—before giving up on the others and going out to get breakfast.

I found Hedda and Carol at their favorite coffee place, a fifteen-meter brown shipping container with a metal shutter welded over the front. Each morning the proprietor opened the shutter and set up the awning, unfolded the tables and chairs, and placed the double-burner propane stove on top of an old oil drum. With that, the Thai Fun Café was open for business. Hedda had befriended the proprietor, a woman with two young boys, saying that she was an artist and would paint a mural on the container free of charge. The woman, who was probably forty but looked sixty, her body knotted from a life of hard work, likely pretended not to understand. Hedda showed her sketches of a stylized phoenix—the image daringly reminiscent of a dancing Garuda, a humanoid bird and the national emblem of Thailand. The woman surely nixed the project out of the clear desire to keep her business—the people here took their patriotic symbols seriously.

As I approached the Thai Fun Café now, I could hear Hedda and Carol arguing in German. I pulled up a chair as Hedda called Carol a *besserwessi*, a word I only knew because she used it so frequently. Carol playfully stuck out her tongue. My arrival ended their feud, and they switched to English.

"Yehuda, good morning."

"Big plans for the day?"

"Yah, come with us. Pra Buddha Teepangkorn," Carol said, enunciating the words carefully. "A giant gold sleeping Buddha at the top of a hill. Lot of statues. Great view of the island."

I ordered a plate of noodles, listening to Carol prattle on about the ten precepts of Theravada Buddhism, how she was and wasn't a believer, and what was the Jewish response to Buddhism anyway? I worried that I needed an answer, but she filled in the blanks herself as I drank my coffee.

I didn't return to the bungalow until the evening. Tager and Ostrov sat on the veranda, looking haggard from the night before, with dark circles under their eyes, their movements slow and deliberate. They were in good moods despite their appearance, and waved and smiled when they saw me.

"Stories to tell?"

Tager grinned. "After you bailed, I went with Frida and Carina to Waldo's. Met some Brazilians, showed me a little trick." He got up and went inside. I followed, hovering in the doorway as he rummaged through the pockets of the shirt he had worn the night before. Finding what he looked for, he cocked his head in my direction. "Ever hear of chasing the dragon?"

Tager motioned me over. "Check it out. A pinch of crazy H on the foil, lighter underneath, then hoover away when the sizzle starts, and you're golden."

"Heroin? Are you out of your fucking mind?"

"You partied opium like no one's business. No needles. Just boys having some fun. An experiment."

Ostrov came into the room. "Barkeep at Waldo's is the man."

Tager and Ostrov had established a system between themselves. Tager carefully opened a folded paper packet while Ostrov readied a square piece of aluminum foil several centimeters in diameter. He handed me a straw and put a few grains of brown powder on the foil before sparking a plastic lighter and putting the flame underneath. The heroin crackled, and I caught the vapor in the straw, inhaling for all I was worth, not believing that I would consume enough to achieve any noticeable effect. I held my breath, sitting back on the bed before exhaling, the heavens opening with an explosive force many times magnified from what I remembered of opium.

"See? What'd I tell ya?"

We indulged in our passion earlier and heavier in celebration of the king's son's birthday, and relished the I-don't-give-a-shit spirit by pretending to involve the Thai royal family in our debauchery. After the first puff of heroin, pot became irrelevant, merely a soft distraction to help pass the time between episodes of the more serious stuff. We bought heroin regularly and cheaply enough that we didn't think we would ruin the rest of our trip. Still, things added up, and with economy in mind, we left Uncle Fang's and moved from the beach to an inland cluster of bungalows—cheaper and farther away from the general tourist population. We understood that we were playing with fire, and made a point not to smoke every day. But the off days grated like a silent shriek, so entirely devoid of content. We doggedly clung to our vision of paradise and went through the motions of diving, hikes in the hills, and the company of others in the bars. Hedda and Carol had departed back to Germany via Nepal. I missed their companionship and self-confidence in their worldview—universal in accepting all of humanity but rigid in how one should express such a philosophy.

Our bungalow was part of a holiday compound called Camp Sanuk. The name was painted in black letters on a termite-riddled, gray plank a meter long, propped up by a small pile of rocks by the roadside and covered with vines. The eight bungalows were crude affairs, arranged in a circle in a clearing in the jungle, with soft palm lumber radiating splinters and rusted tin sheets for the roofs. Inside, you could see how the wood had warped from multiple sun-scorchings and downpours, and did a poor job of keeping out light, rain, dirt, and bugs. This last point might have been a problem, but the cots had mosquito netting, which made the situation bearable.

Near the road, a cement building had two bathrooms with shower stalls, and a communal kitchen with random plastic plates and utensils, a few dented pots and pans, and a single gas burner caked with char and grease. Outside the kitchen, two weathered picnic tables sat beneath several palms heavy with coconuts. Ostrov started the joke of wagering who a coconut would fall on and when, forcing us to acknowledge the danger.

We paid our money to the round Mr. Atitarn, who asked no questions and was quick to leave after receiving the cash. He appeared only a few times a week to collect rent and haul away trash. Our command post naturally became the bungalow porch, where we spent countless hours waiting, watching, calculating our next trip to the village as if it were a commando strike. We called the porch our *zula*: an army term for a place to kick back and relax without concern for regulation or propriety.

"Dude, think it's time to go to the village?" Tager said, giving voice to what we all felt. I looked at Tager and Ostrov; we were all coming slowly out of our own trances, feeling dissatisfied and antsy.

"Get stuffed," Ostrov said, but I couldn't follow what he spoke to.

I understood that we had arrived at the place where everything appeared to be bullshit, save for the few hours of bliss we parsimoniously awarded ourselves. I knew by our pale skin, our diet of a few bowls of noodles and endless chocolate bars that a change was needed. But the thought drifted away quickly as other concerns loomed.

Earlier, before the party started, I completed a letter to my parents. I remembered sealing the envelope, affixing the stamps, and placing it in the slot of the yellow mailbox in the village. Now I couldn't remember what I'd written or if I posted a blank sheet of paper. I shook it away, figuring that I had told the folks the jungle was green, the sea blue, everything so fucking perfect.

The other residents of Camp Sanuk were the batik-and-beads set, sojourners who sought economy while studying Buddhism or martial arts, or just reading stacks of books. Many, like us, wallowed in nothingness and fought off boredom with various activities, tactics, philosophies, and chemicals. I made a point to ask any newcomer his or her name and chitchat around the kitchen—but many wanted to be ignored, and I could respect that. Despite the less touristy crowd at Camp Sanuk, there was still turnover, even a time when the only other occupants were a family from the Netherlands. The couple and two girls, ages six and nine, looked beaten-down by the climate—especially the parents, who labored in the heat under the daily chore of shopping for and cooking vegetarian food. No matter what they threw in the pot, it always looked the same when it hit the brown rice. Tim, the father, was in his early thirties, and wore a stringy goatee so long and narrow that he kept it folded in an orange knit sack, dangling from his chin like a wattle, his amber dreadlocks tied in place with a tattered strip of maroon cloth. He told me that he was on holiday, saying this with the grimness of a death announcement. He also revealed that he had been traveling with his family for a year and a half. I knew I'd learn nothing from Tim and his wife Henrice, and was content to nod when we passed and leave it at that.

I thought about Tager's suggestion of going to the village but wanted to save the activity for later. I stood up and found my towel and water bottle as I prepared to walk to the ocean for a swim. One of the side effects of our lifestyle was muscle soreness, as if we had finished a tough round of calisthenics. Swimming in the warm sea helped me feel almost normal. I went inside the bungalow and rifled through my pack for the sunblock. I heard several voices outside, and Ostrov giggling. I looked up to see a local dog run off.

"Share the joke," I said, figuring Ostrov was back to his schtick of voicing the dog's internal monologue. He shook his head.

"Check it," Tager said. "Israelis. I hear the *evrit*."

The new arrivals carried colorful backpacks with all sorts of smaller woven purses and bamboo mats strapped to the outside. They wore brightly colored baggy cotton pants, tie-dyed

T-shirts, and sport sandals. The men, unshaven, had long hair, two with ponytails. One girl had long black hair; the other looked like she had shaved her head that morning.

"*Am Yisrael hai*," Ostrov said, frowning.

We were sinking into a morass. Finding others who potentially understood—who could relate to our state of mind, what we had been through in Israel, what we were going through in Thailand—appealed to me.

We watched as the group set down their packs and explored the kitchen block and area. After several minutes, the thin bearded guy walked over to Mr. Atitarn and counted out bills. Mt. Atitarn pointed at the three bungalows adjacent to ours.

"I'm going to the beach," I said, aware of the glances our way.

"Good idea," Tager said, picking up on the vibe that the newcomers might want to chat and then be alerted to our utter idiocy.

We stayed away for several hours and returned after dark when the grinding pit of sobriety became too strong to ignore. Weak with heads aching, we showered and ate chocolate bars. I didn't have the energy to do much of anything, and by appearances, neither did Tager or Ostrov. Despite the early hour, the best plan—the only plan—was to lie on our cots under the netting and stare at the shadows on the ceiling and pray for the release of sleep. We could hear the new arrivals in the kitchen laughing and carrying on—the hard-edged Hebrew pop songs drifted into the night from a CD player. Part of me wanted to join them, but the other part wanted to wait until a better impression could be made.

"It's the fucking souk here," Ostrov said. "Might need to get them to shut up."

"Don't think I could sleep, even if silence," Tager said. "Let them have their fun."

The voices and music continued long into the night, and became a surreal pastiche of sounds and images, integrating into the background of lucid dreams.

When the sun came up, I pulled myself to my feet, believing I hadn't slept for five minutes the entire night. Ostrov and Tager had fared no better, and with our combined rustling, we were soon all dressed and standing in the yard. We went to the kitchen to make coffee but found all the cups and dishes, including the coffee pot, sitting unwashed on the counter, most covered in the fluorescent orange residue of congealed coconut curry. Many cups had cigarette butts snubbed out in them—a particular irritant for Tager, who muttered, "Assholes."

We walked to the village under a punishing sun and sat at a busy café, feeling like ants frying under a magnifying glass. The other customers sat around us and read guidebooks, wore fanny packs, and radiated earnestness at the challenge of being in a tropical wonderland, their day a schedule of well-measured pursuits. Our tired faces, scraggly beards, and shaggy hair—all tufts and wings crawling out of ball caps—made us stand out. We ordered coffee and pancakes, and I forced myself to eat, knowing I needed food. The pancakes and weak cane syrup didn't taste right; chewing and swallowing became hard work. I felt the junk molecules in my blood demanding to be reanimated to the potency that they had enjoyed the day before.

"First order of the day is to resupply," Tager said, staring a hole into his uneaten breakfast.

"Today's for culture and education, *habibi*," I said.

"This way we'll be good to go for tomorrow."

"Let's lay off a while—economize." I looked at Tager and Ostrov, who loudly said nothing.

"Thousand *baht* worth. That's, like, forty bucks. No big shakes," Tager said.

I took off my hat and ran my fingers through my hair and scratched my scalp. If this trip was to indulge ourselves and have the time of our lives, something had gone seriously wrong.

Ostrov tapped his front pockets and the space under his

arm, as if reassuring himself that his wallet and passport were all where they were supposed to be.

"You sure you're not Catholic?" Tager asked.

"I'll see you guys later," I said. "I'm going for a hike, to see the mosque in Ha Thanon."

"Get serious," Ostrov said. He squinted at me as if he intended to say more, but slumped back into his chair.

I didn't know why I had said I was going to the mosque, for I couldn't have cared less about seeing minarets or conversing with Muslims. I understood only that I needed to get away from Tager and Ostrov—break free of their gravity. I stiffly stood up and walked away from the café, vowing I would make this trip if only to fill my day with something other than the void that consumed our lives.

After twenty minutes of walking, I felt like shit, but took pride that I had left the vicinity of Lamai Beach, which had become a black hole. Two-story houses, blues and pinks, gave way to lush open country with groves of palm, teak, and mango trees. I passed mosaics of hand-tilled vegetable patches, remote guest houses, and small temples with clusters of monks in orange robes praying or farming. I sweated and cursed, drinking my water, and waved off taxis that honked at me inquisitively. My distaste for Tager and Ostrov's travel program grew, my black thoughts grinding on the noisy new arrivals.

I remembered in Israel when the three of us had planned a day on the beach in Herzliya. Still in the IDF, we looked forward to a day of not being soldiers. Tager, in one of his uncle's trucks, picked me up in Bat Yam and then turned around to get Ostrov in Ra'anana. We pulled off the Ayalon Highway onto city streets, joking and laughing, feeling life's potential in being able to decide for ourselves how to spend a sunny spring day. We entered the stop-and-go of Ahuza Street traffic, where a repair crew forced two lanes to merge. Several cars in front, a fancy Volvo sedan refused to let a battered yellow Mitsubishi into the lane. The Mitsubishi driver honked and gestured, but the Volvo did not yield a millimeter, the driver broadcasting an angry scowl and an imperious thumb jerked rearward. After several long horn blasts, the Mitsubishi tried to bluff his way into the queue, figuring his shitty car would force the issue. If brinkmanship was the intent, the threat played out, as the Mitsubishi's bumper smashed the plastic lens of the Volvo's front left headlight.

The Volvo driver, a bear of a man in his mid-forties wearing a collared shirt and slacks, got out of his car, jogged over to the Mitsubishi, jerked open the door, and landed well-aimed, forceful punches to the driver's head. The smaller, older man, who looked like he worked in a bakery—he wore clean, white work clothes—struggled to deflect the blows. A delivery driver on a Vespa put down his kickstand and ran over to tug tentatively on the Volvo driver's arm.

"Shit. Check it," Tager said.

"We're going to be here all fucking day," I said and got out of the car. I walked toward the fight, half expecting the driver to fire off a few more punches and then move on. I heard the truck engine shut off, and Tager appeared at my side. I didn't need to explain: we would put an end to this sooner rather than later. The frustration of the army boiled up—how nothing we did made any difference. All the endless patrols, all the tedium—none of it contributed to a better place. As we approached, my mind was clear—time to put out the fire.

Drawing near the Volvo driver, we heard his curses as he spat them out in rhythm with his punches. "I'll teach you to fuck with me ... your fucking life ... fucking car."

I pushed past the delivery driver and grabbed the man by his shirt and belt—then heaved him backward. Tager and I stood between him and the Mitsubishi.

"Did you see what that *mamzer* did to my car?" the man yelled.

"Stop being an idiot," I said.

"Fuck you," he said, trying to push us out of the way. Sometimes all that was needed was an exit with honor, but this guy wanted to continue the beating. I stopped him hard with a forearm push to his chest. The man backed up and for the first time took inventory.

Ever the actor, Tager extended his left arm forward and flicked his fingers toward himself, the martial-arts-film challenge. We were skinny kids compared to this guy, but I had approached the place of no return, understanding plainly what pain and suffering looked like, even if it was my own.

"We'll kick your ass from here to Afula, you piece of shit," I said, making sure he got the message that we weren't going anywhere.

The driver looked at us with narrowed eyes, his chest heaving with exertion, his mouth open like a fish gasping for air.

"Go call the police, the prime minister, your mother," I yelled. "Move your goddamned car."

A shadow passed over the man as he became aware of a new notion. He straightened up and smoothed his shirt. He walked back to his car, stopping twice to point a finger and shout a few more obscenities. Beat by beat, the tension deflated. Tager grabbed a handful of ice from the cooler in our truck's storage compartment, and offered it to the Mitsubishi's driver. The man said he was okay, and after pacing in the road, loudly contemplating filing attempted murder charges, got back into his car.

Sick and sweating, I bought a two-liter bottle of water and guava pieces in a plastic bag at a roadside fruit and vegetable stand. I saw the mosque in the distance with its green turnip-like roofs and golden spires bearing the crescent moon with the star. As I approached down a dusty street, passing open-air stalls selling all manner of produce, meat, and seafood, the fish odor prevailed. I discovered countless metal racks of drying fish near the water. I walked past the mosque's front gate, the courtyard empty, a sleepy cleric sitting nearby wearing a simple white *shalwar kameez* and a skullcap. I nodded a greeting, but he didn't acknowledge it. I went down a few nearby streets, scattering chickens, being casually regarded by men and women sitting on cushions in the front of their shops and homes, while caged birds and TVs added to the noise left by passing motorcycles, cars, and tuk-tuks. Ha Thanon had little development or tourist attractions, evidenced by few signs in English and almost no cafés. Women and girls in hijabs passed me by and I wondered what they saw—friend or foe? I tried saying *"as-salaam-alaikum"* a few times, with no reaction but a quickening of their pace.

After passing through the market, I went down to the beach to watch the last of the fishing boats arrive and unload their catch. The locals didn't give a shit that I passed through their midst. They got on with their business and left me to my silent existence, neither an attraction nor deterrent.

I started back toward the road, considered taking a taxi, but decided that the physical challenge of walking would be my penance—for what, exactly, I couldn't say. My head throbbed, and my joints ached as I began my trek. I looked for the sermon in what I had experienced—the raids and searches in the army, the drugs, the travel in Thailand. The multiple choices hung in the air in front of me and invited me to pass judgment or create a moral to my story, but nothing surfaced, each thought one in an infinite pool of memories and images. No conclusions, no resolution. I walked past an appliance store, an animal feed store, and yards stocked with agricultural machinery and boat repair supplies. I passed monasteries and meditation centers, monks and field workers, and found in a few smiles a reminder that nature, life, and chance didn't always insist on a bad outcome. I stopped to rest every few minutes, sipping my water and stifling an urge to vomit. The walk had taken me an hour—going back to Lamai Beach would take twice that. I planned to stagger back to our camp at the end of my endurance, the effort cutting through the fogged consciousness and deadened emotion.

The last kilometers to Lamai Beach brought a headache so severe it warped my vision with every beat of my pulse, my junk-tightened muscles and joints aching, sending spasms of electric pain down my legs. Once I reached the village, I sat at an open-air restaurant and ordered a soup with squid, shrimp, fish, cellophane noodles, and a spicy broth. I finished the bowl as if in a dream before sitting back and looking at the harbor.

When I returned to Camp Sanuk, I found Tager and Ostrov on the veranda of the bungalow, both in a sleepy stupor. "What's the celebration today?"

"King's son's birthday," Tager said.

"That was yesterday."

"He has another son," Tager said, a smile spreading across his face.

I sat down and put my feet up, watching the Israelis sitting around the picnic tables drinking coffee and smoking. Two of the guys sparred with each other in imitation of the Muay Thai fighting style. The thin guy sat at a table with a young local girl who earnestly pronounced Thai words for him to repeat. The girl with the shaved head came out of the kitchen with a pot and asked if anybody wanted coffee. I massaged my feet and popped a blister with my camping knife before pouring water on them.

"Kobi has a new friend, naughty bugger," Ostrov said.

"Who?"

"Jerry Garcia's younger brother," Tager said. "The guy with the whore. Had a chat while you were out. They're all just out of the army, too. Nahal *jobniks*, or something. Kobi and the two girls are from a kibbutz in the north."

"Thai girl, what kibbutz she from?" Ostrov asked.

Despite my purification march, I felt like shit for the next couple of days, not believing the heroin had caused so much damage. Every second of every minute, I wanted to smoke a few puffs to take the edge off, but always found a way to resist. For all my cold sweats and curses, Tager and Ostrov looked on, distant and uncomprehending, almost amused at my suffering, never seeing my contortions as a road they would walk. I was a raw nerve in all ways, as both light and sound pierced deep into my brain and caused crushing headaches.

As I regained my strength, I went to the beach to sit on a bamboo mat to read or lazily take in the view of the sea and sky. Despite the perfection of paradise, everything annoyed me—reading or not reading, talking or silence. In the evening when I lay down on my cot, the Israelis would start their evening of cooking, playing music, drinking rum, and smoking pot. I had given bonhomie a shot. I introduced myself and learned everyone's names and asked where they'd been, what plans they had. Of course, we talked about our national service, what we did in the IDF, people we both might know in common, relatives, soccer teams, favorite television shows. I presented myself as a decent human being who deserved consideration and hoped they would be less noisy during the night.

The group appeared happy to know me. The girl with the long, dark hair, Batya, broke into a big smile when we learned I had served with her older brother in Lebanon. For a moment we all unselfconsciously shared our complaints and insights about Thailand. After a day, judgmental tones and small comments crept into our conversation, especially after I explained where in the West Bank I had served as a Golani soldier. When Itamar, from Ramat Aviv Gimel, offered me a joint, the girl with no hair, Vered, said, "He needs a beer. Give him a beer. After all, he's Golani." The remark was tinged with sarcasm.

The group had studiously avoided the combat units, Itamar and Vered skipping the IDF altogether. Ostrov couldn't get his head around this and spent an hour asking me in private what could have possibly transpired to get excused from the IDF. I told him what Itamar and Vered had told me, and how they had bragged about the simplicity of the act. Both had appeared at the intake base in disheveled clothes, and exaggerated whatever emotional problems they suffered from, as they had been seeing therapists in high school. All of them viewed our service in the territories as complicity in propagating absurd nationalistic aspirations and general cruelty. I saw this coming, for the group had the careful look of people who defined themselves by their oppositions. At Camp Sanuk, they were the guardians of cool and would share honor with no one.

No one save Mary, the Thai girl, who everybody welcomed. They called her *achot*—sister. Mary enjoyed the new foreign name and repeated it softly after somebody said it, trying it on as if it were a new piece of clothing. I was impressed how she so effortlessly fit into the group. One minute Kobi led her into a bungalow for fucking; the next she sat in the kitchen laughing and cutting up vegetables with the others.

I knew I had the right to lounge around the picnic tables in the evening if I wanted, but I understood what it would take to get me back to the place I wanted to be: no partying—no pot or hard liquor, just two beers around dinner. This ensured that every night I would toss and turn on my cot until the group decided to get some rest. I tried asking them to move or turn down the music. "Don't worry, sweetheart!" was thrown back, and the noise only got louder. After complaining to Moshe in the daytime, he told me, "Everyone does what he likes here. If you like quiet, go find the quiet place. We paid our money, just like you. That means we'll have a party."

These comments burned my gut, hardening into something tangible after a week as I rolled from side to side on my bunk under the mosquito netting. One morning I awoke to find the family from the Netherlands packing up. I walked over to the pile of duffel bags.

"Leaving, Tim?"

"Time to go."

He loaded his family's gear into a tuk-tuk and was soon down the road in a cloud of black smoke, the girls giving a few studious waves. I didn't think they were sad to go. They were accustomed to frequently moving, probably feeling that their duty was to mirror the dour demeanor of their parents.

"The Dutch family just left," I told Tager, and conveyed with dark looks that their departure was connected to the behavior of the other Israelis.

"Bummer, I guess. Never did say too much to those folks."

"We're here, in the jungle, this remote place, and it's Tel Aviv rules. A giant fuck you, all over again," I said, kicking the leg of the chair on the veranda. "Stupid, arrogant idiots. Make our lives miserable just because they can."

"Would you feel better if those assholes were from Paris, New York, or Moscow?" Tager asked, looking at me with his dead pallor but unblinking and direct. Oddly, his expression and tone appeared normal, which irritated me further. I couldn't ignore his opinion because of incoherence. I caught him at the changing of the tides, and he sat at rough equilibrium.

"Why take this whole thing so personally? So ethnically? Israel isn't Zion. It's not a concept. It's a place. Like any other. With good people and bad. Just because you've got such a goddamned shit temper, you've convinced yourself half the country's plotting against you."

"Your mother's cunt!" I wanted to be done with every last one of them. I grabbed my belongings.

"I'll come too," Tager said. "We can meet David in town."

As we walked, Tager appeared weak and struggled to match my pace, and I conceded to myself that I shouldn't be angry with him for defending the Israelis. I knew that he was full of shit, and had I been sticking up for the Israelis, he would have been tearing them down twice as strong. "C'mon, man, give up the partying. Then we'll kick their asses. They've got it coming, and you know it as well as anyone."

"I am. I have. I'm just doing a few grains here and there to get over the rough spots. But there's four guys, ya know."

We found Ostrov idly shopping for a paperback before we went to our usual open-air café. We all ordered noodles. Tager and Ostrov picked at their food, slurping the broth but leaving plenty uneaten. I finished my food and ate what remained in the others' bowls after getting the nod.

That afternoon, we went to a lagoon, and I went snorkeling, swimming a few hundred meters to the edge of a coral reef where I practiced long dives. I luxuriated in the flow of warm water over my skin, and saw reef sharks, manta rays, puffed-up yellow-and-black lionfish, and massive brown-and-white groupers. As expected, when I returned to shore Tager and Ostrov were gone.

Back at camp, I showered and ate a Nutella sandwich. I found Tager and Ostrov drowsily sitting on the veranda, sunk into their chairs. They looked at me as if I was a ghost passing and said nothing. I put on my clean shirt and went back to the village to sit in a pub with satellite television. I sat at the bar and felt a sleepy satisfaction as I waved away solicitations for sex, gems, and drugs. After a few minutes, all the hustlers had made their pitches, and I sipped my beer unmolested, my head sharp and clear. I watched BBC World Service and saw images of European politicians, Africans in fatigues carrying Kalashnikovs and rocket-propelled grenade launchers, and Jerusalem. The camera panned across a burning chassis of a car, rescue vehicles, stretchers, and men wearing *kipot* and beards, rubber gloves, and reflective vests, picking up body parts near an outdoor market. Another bomb blast. I immediately thought of my family, figuring they would be okay, as Jerusalem wasn't in their usual field of travel. I felt lucky not to be in Israel, not to have to process all the pain, hate, and fear that the bombings instilled. But that didn't stick, and I wished I was home just so I could relax in the thought that there were people like me close at hand, people who wouldn't get lost in useless meandering when the order came to kick in the door. I felt ashamed and small, guilt washing over me, the crying children in front of me again. All these contradictions, swirling around in my head with no resolution, conclusion, hope of transcendence. I finished my beer and recognized myself as an official lost soul. I accepted that this must be the fucked-up natural state of adulthood.

I walked back to camp feeling restless and bored. At the bungalow, Tager and Ostrov lay on their cots, the other Israelis shouting to one another over the loud music. A few other shaggy travelers enjoyed the scene and lounged around the kitchen block. I went to the veranda. "Quiet! You pieces of shit!"

"We'll vote on it in the Knesset," a voice shot back, bringing bawdy laughter and cheers.

I quickly walked over to the picnic table, the center of attention, as a cooler sat there with the CD player. Nobody paid any mind until I had the boom box high over my head and hurled it to the ground, shattering the plastic casing and bringing abrupt silence. Kobi ran toward me waving his arms and yelling something I couldn't make out. I turned my shoulder toward him and fired my fist at his hairy face, sending him to the ground. Moshe came at me next. I'm not even sure he was going to hit me, for he didn't adopt any of the usual fighting stances, but I planted my heel in his gut for good measure. I flung the cooler against the cement wall of the kitchen in a violent cascade of bottles and ice, aware that those assembled watched my destruction in a stupor or in a firm commitment to self-preservation. I spied Itamar holding his guitar and ran over to grab it.

"Not the guitar," he pleaded as I struggled to rip it from his hands. "You broke the CD player. You win. Enough!"

I stood there, arms at my sides, breathing heavy, almost disappointed that the fight was over and nobody would challenge me further. The others could have all rushed me at once and beaten me bloody, but they stood there unable to meet my gaze. On his feet now, Moshe muttered insults and looked at the ground where the CD player lay in pieces.

"Get the fuck out of here," I said. "Now!"

With that, the group packed up and left. I continued to breathe heavy, exhilarated by my daring, almost positive that what I'd done was justified. I wanted the feeling to last, for I needed assurance a little while longer—just long enough to get me to the next station, to let me know that I was still the same person I had been before leaving Israel.

PORTLAND ZIONISTS UNITE!

OCTOBER 2015, NORTHEAST PORTLAND

GARY

THEY WERE THE first Jewish people I knew in Portland. I met them because I'm a property manager.

Well, my dad is the real guy, but he now resides in Tempe with his fake-tit second wife—all suntan, facelift, and vodka martini. So I'm now the dude for the duplex on Tillamook Avenue, at least while I work on my associate's degree. I forgot to sign up for any classes this semester, not that anyone's checking.

I do the usual: finding tenants, yard work, bills, rent, repairs. It's not like I gave Steve and Ruth the lease because of their religion, but it made them sort of special, like people who know stuff you're supposed to know but don't. My mom always told me I was Jewish because of her, but that was where the education started and stopped. I suppose I've learned more about being Jewish from watching *Seinfeld* reruns—which is a sad state of affairs even for one so academically uninclined.

I have a roommate, Carl, who rides tweaked kid bikes down from the zoo and creates other mayhem in the name of art and experience. He's twenty-one, same as me, and comes from Bend, which is a more happening place than where I grew up but still not so big that he has anything major over me. With him on board and the income from the other unit, I can cover my bases and do that which doesn't necessarily need doing. Carl and I are well-suited, sharing an addiction to killing zombies in the game *Call of Duty: Black Ops.* I know it's an old game, but the heart wants what it wants. The post-zombie-apocalypse Pentagon is our preferred venue. Carl usually plays Robert McNamara while I'm Fidel Castro.

Steve and Ruth, a couple in their early thirties, have been the renters since July. I knew they were Jewish because they had bumper stickers to this effect, or at least about Israel. I put a few questions about being Jewish to them both, and each time received an answer so long I couldn't follow—something about culture and parents and things being different in Israel. So they're Jewish, but with a level of qualification beyond what I can fathom. They're good with me asking general questions, but I now only ask Steve, because if I ask Ruth, she'll talk for twenty minutes before coming up for air. She's the undisputed expert, having gone to Jewish day school through eighth grade, done stuff at an actual synagogue, and visited Israel.

Until she moved in, four months ago, she taught Hebrew to little kids at the community center on the west side of town. Now she works part-time in the community center's administrative office in some capacity. Steve sells financial products, so he's a busy guy and just gives the skinny to my questions. I think about dudes like him, like I might have turned out similar in an alternate universe, wearing suits, doing important shit, carrying a briefcase full of urgent documents. I can learn from him, as he gets things done in a way that guys in suits do things—moving fast and efficient—not the endless grasping and pondering that plagues my waking hours. Steve is ambitious; he'll just whip it out that he'll do something and *booyah!*

If it doesn't work out, he shrugs and moves on. He works in an office tower called Big Pink in a slick world far removed from my mossy existence.

Despite this chasm between us, we're all typical for the neighborhood. We have our bikes and share a community-supported agriculture order. I actually eat my share and can see what Steve and Ruth throw out in the composter.

Regarding the bikes, Ruth has a step-through indigo fixie with plastic flowers on the handlebars that she rides to the University of Portland for her nursing program. I helped set it up after she brought home most of the parts from a garage sale. She borrows my floor pump and chain lube occasionally, sweet talking me into a repair when necessary. I like doing things for Ruth, as she's a nice person in the way that people show each other small kindnesses. Steve is a different story. He can be a good guy, full of stories and energy, but it's easy to get on his wrong side. I once told him his full-suspension mountain bike, with tires so over-inflated they hummed on the pavement, was a poor choice for the urban errands he mainly uses it for. I genuinely tried to be helpful, as I think about bikes and optimal setups on a daily basis. He narrowed his eyes and smiled a lopsided smile, "Well, you must be King Shit of Fuck Mountain." I didn't take it to heart. He's got his vision, same as everybody else.

Because it's an American Craftsman duplex, which means it's old and hexagonal bathroom tiles are supposed to make up for the lack of electrical outlets, I can hear their clock radio go off every morning at six. *It's six o'clock, the news is next!* Mr. NPR crows every weekday. I go back to sleep, but I worry that if I ever have a girlfriend, Steve and Ruth will hear the wolf screams of maximum coitus—or the sounds of embarrassed frustration, as well could be the case. I am confident that if Steve learned of any triumph or failure, he would have a field day teasing me. He comes from the East, Crouton on Hudson perhaps, somewhere with a pedigree. I grew up near Sheridan, Oregon, a place out in the sticks and best known for its federal correctional institution. So Steve would say something like, "Dude, you must be hung like a bull elk" or whatever his concept of rural Oregon stupid might be. Steve can say "pussy" or "vagina" like it's nothing, even to Ruth. Not me. We've all got our hang-ups. Steve notices this stuff, how I look embarrassed when he talks about women, and says no wonder I have no girlfriend. Because of this, he's always telling me sex stories— not all of them involving Ruth. He pays for it, though.

Yesterday I was pruning the roses in the strip between the sidewalk and the street. Steve pulled up in his yellow Nissan Xterra—the guy should ride his bike more, as he doesn't look too fit, his breath often sour from nighttime beer. But he's a doer; nothing slows him down. He is good-looking in a New York-detective way—square jaw, thick dark hair parted on the side, but eyes kind of too close together, giving him an odd look if you're in front of him. Some days he doesn't want to meet my eye; others, he's my best friend. Today he wanted to talk.

"*Gaaar-weee,* had a wild day. Really."

"Sell lots of term?" I picked up this was his most popular product even though he talked a good game about mutual funds and blue-chip portfolios. He had written me a policy soon after moving in. Steve accomplished this by saying he wanted to hang out and play *Black Ops*, JFK being his character of choice. He knew the game in several permutations and played with skill and intelligence. During play, he gradually shifted conversation away from weapons and strategy. He pointed out why life insurance made sense and artfully omitted that I would be super dead if the policy ever paid out. I planned on making a payment, but Carl as beneficiary killed the notion this was an important thing to do.

Steve walked over to me in a loose-limbed amble now, wearing a light brown suit with an amber and red striped tie, a

U of O pin on the lapel. "So I met this girl from my networking group for a meeting ..." He was smiling and looking at me conspiratorially. "Because she sells a weight-loss product, she works out all the time—total gym rat, wears a sports bra everywhere."

He was pursing his lips together as if trying to be delicate or philosophical, but I could tell he was pretty amped up. "She wears these leggings ..." He took a breath. "Her ass looks like two hard-boiled eggs in a handkerchief."

He let that one sink in, knowing that I had nothing to top it. He was about to continue but then waved the thought away and took a moment to compose his thinking. "This girl, let's call her Betty, full-on Oprah flower who blossoms in a be-yew-ta-fool transformation. Unhappy, fat Nebraska teenager. Stint in the Marine Corp as MP. Iraq. Where she had to do all this crazy shit searching under hijabs and almost got blown up twice. Unhappy marriage to psychotic soldier. Then divorce. Weight loss. Better living through healthy food and exercise. Older than me by a few. But get this, she wanted a long-term care policy."

"For when you're old and shit your pants?"

"We're talking at her house in Northwest. She started all serious asking about cost of respite care, an aging relative. Then she just started to drift." Steve took a breath, his face going slack as if suddenly unclear about what had happened next. "Tells me about a breakup, this other guy, everything so goddamned complicated. And I'm looking at my watch, wondering what we were talking about anyway. She gets up for something, then comes back buck naked."

"Things like that don't happen," I said and shook my head, confident in my disbelief but aware that what he had said was most likely true. Compared to Steve's life, mine felt like an ancient place and time. I lived and breathed in the same house as him, yet I couldn't comprehend that he described a reality—a Portland—I shared.

191

"Racing stripe," he said, glancing down, and then rolling his head back like he was the king. But his eyes weren't smiling. I guessed that this would be when Steve raised his hands and called for high-fives—but he looked off, sadness and confusion flitting across his face. Steve told me he loves Ruth, but they weren't married. I gather she had her doubts, too.

I looked at Steve, waiting for more detail, clarification, or even remorse—some clue to what it all meant. After a long pause, he said, "These things are like charity." He shrugged his shoulders, squared his suit jacket, and walked into the duplex.

I couldn't figure out what he meant. Did he mean the girl was sad and he cheered her up, or that a random gift had been bestowed on him? I figure my not knowing had to do with why I didn't have a girlfriend. I shook my head in wonderment at how other people got on in the world. No big mystery, for later that evening I heard Ruth scream, "I smell her on you!" Then the fireworks started—doors slamming, loud bumps, and the sounds of ceramic or glass smashing.

The next day I was in the basement where the communal washer and dryer resided, changing out the furnace filter. Ruth came down the stairs and put her basket down on the dryer. She was wearing turquoise yoga pants and a black T-shirt with gold Hebrew letters on it. Ruth brusquely poured out the detergent and threw clothes into the washer, looking like she had a bunch of stuff to do. She was a good-looking woman, just a bit over five feet, big hips, big boobs, with dark frizzy hair that when unleashed went every which way. Her long, angular face accentuated her dark eyes and amplified whatever emotion steered the ship. When she smiled, it was like the sun coming out, large and gap-toothed. She had grown up on the west side of Portland in a fancy neighborhood. When we talked, she liked to imply that she had smoked a lot of pot, but now was getting serious with her life.

"What up?" I asked.

"Getting it done," she said flatly.

I put the furnace sheet metal back in place and crumpled up the old filter.

"Hey, can you help with something, Gary?"

We walked up the stairs to her side of the building, coming up through the kitchen with the fifties-era stove and original cabinetry. I looked for things that needed attention. If I could spot them early, Ruth wouldn't bother me at seven in the morning with a shrill tone. All appeared as it should. They had this big "hand with an eye in the palm" artwork on the wall in the kitchen, and it needed something more than a thumbtack to keep it up, but that wasn't my concern.

Passing through the other rooms, I noted everything was tidy save for the spots where Steve liked to sit: half-empty coffee cups and *ESPN The Magazine*, a microbrew bottle on a side table, pamphlets about disability insurance.

"We've got this big-ass TV in the bedroom," Ruth said. "If you grab one end, we should be able to move it down here pretty easy."

On the second floor, the futon couch I had helped assemble had been made into a bed, Steve's clothes strewn upon it. Ruth caught me looking.

"Does he tell you stuff?"

"He told me how you met—you were teaching English to Cuban and Burmese teenagers when Steve was getting his MBA in Eugene," I said, and hoped this would suffice. I figured she meant knowing about him getting some on the side, or that he slept in the doghouse, but I didn't have the chops to go that route. Again, I realized how clueless I was. My old man once told me never to get involved in a boy-and-girl fight. I used to think that this simple advice served me well, but now I believed I had turned away from life dramas that would deepen my wisdom. My mom often said she hated any niceties that whitewashed the complexities of life. She always said she was a resource for me, that I could ask her questions about the world, relationships, women. But when I took her up on that, she just talked about the divorce and how she was handling it, even though it had happened over ten years ago.

In the bedroom, Steve and Ruth had a forty-inch television that wasn't so heavy, just big—it sat prominently on top of a dresser, dwarfing all else. The queen bed with fancy coverings made the room look like a resort hotel I had stayed in when I was little kid and my parents were still married. I felt proud to have given the interiors a fresh coat of paint before Steve and Ruth moved in, like I was an adult who knew how to act with other adults. We unplugged the black boxes and carried the television downstairs and set it on the floor in front of the fireplace. The massive black rectangle of a television prompted me to reconsider my having given up cable. I had thought not having cable would help me focus on school, but I ended up just watching the same shows on my laptop.

Ruth seemed to cheer up with the thought that Steve would now not have any reason to enter her bedroom. I understood in spades that it would not be wrong to start getting organized for the next tenants. Interviewing new tenants was the part I hated most about my situation. I couldn't tell shit about human nature or character, and people always took advantage.

"Need any help hooking up the DVR or cable?"

She shook her head, and I turned to go.

"Hold up. Here, take one of these," she said, and put a flyer in my hand. "There's a program about Israel coming up. Two former soldiers will share their views about peace between Israelis and Palestinians. Some friends are going to this; we can go out for drinks after. Should be fun."

I had told Ruth that I was Jewish, in the sense that my mom was, and this is how it was supposed to work—not that I knew even the FAQs. Ruth had been getting me interested in Israel, and I warmed to the topic as I grew embarrassed by my provincial life. So many people my age had passports and jumped on a plane to backpack Nepal or run a marathon in Turkey.

When they had moved in, Ruth and Steve had a small party. Over wine Ruth told me how she spent the summer between high school and college on a kibbutz, where she had her first romance. When she said this, she threw her head back and laughed in an exaggerated manner. She looked at Steve, who wasn't amused—always feast or famine with these two. Later that evening, she introduced me to her friends, mostly women, from her life as a Hebrew teacher and staffer at the Jewish community center. She lightheartedly called each Jewish connection a member of her Portland Zionist group. Most weekends she rallied the Portland Zionists to do yoga together and then go out for breakfast.

Soon after Ruth and Steve had moved in, I went with the Zionists to the Jewish film festival. Steve had backed out at the last minute. The film was a kicker, about this really Jewish dude living in Jerusalem who dressed like an old-time Quaker and couldn't throw out uninvited houseguests because of God's bizarre commandments. Ruth's friends were cool but kept asking personal questions, like if I considered myself a spiritual person or what my philosophy in life was (even now, I can't begin to figure this one out).

Things reached a low point when Ruth asked in a stage whisper if I wanted to date any of her friends, girls or boys. It pissed me off that I radiated no heterosexual energy—I understood that this was what politeness meant, but still. Under cross-examination, I admitted I *was* looking for a girlfriend. I wanted no set-up from Ruth but figured no one else was throwing any crumbs my way, so I should suck it up and be happy to get some help. Eventually I met this girl, Orly, through Ruth. Things started okay, and there was a feeling of lightness when I learned we both pretended to be vegetarians, but I didn't keep up with politics—local, national, galactic, whatever. I never got to where I could show her the areas where I shone as a human being. I was a fucking moron, for when I thought about what exactly those things might be, I realized I was lost. The answer that first bubbled up was that I thought of myself as a mindful person who walked gently on this earth—yeah, try saying that with a straight face. The big victories in my life had been the stuff of a fleeting moment, barely the blink of an eye. No prizes, awards, achievements— just a flicker somewhere that life didn't suck.

When my parents were married, my mom worked as a clinical psychologist with the Federal Bureau of Prisons. When people asked about her job, she'd tense up, saying she was part of an interdisciplinary healthcare team, administering a variety of psychological assessment techniques and treatments. Later, when she chucked her PhD and hospital training to work in agriculture, she would say that her former job was to provide the violent inmates with the lobotomy pills and be done with it. Mom admitted she was a depressive person, but this self-awareness wasn't enough to keep things going with Dad, who was more a "bon vivant," as he liked to call himself. How the two ever got married is a story, but the short of it was that they met climbing at Smith Rock State Park one summer. They weren't together then, but hit it off, kind of, because they camped near each other and did some sort of campfire *kirtan* and had long conversations under starry skies.

Five years later, when Mom had her first prison job in Lompoc, she looked Dad up because he was the only person she knew in the western United States. He worked as lifty in the ski industry but had bigger plans. He had scraped up enough cash to buy a derelict house in Mosier, Oregon, and fixed it up himself. In the summers, he lived in a room in the basement and rented the place out to windsurfers and tourists as best he could. When Mom found him through a mutual friend, he didn't need to think on it too long, packing up his Ford Bronco and driving to California. I saw a picture of this beloved vehicle, with a cracked windshield and looking like it barely survived the Paris-Dakar race. I don't really know what brought them together, and nobody was talking now, but I came along in 1994.

In 2007, when Mom went through her "life reevaluation," as she called it, terminating her contract with the prison and starting a new direction, Dad moved out. I spent high school not doing much of anything except getting by. Mom had been strident about me learning things and understanding the world, but after the divorce, I was supposed to be my own person. My graduating class at Sheridan was fifty-five. That year was a record, with only one dropout, but graduation didn't feel like any achievement. I keep going halfheartedly for college classes, hoping to figure stuff out. I knew I needed lots more self-improvement.

Riding my bike back from the Bicycle Repair Collective where I rented shop space to work on my ride, I felt good about life—this was what having a customized bicycle tuned to perfection did. A well-lubricated chain took one random element off the list of things that conspired against you. The weather was shit—a dark day of mist and rain—so I figured I needed to stoke the mood and stopped at Aztec Willy's for a beer and chips. I wasn't long being drinking age, so I still got a kick walking up to the bar and ordering. I strode purposely into the bar, suddenly aware of Steve's riveting glare from his perch on the far end. His tie hung loosely from his collar, and he appeared to have settled in to watch a football game on the big screen behind the bar.

"Gary, you're the man. No cares, responsibilities. You just live to party," he said, ordering a pitcher of margaritas.

"Can hardly run my car I'm so broke. I dress like a thrift-shop retard. You're the dude who's blessed."

He gave me a quick once-over and returned his attention to the game. I thought he would reject my assertions, especially about the clothes, as I wore last season Patagonia with only a single duct-tape repair on the jacket. Apparently not. His face flexed, perhaps because I knew about his recent issues.

"Ruthie's my girl all right," he said, not taking his eyes from the screen. "She's the one. I want her to understand me the way I understand her. When that happens, I'll just grab her and run to Las Vegas or Aruba."

I didn't know if I was supposed to follow up, or if this was the place for a philosophical nod or wink.

He poured the drinks. "I want her on my team. Every single time I need her help, it needs to be explained in minute detail, then negotiated, agreed upon ... I want loyalty, home fires burning, straight shot of support love."

I sipped my drink and tried to look pensive. Whatever Steve was talking about, it was beyond me.

"I wanted her to come to a fucking office event. She said it would be boring. *Of course it would be boring!* But it's my life. She's going to be a nurse, doing her shift, going home, making pottery, doing whatever the fuck she wants. There's a fusion of life and work with me that defies strict explanation."

Earlier in our relationship, Steve had shared that he had gotten a history degree and MBA from the University of Oregon, telling me in the same breath he had been recruited to play football but got injured. Later he forgot that lie and, in a more thoughtful moment, said he had tried for a walk-on but got cut. He wasn't that big or strong, standing a couple of inches short of six feet. His voice made up for it, for when he spoke he sounded dead-on big and professional, even when talking shit. Now, as the alcohol limbered up my brain, I realized that he thought he had a chance at playing Division I ball, which made me believe he could be equally unrealistic about other things.

"She said she was moving out. I told her I wasn't giving up on us. We're not together, not apart. Probably just playing me for rent."

Rent checks came from him, that part was true.

"I remember how it was early on. So much fun—no complications. We'd have hot monkey sex, watch old movies, crack jokes about our overbearing relatives. Now it's all about having to be on some exact frequency—her frequency. I have a frequency, too."

He spoke mostly to his drink and occasionally glanced at the game with the transcript running at the bottom. I tried not to take his words too deep. I knew he could turn on a dime and slap you down for no real reason.

We drained the pitcher and walked home. My mind drifted to thinking about sitting in my tapestry-covered lounge chair and firing up the Xbox for a round of *Black Ops*. Steve asked me what teams I followed in a lame attempt at banter, as if suddenly alerted to my presence, but it didn't work. Mostly we walked in silence.

"So you're going to the event about Israel?"

I nodded.

He shook his head, "*Gaaaar-weeeeeeee.*"

The next day, I awoke with severe cotton mouth and a headache. Three drinks and I was toast, no big news there. The NPR alarm didn't even register, I slept so hard. I rose up and made a pot of tea and eventually got myself running. When

I was hungover I wanted to be productive, like I would make up for being wasted by living a more purposeful life. I put on my outside work clothes and jammed a beanie far down my head and went into the backyard. I slowly raked up the dead leaves around the composter and cut back the rose bushes and hydrangeas for the winter. Despite the easy work, I breathed hard, the vapor condensing in clouds that lingered for a few seconds. Mindless movement felt good, as I wasn't in the mood for interactions with planet earth.

"Gary, hey. There's someone here I want you to meet."

I turned around, and Ruth and another girl were on the back stoop, light-colored hoodies over tight yoga clothes.

"Gary, this is Shira. Sorry you have to be Schleppy McSchlep when you meet. Shira, believe me, he cleans up nice."

I tried to snap out of it. "Hello. You going to the event tomorrow?" I said, happy to land on a point of reality.

"Sure. See you around," Shira said, looking slightly embarrassed. Slender, no makeup, with dark hair and complexion, she appeared to be my age. Ruth followed her into the house, arching her eyebrows and cocking her head in my direction. I didn't need the look. I got it—Shira was totally hot and available. All was up to me. I wanted to cry or run away or, more likely, go up to my room and smoke a potent bowl of weed. I promised myself that I would read the brochure, go to Wikipedia, practice saying words I knew I couldn't pronounce, learn about the wars and neighboring countries. I needed humbly to gather my forces for the event, hoping to be less stupid than I otherwise would be.

I heard a car start and figured Shira had gone. I went to my side of the duplex and carefully removed my muddy clothes. I found the couch and loaded the bong. Carl sat at the breakfast table absently picking at a plate of potatoes, having already indulged.

I liked Carl, as he upheld the basic tenets of friendship

and gave my insecurities security. We were equals on many fronts. He was a good piece of work with long, unkempt brown hair not too groomed or ratted out, a wiry frame with oddly bulging packs of muscle here and there, and a vibrant, open expression most of the time, indicating that he was agreeable to hear your thoughts even if they weren't fully formed. He had a skinny vegan girlfriend, Sapphire, who worked summers in a cannery in Alaska—that job gave her enough cash for veggies the rest of the year. She was pretty in a country way of wheat and kale but looked like hell when she came back from Alaska—all bug bites scratched raw and dark circles under her eyes. Shy and quiet, Sapphire bore the world lightly, even if she dismissed some of the things Carl and I were into. In my mind, she was the litmus test, for I figured I had the game to handle a girl like her. She would ask Carl what he wanted to do in a slow, cheerful voice that let him know it would be okay if he didn't have the answer right at hand. People like Ruth and Steve were moving twice as fast as me.

I lay back on the couch and thought about the event the next night, wondering if I wanted to blow it off, dial it in, or hack through it with my usual grace of a spastic child on ice. I worried that Shira would be a strident class-president type who drove a Honda Civic. I drove a Honda Civic, but for me it was different. I inherited the car, or claimed it as my inheritance, or was borrowing it. Mom never clarified this and often hinted that if something forever unsaid didn't happen, she would repossess it. My parents still fought about everything.

Carl stumbled into the room, found the remote for the TV, and groggily looked for an Xbox controller. He gave up and fell into a chair, making an oddly gleeful sound as if he had completed a tough task.

Carl had spent much of his upbringing ski racing. He had gone to training camps on Mt. Hood in the summer and worn those fancy racing suits that look like high-tech long underwear. He told me he wasn't going to race in college, should he ever get to a school with a team, much less represent anyone anywhere on skis. Like me, he sporadically attended the Killingsworth branch of Portland Community College, which is where we met. He smoked way more weed than me and owned five bikes of varying repair and several cartons of parts. One time, on a lark, he rented time at a maker space and used an acetylene torch to alter an old steel frame, making drastic cuts and assembling the tubes with sloppy brazing. He made his own strange handlebars as well—a real Franken-bike. He borrowed some crazy-fast wheels from a skiing buddy— they were like four grand wheels, carbon fiber with only three machete-like blades connecting the hub and the rim of each wheel—and he rocked it. Took second in his age group in the Cascadia 50K Time Trial. A podium finish complete with award-ceremony honeys who gave him his trophy and prize money. He stood there big and glossy, like a photo from *Bicycling* magazine, wearing his race jersey and sunglasses, holding his trophy high over his head in one hand, the winner's swag in the other.

I thought differently about him for a while, but he kept doing bong hits before going to work at New Seasons supermarket, so whatever brilliance shone forth at that instant was quickly hidden away. I was of the same ilk, having my brief flashes but not knowing how to make use of any budding skills. When Carl put his bike together and suited up for his ride with seriousness and aggression, I could still see the boy who dreamed of being an Olympian.

"There's a visit again in a few days," Carl said. I had forgotten he was there. "Major scrub-down and all that."

"No prob," I said, knowing most of the stuff lying around was Carl's. "Jesus is coming, hide the bong."

He smiled. He told me his parents, Jeff and Sue, had gotten all Jesus-y. They seemed like the types who went to

202

church to put a good face on something bad they did habitually. Although I'd met them about five times, there was still this formality. I figured Sue wanted to drop F-bombs and suck back whiskey sours, but her face was stiff and unyielding. Jeff took Carl and me to dinner a few times, and he was more relaxed. He worked road maintenance for Deschutes County for a good number of years, and could make a discussion about road surfacing funny as shit.

Sue always asked about my mom. I didn't know what to say. Initially I gave them the low-down, explaining that she worked as a tenant farmer after the divorce and now managed the McMinnville farmer's market. Now I would just say that she was fine. Jeff liked to ask questions about my dad's rental properties in Hood River, Bend, Astoria, Reedsport, Lincoln City, and Government Camp. I made Jeff laugh when I told him Dad had a condo in Maui but I wasn't allowed to stay in it. Dad goes to these places to do the larger maintenance projects himself, but mostly he was tied down with Marla at the B&B in Tempe.

Sue asked me about my religion. I said I was a non-practicing Jew, something I'd heard Mom declare, but I knew there was more I was supposed to say.

"Gold-tipped Siamese temples," Carl said.

"Huh?"

"Ruth's friend," Carl said.

I shrugged. "You and Sapphire have it out?"

"We're making ratatouille later."

"No worries. I'll be going out."

I thought about getting up. I conjured images of things I might do—tool organization, moss eradication—but then lay back and fell asleep. When I woke, Carl was gone and my back ached.

Often I thought no one had the problems I did—but when I stopped and thought about it, really knit my brows together, I took a second to realize that everybody had the same problems, though perhaps not to the same extent. What to wear, what to say, how to act. At the level of universal confusion, I took solace in my ignorance. One teacher said that whatever a person does, whether it's making cheesecake or selling ditty wipe, our purpose and responsibility was to show up and do whatever to the best of our abilities. I took this to mean I shouldn't feel bad about dropping out of community college and choosing a path of serious self-discovery.

I looked at the clothes at my disposal, all thrift store scores: the Dacron disco shirt, the bowling shirt with "Earl" over the heart, the baggy wool sweater. Shira was an ethnic, so I should play up my redneckism rather than enrage the gods by trying to pass as a hipster sophisticate. This made me feel good, like I'd finally gained some knowledge of self. *Fuck, I'm an idiot* was the reaction as I looked in the mirror.

I pulled the dark sweater over an orange T-shirt and checked myself. I had gone online and searched Wikipedia about Israel, ignoring everything except "Criticism of the Government," a link that took me to a page flagged with concerns about neutrality and questionable editorial content. I figured this was the meat. As I read, several streams of experience came together: a political science class a year ago where this red-headed dude talked about historical injustice to the Jewish people while this girl with a pierced nose and expensive laptop rolled her eyes and squirmed in annoyance; seeing a bearded guy wearing a T-shirt with a clenched fist surrounded by a six-point star, the wearer telling me in no uncertain terms that Israel would kick all the asses of the world combined, and saying it in a way to let me know my ass, too, was on the list. Reflecting on what I'd read and seen, I knew I could identify the major players in the discussion, and with that, I let my thoughts drift on to Shira.

I ran my fingers through my hair and leaned forward, reflexively sniffing my pits. I had showered early in the day but wasn't sure when the sweater had last been washed. All seemed okay—not that the pullover smelled clean. I reminded myself that should history repeat, should probability continue to assert itself, the odor of my clothing would have no bearing whatsoever.

I paused and stilled my breathing, for a second hearing laughter from Ruth's bedroom on the other side of the wall. A spasm of self-consciousness washed over me with the thought that she may have heard my primping and creaking floorboards and assumed I was masturbating. The laughter became giggles, and I heard Steve's voice in flashes. Ruth exclaimed loudly, then more laughter and what I thought was weeping but which turned out to be the sounds of love, or at least good athletic sex.

I went downstairs. Carl and Sapphire cut up vegetables, and the Dave Mathews Band played loudly, covering the noise of frying potatoes. "She won't admit it, but she loves Black Sabbath," Carl said, and shot Sapphire a look.

"I am Iron Man," I intoned, trying to sound like the guy in the song.

Sapphire smiled, having recovered nicely—her almond face fresh, her bare arms free of scabs. *"As if!* I'd be happier if we'd listen to more Sabbath. Enough of the jam bands."

I dropped into a chair and looked at my hands. I didn't feel precisely clearheaded, but my eyes were open and of regular coloring.

"Gary's got a date tonight," Carl said.

"Treat her right," Sapphire said and turned to look at me more critically. I wanted her to say what was obviously wrong with me, but she turned back to her cooking without comment. Carl dressed no better, but then again, he had that mountain kid "shred 'til yer dead" charm I do not. Carl still did shit like ride his skateboard off the first eave of the roof, landing it sweet first time with no pads or helmet. Sapphire might groan at misplaced testosterone messing up the world, but she stayed over after that one. Carl pushed me to skateboard more with him, and I once again took it up. I was not as agile, as I sported a build like a big potato. "You have a big refrigerator," Mom liked to say about my barrel chest. "Too much agricultural work and not enough high-altitude training," I'd tell her.

Six thirty came, and I stood up. "Wish me luck," I said to no one.

I walked outside and knocked on the other door. I saw, through the window curtains, Shira and Ruth on the couch sipping red wine. Steve yelled "Yo!" and I walked in. He stood by the fireplace, so I sat in the rocking chair. "Here he is, our landlord," Ruth said, looking relaxed with her bare feet tucked up under herself.

"Shalom," I said, making myself laugh, Ruth and Shira joining in.

Ruth gave a mock startled look of surprise, "Shaloha!"

Steve handed me a beer, and I took a big swig—I couldn't escape the feeling that the evening would be challenging in the usual ways I dreaded. The plan was to hear the activists hold forth at the Unitarian church and then go out for drinks.

Shira looked sweet, wearing a trim, blue base-layer top that showed off her figure, that hand-with-an-eye-in-the-palm thing on a gold chain around her neck. As I sat, I noticed bits of green in her hazel eyes. Her thin lips continuously moved even if she wasn't talking, which made it impossible to decipher her mood—one minute playful and light, the next judgmental and caustic. Her black hair hung loose around her shoulders, and she moved with the casual discipline of one who practiced yoga daily. I wished I had replenished the thin amount of THC in my bloodstream. I couldn't say exactly if I wanted weed to calm me down or spike my mind to unexplored thoughts. Pretty girls like her made me feel like a foreign species, craven in my desire and forever unschooled and unknowing. As usual, I had to wonder if I wasn't too hard on myself with all the self-recrimination.

"You ever been to Israel?" I asked her.

"My dad was born in Jerusalem. I visit the aunts, uncles, cousins every other year or so," Shira said. "I was there last year."

"The holy tongue *evrit* is pretty cool," Steve said, "but all the Israelis at camp would swear in Arabic."

"She'll tell you to go to hell in Hebrew just fine," Ruth said, rolling her eyes that this was the first thing in Steve's mind, "but your bar mitzvah training didn't give you the tools to understand."

Shira rose to the bait and said something with hard grating noises and a provocative hand gesture. Even I got the picture. She said she had recently graduated Portland State University with a computer engineering major.

"You a gamer?" I asked, betraying a nervous excitement that things could get interesting.

"I needed a practical major," she said. "I'm pretty good at coding, but when I think about the whole tech scene, work, a job, it's like, give a woman a program, frustrate her for a day. Teach a woman to program, frustrate her for a lifetime. Maybe I need a job without a screen. Who knows? What about you?"

"I'm working at property management while I finish my associate's degree in business studies." I felt good for reciting the line with requisite seriousness.

"Gary, here, is great with home repair. Nothing comes up he can't handle," Ruth said.

"He's got the plumber's crack to prove it," Steve said with a smirk. I was happy nobody laughed.

Ruth alerted us that it was time to go, and we drained our drinks, put on coats, and ambled out onto the sidewalk.

"So the guys speaking tonight—one wants peace, the other to keep the occupation as it is?" I asked.

Shira's face contracted into an expression of annoyance. "Well," she said, a tone seeping into her voice, "one of the guys will present the minority view of why we should make peace with the Palestinians now. The other guy will no doubt make the more logical argument that peace shouldn't be made because the current situation is too dangerous, the Palestinian leadership too deceitful. Yeah, I mean, I don't like everything the Israeli government does, but people here have no right to criticize. They've never been to Israel, don't know any Israelis or Jewish people. They read something on a website, see pictures that could come from anywhere."

I felt myself slipping into that place where I couldn't gauge what exactly she was talking about. She had this background, these visits to a foreign land, and I had what?

We walked into the church, which I learned housed a Jewish congregation when the Unitarians weren't using it. Two columns of pale wood pews defined the sanctuary, which looked like it could fit sixty people. The varnished wood timbers sported elliptical lighting fixtures that shed a yellowish glow on the scene, reminding me of a sepia photograph, and adding to the notion that we were doing something traditional and important. At the front of the room, wood paneling showcased a quilted tapestry of Adam and Eve, an apple suspended between them in a gender-neutral way, as Ruth explained.

We took our seats in the second row, as we had arrived a few minutes early. Ruth found a few other members of her Zionist yoga group and waved them over to sit with us.

When the program started, a tall, middle-aged woman in a dark dress and an embroidered yarmulke that covered most of her head walked onto the pulpit—set with two chairs with a wireless microphone on each—and introduced herself as Rabbi Miriam. There were mostly grandfather and grandmother types in the crowd, with a smattering of younger people—I'm liberal with the term "younger"—raising the question of why I had bothered. Sure, I had no social life, but I wasn't required to subject myself to this.

We walked a few blocks to the Starday Tavern, a place that looked like a transplant directly from Sheridan: all beer lights, ripped vinyl, video poker, rough wood, faded posters from decades-old rock shows, and bad oil paintings of horses for sale on the walls. We got our drinks and settled around a table.

I should have realized the evening was going to be a bust when the program started and the two former Israel Defense Forces soldiers came out and took their seats—paunchy middle-aged men with looks of serious fatigue. One guy was smaller, bald, with delicate glasses and a goatee and mustache. He wore black jeans and a blue shirt, vaguely resembling what I thought a communist of the last century should look like. Tall with curly brown hair, the other guy had my heavy build with a thick neck and arms, like he enjoyed lifting weights. He looked more put together, with dress slacks and a collared shirt.

I hoped for an experience better than the movie I had seen with the Portland Zionists. I wanted stories of adventure and daring, raids and firefights, altruistic heroics in the pursuit of a higher calling. Instead, a salad of Hebrew washed over me as well as the Ottoman Empire this and that, Balfour Declaration, status of residents of East Jerusalem, Arab Peace Initiative, Green Line, demographic trends, Apartheid state, and a million recitations of the world "Jewish"—no battle stories whatsoever.

As Rabbi Miriam asked questions, the two men on the pulpit embarked on a heated exchange over points dealing with what words were permissible to describe present-day Israel, who was the biggest purveyor of "delegitimation"—whatever the hell that meant—and the true nature of occupation. Things almost got interesting when the big guy suggested Zionism was prohibited from the curriculum at the Jewish school. When this happened, a teacher from the Jewish school, who sat in a pew in the audience, felt compelled to stand up and set the record straight.

The only thing of value occurred as things began to wrap up. The commie-looking guy was asked why he felt the need to express his views about making peace with the Palestinians, as failure seemed preordained, since all the politicians, both in the US and Israel, were intent on maintaining the status quo of military occupation of the West Bank and Gaza. The guy went way off topic, talking about how a person lives his life with the thought that what's past is over. He mentioned how he became accustomed to kicking ass in the army, promising himself he would be a different person in civilian life but unable to do it. Too many bad memories, spending all day wishing for a do-over. He concluded that no amount of hoping or praying could undo what had been done. So when he got up in the morning, there was just one thing left, the only thing he could do, the only path that made any sense; he acknowledged the person he was and tried to be the best person he could. Advocating for peace was his way of doing this.

I took his words to heart. What if there wasn't any real point in endless self-recrimination? What would it be like to get up in the morning and try and live life with the best intentions available, letting all the mistakes of the past be acknowledged but relegated to a corner of the mind where they posed no interference? This thought stood clear of the fog of confusion that otherwise defined the event.

"What you say, guys?" Ruth said. "Ready to bring peace to the Middle East?"

Steve poured himself a beer from the pitcher, a scowl on his face. "The guy, Tager, calling for the removal of settlements from the territories? Give me a break."

"The other guy, Cohen, said it right," Shira said. "Until the Palestinians recognize the Jewish state and renounce terrorism, Israel needs to stand firm against international pressure."

"Why doesn't Israel just make the West Bank its own?" I asked. "Like when the US wanted more territory, you know, it just took it."

"Too many Arabs," Steve said. "Israel can't give citizenship to the Palestinians because then they could vote and Jews would become the minority in Israel."

"Palestinians can't vote?"

"They can vote for leaders in the Palestinian Authority in the West Bank, but elections haven't been held in years and years," Steve said. "But no, they didn't vote for Prime Minister Netanyahu."

"We can talk about something else," Shira said.

We looked at her, perhaps open to the possibility, but nobody said anything.

"I want to show you how small Israel is, how no part of Israel would be safe from rocket attack if the West Bank became a Palestinian state," Steve said, and took out his phone. He unlocked the phone, the screen showing a text message. His eyes lingered to see who it was from.

Ruth leaned over to read the name. "Goddamnit, Steve!"

"I didn't do anything. She's still president of the chapter of the group."

"Texting on a Saturday night—yeah, networking. You sack of shit."

"Ruth, you've got the wrong idea. I've been part of the group for four years. I'm not throwing it away over a one-time thing," Steve said.

Other bar patrons turned to look. Steve and Ruth began having it out right there in the bar, their voices echoing muted rage. The feeling to flee hit me like freight train.

"Shira, let's go," I said.

She stood up with me, and tried to catch Ruth's eye, lend

support, or offer assistance, but got nothing. I pushed in my chair and focused my vision on the door, exiting into the cold night.

I worked around the house Sunday and ran errands, expecting to see Ruth or Steve, but they kept tight and quiet on their side of the duplex. That night I joined Carl on his "zoo bomb," as he called it. Carl had the combination of a lock that unchained a bevy of modified kid bikes at a downtown monument. After choosing our rides, we took the Max to the zoo. Carl claimed to be part of some movement or club where members made art and rode small bikes down hills. I couldn't speak about the art, but Carl dressed for success with a lime-green marching band suit jacket and welder's gloves.

"Got to scream loud," he said as we readied ourselves to descend. "Let those establishment fucks know there are other people in this city."

Made sense. Some traditions had to be observed even if they were stupid. We did the run a couple times, churned through the evening hours pretty good. Surprisingly, we talked to some girls, despite my conclusion from Saturday that I needed time to recalibrate myself before trying to advance with potential girlfriends. One girl, who gave the weird name Keiber, seemed cool mainly for being up for the simple thrill of rolling down a big hill on a small bicycle.

On Tuesday, I took delivery of our community-supported agriculture box, dividing up the celery, sweet potato, and broccoli before knocking on Steve and Ruth's door.

"I haven't spoken with Shira yet. Sooo tell me, where'd you go after the Starday?" Ruth asked. "Come, tell me about your experience."

I followed her into the kitchen where she poked through the vegetables.

"We just went home. To our own places," I said.

"Uh-huh," she said, unpacking the vegetables onto the counter. "You like Shira?"

"Not my type."

"Hah!" She laughed as if I had delivered the punchline of a salty joke. "Here." She wrote a phone number down on a notepad, tore it off, and handed it over. I obediently put it in my pocket. I realized that she had paired Shira with me based on the fact that we were approximately the same age and heterosexual, making me consider if I was a dating crash-test dummy for her friends.

"Steve told me today you guys would be moving out in February," I said. "Buying a house together?"

Ruth stopped fussing with the vegetables. I saw the pleasant mood drain out of her face. "He said that?"

When Ruth had first moved in and I spent time with her working on her bike and helping set up her stuff, she told me about her dad, teaching me the word *macher*—a guy with schemes within schemes, a dealmaker, a fixer. Her dad had been a salesman and was appreciated in the community as a character of a certain ilk. That made sense, as I had the same feeling about Steve. It was one of those things people say: there's a link between your parents and the type you date. Maybe you don't want to fall into a predictable pattern; maybe you don't have a choice.

Ruth looked flustered and shuffled the potatoes around on the counter. "I'm not moving anywhere. Got it?" she said, a hardness creeping into her voice. "Steve can be a bastard, and if that's how he wants to play it he can go to hell. I have resources, so you don't have to worry about who pays the rent."

I retreated to my side of the structure.

Carl and Sapphire sat on the couch looking at their phones.

Carl looked up. "Dude, you ever make it out to Maryhill, on the Washington side of the gorge?"

We all agreed I had the most reliable car, so we loaded up the Civic and pulled out late morning. Carl rode shotgun while Sapphire and her friend Lisa sat in the back. Lisa dyed her spiky hair raven black and wore a jean jacket covered with paint and rhinestones. The design on the back read "Down with the Clown"—it ran across the shoulders with a rough picture of two men whose faces had been painted to look like clowns of the rap group Insane Clown Posse. Lisa had grown up in a small town in Minnesota, and her slender body looked hard and soft simultaneously. She had a few acne scars, four silver hoops on her left ear, and wore an expression that indicated she didn't take life too seriously. She was Sapphire's friend from the cannery in Alaska. She was invited on this outing because she had a connection to the skateboarding scene and knew the course we wanted to bomb.

We counted on better weather east of the Cascades and, as expected, the drizzle stopped when we passed Bonneville Dam. It gave way to sun breaks at Rowena and full-on blue sky by the time we motored past The Dalles.

"What you think? I mean, first he says they'll both move out, then she says she'll stay. Now he's staying, too," I said.

Carl looked pensive. "I thought those guys were older and, you know, had their shit more together."

"Not sure it works like that. My parents could write a thousand-page manual on how to act fucking retarded."

"My dad won't pay a dime for college, even though he's loaded. He says he was raped because he had to pay six years of child support," Lisa added cheerfully. "He sends me three twenties for Christmas and a Pottery Barn gift card for my birthday for, like, twenty-five bucks."

We all laughed. "Woo-hoo!" Sapphire said. "I think you can buy most of a pillow with that wad."

"He makes computer-controlled machine tools in Faribault, Minnesota, and drinks beer," Lisa said, her gaze drifting out the window. "A twice-divorced alcoholic. Bravo for him."

Hearing this made me feel light, like nothing I had going was as bad as what others dealt with. People fell in and out of love, often involving kids and bystanders, but that was the point of it all. Live life, cut your losses, keep going, and hope for better. Carl once said he wanted to be a human air conditioner—inhale all the hot bullshit air and trouble of this world and exhale clear thoughts and pure energy. At the time, I thought he was going Jesus on me, but now I could see his point.

We made it to the top of the speed run, climbing up the northern edge of the Columbia Gorge, and looked down on the barren fruit orchards of Maryhill. The reddish cliff walls and dun vegetation stretched before us, and I pictured homesteaders and covered wagons despite the railroad and interstate. The sky loomed enormous, and I felt that if I looked up too long, a wind gust might carry me up into it. Clouds obscured Mt. Hood, but we all knew it was there, a giant pyramid peering down at us, reminiscent of something unspoken on the edge of our consciousness. Far below, the Columbia River ran black under the bridge we had crossed, and an icy wind puffed gently.

Before arriving at our destination, we took a detour to walk around a replica of Stonehenge. We were thrilled to think it had been built out of celestial freakiness, but in fact it stood to commemorate war dead from a long time ago.

Standing outside the car and studying the road carefully, I felt the smooth blacktop radiating warmth.

The past summer, Lisa had competed here in the Maryhill

Festival of Speed, wearing a set of motorcycle leathers and a full-face helmet, and flying down the course on a longboard. She showed us her gear, the board measuring 34.5 inches with unusual cutouts on the tip and tail, the setup looking hard-core.

Today, the plan was to follow the rider going down the hill in the car so that the person on the board wouldn't be menaced by a driver coming from behind. It was the rider's prerogative to keep in the right lane and avoid oncoming cars. Because it was the middle of the week, in the middle of the day, in the middle of nowhere, we hoped that that the traffic would be light. This seemed right, as we had only seen a few cars since heading up the hill from the river. This was one time when you knew you were a dipshit for going, a dipshit for staying.

Our own Hellboy, Carl, led off, arching graceful curves mostly, skidding to the edge of control on a few of the hairpins. He stood tall and pumped his arms as he rolled out onto the flats, flushed and whooping.

Lisa went next. Sapphire enjoyed gravity sports but hadn't studied this denomination, and so was happy to spectate.

I tuned my trucks for longer than needed before forcing myself to jump on the board and push off down the hill, telling myself I could skid the board to a stop if the speed got too hairy. The perfection of the asphalt, the tunnel vision of going fast, the way the sound of the wind got in your head and quieted the mind all added up to one fucking awesome instant in my existence.

We stayed on the hillside for over two hours, and each of us took two runs, until a sheriff's deputy showed up. I thought the worst, but he politely told us to move on. Thrill-seeking buzzheads bombing the hill were no doubt a common occurrence. Only later did I realize that the deputy might have only been a few years older than me, making me feel I needed to set my sights in life a little higher.

Driving back, the bracing freshness and exhilaration of our

Zen joyrides lingered and we laughed and joked. A few scrapes and bruises and a shredded pair of jeans were the only damage. We stopped in Hood River and ate pizza at a place playing a snowboarding video on a big screen. Seeing the riders soar through the air or plummet down a sheer mountain face further verified the day's pursuit. We gassed the car, bought beer, and found a park off the highway on the west side of town. Sitting on a picnic table, Lisa and I watched the sun sink into the "V" of the gorge, the layers of clouds making it red like on the Japanese flag. Rays of light delineated by mist painted the cliffs and water.

Lisa took a swig of beer. "Carl said you had something Saturday. We all could've hung out."

"I had a thing," I said with a pang of apprehension that I would need to explain the nature of the Israel-Palestine conflict. I fidgeted and thought that even if a geopolitical discussion wasn't required, explaining what had happened and the ideas discussed would still be hard. All of it felt so far away and impossible.

"Cool," she said, smiling.

I leaned forward and kissed her gently on the lips.

She closed her eyes and kissed me back, before opening them and turning away, letting forth a girlish giggle. "What's gotten into you?"

I put my arm around her and savored the moment. A few minutes later, we packed up and headed back to Portland.

"I'm not going to pay you full rent," Steve said.

"What?"

"My commissions aren't coming in as expected. Just need a few weeks. That's fair. I've helped you countless times."

"Definitely not cool." I shook my head.

"You're acting like a total douche."

"You even planning on staying here past February?"

"I'll let you know."

"Your lease is up, if that means anything."

Steve floated around me as I wrangled the compost and garbage cans off the curb and back to their usual spot behind the house. A slow anger burned behind his eyes as he appeared on the verge of laying into me with some new set of problems. He usually wasn't home from work so early but had changed his clothes and looked to be setting out for another appointment.

The porch of the duplex was stacked with cartons—of what, I had no idea, yet nobody had claimed to be moving in or out. I walked back to the front.

"What's with the boxes?"

"Moving some stuff around."

I looked at him, but he didn't meet my eye. A delicate time with tenants was when they wanted their security deposit back before they vacated the premises. They would promise the world regarding cleanup and leaving the place decent, but would usually punt when things got hectic, forcing me to suck it up. Steve hadn't asked for anything yet, but he and Ruth were all over the map with crazy as of late. Ruth had asked permission to have another cable run into the house so there would be two internet and TV accounts on their side of the duplex. She nagged me for days to fix the showerhead. When I got there, I found two shower caddies stacked one on top of the other with a his-and-hers orientation. I didn't need to look in the refrigerator, imagining the duplicate milk and condiments. No one wanted to mend the relationship or see it end.

"Steve, maybe you and Ruth should see a therapist. Talk it out. Get some perspective," I said, thinking about how Mom forced me to attend therapy with her when I was twelve.

He stepped forward and regarded me coldly. I feared things would get heated, but when I looked at his face, I saw confusion and blankness. His hands jumped around, then stayed put. "Worry about your own mental health." He looked agitated that he hadn't come up with a better rejoinder.

I let it go. He appeared to have more to say, but I left him there staring holes in the shrubs and trying to maintain some semblance of control.

Going into the house, I kicked off my shoes in the vestibule. Dad was coming for an inspection of his investment, and I thought I should do something extra, maybe further gardening or push Ruth and Steve to move the boxes to the basement. Dad wouldn't give a shit. The house stood in good shape, the bills were paid, the rent still coming in. "If the tenants are crackpots, so what"—verbatim from the old man himself.

I put on a new pair of jeans—the color a pleasing resemblance to dirty engine oil in the flat light—grabbed a hoodie, and set my hair in order in front of the mirror.

Tonight I would hang out with Lisa, who played one of the Rayman games on a PlayStation 4 and had vowed to convert me. I'd give it a shot. In return, she promised to play Halo for an equal time some night at my place. After gaming, we would head out to hear music or see what presented itself.

I stared in the mirror, trying to fathom what Lisa saw when she looked at me. My cell rang—Ruth. I let it go. Moving down the stairs, I heard rustling from the other side of the house. In the basement, I turned on my bike's lights and opened the door to the street, rolling out and jumping on, Pony Express style. Steve and Ruth's problems would exist in their world, not mine. I pedaled into the evening, glad to have a place to go, free of any pressure beyond a simple estimation of how far I could push my luck.

I imagined February coming and going with no change in status quo. I wasn't going to invest time in Steve or Ruth; the moment in which I might benefit from knowing them had passed. Maybe someone or something would eventually force them to reconcile their relationship, but I had other things on my mind.

ACKNOWLEDGEMENTS

THESE STORIES WENT through numerous iterations and many people helped make them possible. Without the inspiration and support of my family and friends, Portland Zionists Unite! would never have seen the light of day. To all of you—many thanks.

Special appreciation goes to the early readers: Dudley Flamm, Mike Flamm, Fran Adler, and Merridawn Drukler.

Mike Levine provided superb big-picture advice, his comments never lacking insight or wisdom.

A big thanks to Siri Hustvedt and Paul Auster for their encouragement.

A huge debt of gratitude to all my friends in the Portland Jewish community who have supported and advised me through all my trials and tribulations.

For instilling in me the love of good stories and creativity, I'm thankful to Ellen Flamm, Richard Peterson, Beth Wickum, and Dudley Flamm.

Thank you to Janis and Tony Hollombe and Sarale and

Mike Miller and their families for a lifetime of Israel discussions, arguments, and love.

My deepest appreciation goes to my biggest supporter and inspiration—my wife, Robin Flamm—for filling my life with joy, humor, and an appreciation of the absurd. To my kids, Olivia and Jonah: ditto.

Thanks to everyone on the Inkwater team who provided direction—especially Andrew Durkin, my patient and skilled editor.

AUTHOR BIO

ERIC FLAMM was raised in southern Minnesota and studied English literature and Chinese at Lewis & Clark College in Portland, Oregon. After graduating, he worked as a journalist in Taiwan, and then at a startup technology company in Israel, where he became a citizen. In 1996, he was drafted into the Israel Defense Forces and eventually joined an artillery unit as a reservist. In 2001, he moved to Portland, where he still lives with his wife and two children. Since 2012, Flamm has been active in Israel advocacy, including the promotion of a negotiated settlement to the Israel-Palestine conflict. The first chapter of *Portland Zionists Unite!* is based on a short story which won honorable mention in the Writecorner Press Short Fiction Awards.

I

CPSIA information can be obtained
at www.ICGtesting.com
Printed in the USA
FFHW021652011118
49163994-53368FF